BROKEN TO BELONG

Broken to Belong

Charity Muse

ISBN 979-8-9861031-0-5 (Paperback Edition)

ISBN 979-8-9861031-1-2 (eBook Edition)

∼

Cover art & design by Cath Grace Designs

∼

Original songs written and performed by Charity Muse. Song recordings and discussion guide available at http://charitymmuse.com

For Deanna, with all my love.
And to everyone who has hoped to belong.

ONE

DANI WILLIAMS

H ome eluded me. So, what was there to miss?

That's what I told myself, anyway. *Maybe I made my decision in haste. Maybe it wouldn't matter. Maybe it*—no. I would be ok. Something had to give.

If you saw me on the stage earlier that year, you probably didn't notice. I had still laid on the charm. I had still known how to work a crowd. My smile had proved just as infectious. My voice still rang with genuineness. When my fingers pressed down on my guitar strings, the resonating steel had continued to connect my heart to theirs. Music has always been a little magical for me. Somehow, even in the times in my life when I've dissipated into fragments, music still carries me. If I'm being honest, music carried me the most in those times.

Three months before I took the flight to South Alabama, I had realized I was beyond being in fragments, and the magic of music proved powerless. I had become a phantom, moving about the world with a song and a memory—the memory that persisted despite fifty-three therapy sessions, a fog of stolen pills, living on the road most of the year, and enough Irish whiskey to kill a herd of horses. Music, for the first

time in my life, had become a chore. The droning applause had accentuated my numbness. Loneliness and emptiness had pricked at me like a
burr in my shoe—ever present, painful enough to remind me it was still
there with every move and rest.

Oppressive heat engulfed me as I stepped outside the airport doors.
I laid down my guitar case and took a drink of water. "Guess I'm not in
Oregon anymore." *For damn sure.*

"I promise it's usually not this bad so early. It's just a heat wave."
Rachel, the director of the South Alabama Safe Home (SASH) smiled at
me as she took a bag from my hand, and I readjusted my guitar case. The
gray streak in her chestnut hair fell across her cheek as we strolled across
the sidewalk and loaded into her blue 1994 Volvo.

"Well, you all set, Dani?" She smiled at me as she started the
engine.

I nodded and reminded myself why I came: the kids at SASH.
Home had abandoned them, too. But they had found a new place to
belong, because Rachel had created one.

From the periphery of my eye, I watched her as she steered us away
from the terminal and onto the snaking concrete leading to the highway,
her eyes fixed on the road. We had only spoken on the phone twice—the
first time to tell her I wanted to come help and the second to finalize our
plan.

"Dani Williams ... the singer?" Her question had made me laugh;
the hint of a smile returned to my face as I mulled over the memory.

I cleared my throat and looked over at her. "So, I know you said
thanks for coming, but seriously—thanks for having me. I needed a
change of scenery." I bit my lip and looked out the window as my mind
drifted across the last year and what I had gained and lost.

"You can't love me into loving myself, Dani. It isn't like writing one
of your songs." Lauren's tear-soaked words had cut through me as I'd
walked out the door.

Love wasn't enough. I'd tried to numb the pain with more work,
but it had only served to remind me of just how alone I was and how
powerless I was to change that. At first, I'd found some respite in the
greets after shows, but by the end of the first half of my tour,
usted me. The pretending and forced smiling for weeks had

culminated in my going home and spending my three weeks there either drunk or asleep.

Next leg of my tour, I'd stopped hosting the formal times for fans to meet me, but a month in, a girl waited outside my bus in the cold for almost an hour for what I thought was an autograph or a selfie. Instead, she'd thanked me for my music and told me it helped her survive after her parents had kicked her out of her house. I don't remember what I said or how I stood. I do know my stomach became like stone as I listened through the whirring in my ears. She'd told me about the South Alabama Safe Home and how she had found refuge there for a few months until she started college in North Carolina. For that frozen moment, I'd felt something other than the numbness, the ocean of sadness, or my seething anger.

A couple months later, when I'd realized I was in trouble, I knew I had to come see the home for myself. Maybe helping with their annual fundraiser would help me find a sense of meaning again.

For over an hour, we rode in near silence before Rachel turned off the interstate and onto a two-lane highway. I could see for what seemed like miles. I stared out the window at the resolute flatness, the farm homes in the distance, and the abandoned small service stations scattered along the highway that seemed to resonate lost echoes of when the world moved more slowly through time. Not a hill or a mountain in sight. Just fields and stretching trees adorned with emerald leaves and dangling moss.

A billboard came into view at the end of a tree line. A picture of a path with an arrow pointing upward sat above the words "Repent. Turn your back on sin. Jesus is The Way."

The term "Bible Belt" means something very different when you are the one on the end of the lashing, and familiar tightness crawled across my chest as I looked. "What's with the sign?"

"Oh, The Way... Let's get you settled in before we get into that." Her mouth curled upward at the corner, and I nodded and focused on the lush green.

Soon, I felt the car slow down and turn onto a long gravel road. I listened as the tires crunched over the tiny rocks, and I straightened my back. We took a gentle curve to the right around a thick grove of oaks and pecans, and a flicker of shining tin roof caught my eye through the limbs.

Sitting at the edge of a field, the historic house boasted sage green siding and tall windows. A great porch with hanging plants, porch swings, rocking chairs, and a small round table with wicker chairs around it called out a welcome. Thirty-five acres of land surrounded the place, enough to feel like a world all on its own.

After Rachel stopped the car, I opened the door, and a sweet floral scent hung heavy in the air. I stretched and shuffled to the back of the car to unload my things. As I reached down to pick up my guitar, Rachel patted my back. "The kids are going to be really excited to see you."

I looked up to see five residents smiling at me from the porch, along with one staff member. Even though I had stood on the stage for seven years, since I was twenty-one, my hands shook as I took my bags up. I didn't want to let these people down. In that moment, it didn't matter if my guitar was in tune, if I sang on key, or if the song I wrote made it to radio or sold lots of copies. What mattered was that I was there, that I was me, and that I would do my best to help out.

When I reached the porch, they greeted me with hugs and hand-shakes, and the pounding of my heart eased. Rachel stepped to the front door and opened it up to let everyone walk in. She smiled at each person as they went by, and as I walked in with my guitar, she winked at me and said, "Welcome to your summer home, Dani."

My feet touched the hardwood floors and my eyes adjusted to the interior light. The hardwood floor creaked under my feet, and the smell of cinnamon and peaches filled the air. I breathed in and looked at the soft light coming in through the windows, casting warmth on the plants and stretching to touch the wainscoting. *Maybe I could find some respite here.*

A woman with a small afro, a hoop ring on the right side of her nose, and tattoo work of feathers and music symbols down her right arm came around the corner and smiled at me. "Hey Sugar, I'm Anita, the assistant director here."

"I's nice to meet you. I'm Dani. Well, I guess you know that." I over my words and half-smiled.

"I do." She laughed and touched my arm. "And I'm sure you're tired. If you want, I'll show you to your room." Her easygoing nature set me at ease as we walked up the great staircase together and she opened the door to my room. "I think you're going to like the view."

Two windows faced sprawling live oak trees, one close enough to climb out onto. The other window faced South, with a pecan tree in the foreground and a wide pasture and garden in the distance.

"You have everything you need?" Anita asked.

"Yeah, I think so." I scanned the room and put my hands in my pockets. "Do I need to help with anything?"

"No. Dinner'll be ready in about an hour, so you just rest a spell." She smiled at me and pulled the door to as she left the room.

I chuckled under my breath, "Rest a spell." Rest was more than welcome after all that traveling and the damn thoughts. I rubbed my eyes and shook my arms out at the thought of them, hoping it would bring me back to the present moment.

My bags sat next to the dresser, fine to wait a while to be unpacked. I washed my face, changed into a clean shirt, unbuttoned my jeans, and plopped down on the quilt on top of the bed. My eyes scanned my phone for a song. Eva Cassidy, *Songbird*, Track 1. "Fields of Gold." Much like the fields that surrounded the home. My eyes closed as I listened.

I don't recall when exactly I discovered Eva. It was sometime after that night when everything I had known suddenly changed. But I do know that her gentle yet soulful voice has eased me like nothing else. Her story reminded me of the frailty of life and the enduring nature of music, and that inspired me to write from a deeper place: the place where I ached the most.

At some point as I was listening, I drifted off, but soon woke up to the sound of the door opening. I hadn't heard the knocking, and the door was unlocked. Before I knew it, I heard "Oh my gosh!" and caught a glimpse of someone shutting the door.

I buttoned up my jeans in a hurry, jumped up laughing, and tried to catch her. I opened the door, and she covered her face with her hands. All I could see was her brunette locks shaking from a deep chuckle. She pulled her hands down and looked at me, her eyes the color of a September sky.

"Sorry. I didn't know you ..." Her face reddened.

"Yeah, yeah. Of course." I snickered at her and gave a sideways smile. "It's ok."

She grinned back at me. "I'm Mae. I'm on staff here in the afternoons. Anyway, dinner's ready. Whenever you are."

"Yeah, I'll be right there," I answered her and put my hand on the door frame.

"See you there, then." She smiled at me again as she made her way back to the stairs.

I watched her for a moment, then looked back into my room. *Maybe I could find something here*, I thought before heading down to dinner.

∽

MAE TUCKER

Typical me to start off with an awkward introduction. I've always had a knack for that.

Dani looked like she'd fallen asleep in the middle of changing. *Bless her heart.* Her ease and ability to laugh it off brought a smile to my face as I headed back down the stairs.

I had actually already met Dani, briefly, when I was twenty-one, in an autograph line when she opened for the Indigo Girls. I instantly loved her music, and she struck me as someone who was probably a kind person as she smiled while signing our ticket stubs. Not that I have the best track record with being a good judge of character, but I thought she seemed approachable. Six years later, I still listened to her and clung to the certain gentleness and depth that flowed through her songs.

I needed that sort of feeling, especially in the previous couple of years. Music had always been a bit of a safe space for me. I know a lot of people say that sort of thing, but for me, it's the lyrics, the poetry. When I lost myself to the point of not picking up a pen to write my thoughts, it was poetry in the songs by Emily Saliers and Dani that helped me find my way back into my own. So you could imagine how excited I was when Rachel told me Dani was coming to SASH for a few weeks.

"Look at you smiling." Anita smirked at me as she walked across the hall and toward the dining room. I shook my head and laughed. It felt good that things were light again after so much heaviness the past few months, and since Anita knew me better than just about anyone, I knew she understood.

Between carrying the weight of the tragedy that launched me into agency work and the relationship that nearly diminished me into nothing, I needed a reprieve. Having Dani help with our summer fundraiser burgeoned with the potential to give me just that.

Soon Dani walked into the dining room, and we all sat at the spacious table. She smiled at me again before taking her seat. I scanned the table, and all five of the residents talked and laughed together.

I like to think that every smile, every laugh, and every moment of joy a resident feels acts like a fault line, cracking across the pain they carry, reaching down until it's only their true selves that remain, unfettered by the deep loss they've been through. That night was no different as I watched them smile and laugh with ease along with Dani.

After dinner, we piled into what we affectionately call "the family room." Dani plopped herself onto a vintage couch with two of the residents, and I stood by a window, taking in the soft orange glow from the setting sun filtering in the room through the window sheers.

Sebastian, a poetic soul and one of our longest residents, sat down at our old upright piano and started playing—his usual evening routine. He pushed his hair back out of his eyes and sang two verses of "Hallelujah."

When he was done, Dani stared at him in silence for a moment. "Dang. That was incredible."

"Thanks." He offered a shy smile and pushed his hair back again. "I think it's your turn now."

She looked at him a moment before her signature wide grin spread across her face. "Ok, but you all have to sing along."

Dani skipped up the stairs and soon headed back into the room, guitar in hand.

She looked at us and curled her mouth upward before looking down at her guitar and play a few chords we knew well. Tom Petty's "Free Falling."

We sang along, and afterward she played "Jackson." When Dani put on her best Johnny Cash impersonation, alternating with her best try at June Carter Cash, we all erupted into laughter.

My eyes locked onto her as she played, her hair sweeping over her eyes at times, the definition in her arms deepening as she strummed, electric. I averted my eyes to stare out of the window again, focusing on the long shadows of dusk instead of her.

When it was time for the residents to go upstairs to bed, Anita and I went to the kitchen to open a Malbec and walked back with glasses for Rachel and Dani. We stepped out onto the porch and all sat at the wicker table together.

Dani stared down into her wine, her coffee-colored hair appearing even darker in the fading light as it draped across one side of her face. I wondered what she was thinking.

"I think it's safe to say everyone likes you, Dani." Rachel smiled as she took a sip of her wine.

"Yeah, I haven't seen everybody that relaxed in a long time. I think this is gonna be good for all of us," Anita said.

I looked at Anita, remembering what we had gotten in the mail. "Anita, did you tell Rachel about what we got earlier?"

"No, I didn't." She looked at Dani and then at Rachel. "It's another letter from The Way."

"Shit," Rachel whispered.

"The Way … wasn't that the billboard we passed?" Dani shifted in her seat and then sat forward. "Maybe you should tell me about it now."

Rachel looked down into her wine a moment before looking at Dani. "You know how I told you we have protesters show up at our events?"

"Yeah, and you said it's been getting worse?" Dani shifted in her seat and tensed her back.

"Right," Rachel answered her with a sigh.

Anita filled in the silence. "The Way is a local church—a Southern Baptist one, with several locations in Alabama. With a quick first glance, you might think they are progressive."

Dani peered at her glass. "What do you mean?"

I cleared my throat and spoke up. "The senior pastor, Lenny, drives a Harley and has tattoo sleeves. Most of the leadership has tattoos and piercings. But it took us just one visit to the church several years ago to confirm that the image is only a front. They push some pretty hardline views on gender roles, and in the past couple years they've been coming up against SASH in every way imaginable."

"What ways? Am I safe here? I mean, this isn't exactly what I signed up for." Dani's voice sounded quiet yet firm.

Rachel leaned forward, her hands interlocked. "About once a month, Lenny writes long editorials in the paper about how what we really should offer is what he calls a 'reparative program'—essentially an ex-gay sort of operation. He and about a dozen or so members have taken to showing up at our events the past year. They hold up signs and try to talk people out of giving to us. It's gotten a lot worse the past couple of months." She bit her lip. "They'll probably show up at the benefit when you play. I should have warned you about it before you agreed to help us out."

Dani stood up and downed the rest of her wine as she walked over to the banister and leaned against it.

Rachel's eyes met Anita's and mine a moment before she turned toward Dani. "If you need to change your mind, Dani ..."

"No."

"Are you sure?"

"I'm sure." She nodded and then turned around with a sly smile. "It wouldn't be the first time I've dealt with hecklers at a show. Besides, it's just one night. Of course, it's ok. There's no reason to turn it into something that's bigger than it is."

"It's true. I'm probably making a mountain out of a molehill." Rachel took a sip of her wine, and Dani laughed and walked back over to the table.

"That must be some more of that Southern-ese." Dani's eyes met mine as she chuckled, and I let them linger a moment, taking in the depth of their green.

Warmth rushed to my cheeks, then the pain hit again.

"It's getting late, and I better head out." I got up and walked inside to grab my jacket, helmet, and keys.

Riding Sage, my CB750, usually gave me a chance to process and unwind as I steered along the pavement. But this time, as I picked up some speed and the wind caught my hair, I bit my lip and swallowed to hold back tears. The scents of privet and honeysuckle and the silver glint of moonlight on the fading blooms of wisteria invaded my senses and took me back to early last summer. I could still feel Heather's arms around me as we cruised the back roads in the lingering evenings. That was the prime of our relationship, before she shattered my heart, leaving me to ride the difficult roads alone and wandering in the searches of the night. Funny how after that time passed, I realized how much that image fit our relationship. I thought I was driving and steering my life, but her grip was more than that of a passenger.

Coming back to the present, my mind flashed back to Dani's eyes meeting mine, and I worked to concentrate on the road.

I decided to take a different way home and pulled into a gravel lot by the lake. I got off my bike and left my helmet on the seat as I ambled to the water's edge. The night song of crickets, tree frogs, and the call of a barred owl in the distance filled the air as I stooped down to pick up a few smooth stones and ran my fingers along their edges.

My voice trembled, *"I don't know"* through a sigh as I began to sort through my thoughts. Dani's presence felt familiar and comforting yet disquieting. And though I felt immediately drawn to her, a strong urge to keep my distance permeated my mind. Probably for the best. For both of us.

I skipped a stone and watched the moon dance upon the ripples in the water.

Have you ever noticed the way the moon changes? Not just the phases, but where it is in the sky on different nights at the same time. Whether it's the waxing crescent, waning gibbous, or first quarter, it's the same cycle. The full moon always makes its rise at the same little hill over the lake, and when I step outside in the mornings, I can catch it before it descends again behind the trees down the road.

I closed my eyes.

What happened with Heather can't happen again. I can't trust myself. Not yet.

I skipped two more stones before I placed one last stone in my pocket in case I needed to ground myself again.

After riding the rest of the way home, I went inside my house and drank a glass of water before heading to bed. As I lay and watched the stars through my window, I replayed my day, just like always.

My thoughts took me from an early morning walk, to my mid-morning writing, to my workday at SASH, and Dani.

Then my mind turned to the ride home, and my memories of Heather, and the beginning of our relationship, walking in a golden field together. Knowing I couldn't sleep yet, I pulled up a song: Eva Cassidy's "Fields of Gold."

Under the glow of my lamp sat a picture of me with my childhood best friend, Rebecca, our faces frozen in time as fifteen-year-old girls. I opened my journal to jot down a few lines.

Could it be possible to reclaim the pebble that danced on the shimmer of moonlight?

Can hope be found, remembered, or even rescued? Even now?

I hoped so. Hope was what I needed to remember most, no matter how elusive it seemed.

Two

DANI

After a hard sleep from all of my traveling, I still woke early enough to see the gray of the morning. I got up out of my bed and crossed the creaky floor to look out the window. Mists rising from the fields beckoned me to come outside for a breath of air. I changed into a pair of jeans and t-shirt before creeping down the staircase. Just enough light came in the windows for me to see. More than once, the steps beneath me groaned, and I paused, not wanting to wake the others.

As I stepped outside, crisp air made its way to my lungs, and I closed my eyes for a moment to take it in, letting the cool clean breath awaken me.

I opened my eyes again and sat down on one of the porch swings, staring across the land, thinking of the day and night before. As I listened to the morning sounds of birds, I tried to just be present, a never-ending struggle for me in my overthinking. When I'm too still, the memories have a way of catching up, another reason I found myself on the road more often than not. Some people might call it running from my demons, but I don't care for that kind of imagery. I think it's more like trying to outrun the shadows that form at nighttime. You can see it coming, expect it like clockwork, but there's nothing you can do to fully escape it.

Before the painful moments started playing like a movie reel, I heard gravel crunching under tires and looked up to see Rachel's Volvo heading around to the house. She parked and got out of her car then headed for the porch, newspaper in hand.

"Hey, Dani. Is everything ok? It's still really early."

"Yeah, I just couldn't sleep." I looked up at her and shivered as a breeze kicked up. "Wasn't it hot yesterday?"

She gave a short laugh. "I'll make us a cup of coffee."

"That sounds great, actually."

She set her paper down on an end table, and went inside. A few minutes later, she walked out with two cups of coffee along with a blanket for me.

"Blackberry winter," she said with a faint smile as she sat next to me.

I took a sip of my coffee and raised an eyebrow.

"It's cool weather in spring. The blackberries need it to bloom, so that's what we call a cold snap around this time of year."

We rocked gently in the swing a few moments, silent as the mist took on a golden hue.

"Dani, are you sure you're ok to stay? I feel like I should have been more up-front."

"I'm here. It's ok. I don't want to let you all down. I can handle it." I held my coffee close, and we rocked some more.

"Do you know why I started SASH?"

I shook my head and met her eyes.

"When I was fifteen, I had fallen in love with my best friend, and since my parents loved her so much, I thought that there was a real chance for them to understand at least a little. But I couldn't have been more wrong. My parents told me I had two choices: I had to change or leave. They sent me to a place in Birmingham called 'Sin No More'—it was a 'pray the gay away' kind of place."

My insides tightened, and I shifted in the swing.

"I wasn't allowed to talk with any of my friends, and I got taken out of school. Just before I left for the program, my parents stood me in front of our small church, and the congregation came up to lay their hands on my head and prayed over me—more like curses, really. They asked for God to give me heartache and difficulty, and to do whatever it took to make me see how evil being gay is." She glanced over at me.

"I moved to Sin No More, and it was a nightmare. I wasn't making the changes they wanted, and night after night, they tried to pray demons out of me. I stayed for about a month before I couldn't take it anymore, and I ran away. Then I found out how alone I really was. Nobody would let me in. No friends or family. I had to steal food just to survive. Until I got caught by a woman who saw me hiding some fruit under my shirt at the store."

"Damn, Rachel." I realized I was staring, but I didn't care so much. I knew that kind of pain all too well.

Rachel nodded. "So, that stranger turned out to be a school counselor, and instead of scolding me, she followed me and asked questions, and offered me a safe place to stay. She helped me graduate from high school, get into college, and then eventually a master's program for social work. Now, she serves on the SASH Board of Directors." Rachel turned her head toward me again. "She saved my life. And who knows how many more. But my point is that places like The Way are exactly why we need this home. There will always be people coming against us, but I refuse to bow down to it. Giving people who've been broken down a place to belong is too important to me for that."

I swallowed back the rest of my coffee and looked out across the field through the mistiness in my eyes.

"Rachel, I wanted to come here and help because I believe in what you're doing here, and because I know what it's like to lose everything—just because of who I am. I haven't met many people who know that feeling, and ..." My voice cracked.

"You don't have to talk about it if you don't want to. Your story is yours. I just hope you know you *are* safe here, too."

I wanted to believe her, but I knew from experience that it's the people and places that make us feel safest that can wound us the most. I nodded and stood up.

"Looks like it's going to be a beautiful day." She looked across the field. "I hope you don't mind, but I kind of planned your day for you."

"That's why I'm here." I gave a half smile and then looked at the shifting colors in the sky. "So, what am I doing today?"

"Well your morning is pretty free, but this afternoon, I asked Mae to show you around the property. It should be a perfect day for it."

"That sounds great actually." I took one more look at the morning light. "I better go take a shower. See you at breakfast?"

"You bet."

I went upstairs and opened my guitar case and touched the strings before I closed it again and headed into the bathroom.

As I let the hot water run on my face and through my hair, I wondered if I could handle what was ahead. I got out of the shower and dried off, then checked my phone for messages. I had one from my sister, Jen.

Hey, Dani. Just checking in to see how the first day went. Love you.

I typed up a response but deleted it and instead asked if I could call her later. A few seconds later, my phone rang and I answered.

"Hello?"

"Don't make me come all the way down to Alabama, Dani Williams."

I laughed, knowing my sister would actually do exactly that. It wouldn't be the first time she showed up to rescue me. "Ok, ok."

"Don't ask if you can call me. You know better than that. Just call."

No matter how many times she said something like that to me, I still felt like I was intruding somehow. She had given so much to me already. Asking for anything felt excessive and needy. "Noted. Thanks, Jen."

"Of course. Is everything ok?" She always knows. Even when I don't say a word.

"Yeah, for the most part. Everybody here seems super nice. I think you'd like them. It's just ..." *Where to start without sending off an alarm that I'm slipping again?*

"Just what, Dani?"

"Harder than I thought it would be." I looked out of the South-facing window, silent as Jen took a moment, too.

"Are you ok? Do you need to leave? Maybe it's too much. At least for now."

"No, I mean—yes, I am ok. It's a lot. I'm not going to lie, but I don't think I need to leave. I just need to figure out how to not think about what happened back when ... It's kind of hard when I'm surrounded by reminders."

"I know." Her voice was soft, and she paused a moment. "Well, you can call me anytime. As much as you need."

"Thanks, Jen."

We talked for a little while longer, and I filled her in on meeting everyone the day before and told her about my plans for the day ahead. After I hung up the phone, I looked in the mirror at my tired eyes.

"You can do this, Dani," I whispered before heading down the stairs.

MAE

When I got to SASH at midday, I sat down with Anita at the kitchen table —our routine for making sure we were on the same page. Anita and I had been inseparable for eight years, since we met in college, and she helped me get my position at SASH. I couldn't have asked for a better role or better place to work. Everything was meaningful to me. From facilitating group time, helping with career and college plans, working the garden, and making meals together, it all made SASH feel less like work and more like family.

Anita took out a notepad and looked at me. "So there's not really anything new other than Dani being here. Everybody seems to be doing great with it so far. We had a good morning."

"That's good to hear. Rachel asked me to take Dani around the property today." When she asked me, I didn't have a reason to say no. That was before I had locked eyes with Dani and felt the danger of falling.

"Good. That should be good for both of you." She looked down and nodded.

"What does that mean?" I crossed my arms and chuckled.

"It means I see you Mae Tucker. I see how you still sulk sometimes and how you get lost deep in thought anytime something reminds you of you-know-who, and don't think I didn't see you trying to avoid Dani's eyes. A little bit of flirting might do you some good." She cackled.

I stuck my tongue out at her and laughed back. I wasn't afraid to flirt with someone. I was afraid of my heart reaching across and connecting with someone else's and what might happen if I got it wrong again.

"But for real, Mae. I worry about you sometimes. Are you ok?" The earnest look in her eyes cut across the superficial wall I kept up most of the time. It had become a survival tactic for me the past year. Just like it had when I was sixteen, when I needed it most.

"Yeah, I'm ok. This time of year just reminds me of last year." I took a breath. "With her." I bit my lip.

"I know it can't be easy." She rested her hand on mine. "You've come a long way since then. I'm proud of you, for whatever it's worth."

"It's worth a lot," I said as I stood up and touched her shoulder. "I'm going to go get the keys to the Ranger."

"Make sure you bat those eyelashes at her, today!" she called from the kitchen as I walked into the hall.

I whipped around to make sure no one else was around to hear us before laughing to myself as I walked outside.

I brought the Ranger around to see Dani sitting on the front porch talking with Sebastian. Dani stood up from her conversation with him, and I stepped around and waved. I tried not to laugh again as I thought about what Anita said.

"You about ready to see more of the place?" I slipped my hands in my jean pockets.

"Yeah, that sounds great!" Dani bounded down the steps and over to the Ranger, and we started off toward the fields.

We drove by the garden first. It didn't look like much, since most things had just been planted. Small green leaves and stems peeked out among the raised beds like a barebones statement of purpose, while other beds looked barren, concealing the seeds under the soil and mulch.

After the garden, I drove us in the direction of the orchard. The last of the apple and peach blossoms clung to the trees in clusters of salmon, pink, and white, and Dani smiled as she looked up at them.

As we rode through the thicket to the next pasture, I broke the silence by telling Dani the story of how SASH got the land. A family sold the land

and house early on, just after Rachel had formed the board of directors. They had cut down their price to half of what it was worth, in hopes it would help the home get started more quickly.

"Wow—that's incredible. And probably pretty rare from what Rachel told me yesterday about this area."

"It really is." I looked over at her and nodded. "Well, what do you think?" I asked as I steered us toward the former fence line.

"It's lovely," Dani said. "I love how peaceful it is here." She looked out and took in the view.

I smiled in reply and drove us along in silence. Peaceful was the opposite of what I had felt for a while, but I could just touch the edge of peace when I went out into the fields.

"So, tell me more about you, Mae. I mean, if that's ok." Dani looked at me with one hand on the rail of the Ranger and one on the seat, as if she might fall off if she let go.

"Yeah, of course," I said. "I'm from the northeastern Georgia mountains. I've been at SASH for a few years now. My parents were actually really great when I came out to them, and I know how lucky and rare that is anywhere in the South. So, I wanted to do something good for people who aren't so lucky." I held back the rest, not wanting to bring too much heaviness into the day.

"So, what else should I know about you?" Dani asked. "I think sometimes we get so used to telling our coming out stories to each other, that we don't talk about more of who we are."

I slowed the Ranger down and paused.

Dani looked down. "I'm sorry. I didn't mean to pry."

"No. Not at all. It's just, I didn't realize." I paused. "You're right, Dani. I get so wrapped up in the work we do here, that sometimes I don't see past that when I tell my own story." I looked her in the eye. "And I bet you get minimized even more with what you do—I mean, your music and all."

She smirked at me, "Yeah. That's true, too." She paused a while. "Sometimes I forget, too, and I lose sight of who I really am. The core of me."

We sat in silence for a bit, then I smiled at her. "I'll tell you what. I'll tell you more about me if you tell me more about you. Something that has nothing to do with music or being a lesbian."

Dani tried to stifle her chuckle before we both laughed.

After we stopped, her eyes met mine. "I have a tendency to dive into deep topics when I talk with people. It's just the introvert in me. I can't do small talk."

"Me, too. For sure," I said, feeling my shoulders relax a little.

We spent the rest of the afternoon together, driving around and talking more about SASH. After our ride, I closed up the Ranger in the shed, and we took our time back to the house, our hands in our pockets as we walked.

"Thanks for showing me around today," Dani said with a crooked smile.

"Of course. And thank you for being such good company." I winked at her before I realized what I was doing. I silently cursed as I stepped onto the front porch and went inside.

"I have to go get ready for group time. See you later?" I asked.

"Definitely." She smiled at me again as she headed upstairs.

THREE

DANI

On my first Saturday morning at SASH, I woke up early and couldn't fall back to sleep—my new normal. I slipped downstairs, stepping lightly on the creakiest parts of the steps, and walked into the kitchen. Anita stood there, making coffee and taking out ingredients to make breakfast as she sang, her voice deep and resonant.

"You're up early," she said to me. "You ok, darlin?"

"Yeah, just couldn't get back to sleep. I think I'm starting to adjust to the new time, but still not quite there." I smiled at her as I grabbed a coffee mug. "Can I help?"

She smiled back as she handed me an apron. I put it on and pulled my hair back.

Anita pointed to a whisk and bowl with a faint smile. "So, Dani, what brings you to us this summer? You sure came a long way away, and I'm just curious how you found out about this place."

"Yeah I guess it is kind of a long haul," I laughed. "Someone told me about it, and it sounded like something I could have used a long time ago." I paused and peered down into the bowl. I didn't want to think about what happened. "So, when I decided to take the summer off of touring, I knew where I wanted to go."

"Sounds about right—" Anita looked me in the eyes "—and sounds like the reason many of us are here."

The corner of my lip twitched upward, and I swallowed. My eyes burned at the memory trying to surface, so I focused on scooping flour into a measuring cup.

Anita must have caught on, because she stepped over to the opposite counter and pulled up a playlist. "You like jazz, honey?"

"Hell, yes." I grinned at her and breathed a little easier.

Soon, we immersed ourselves in making pancakes together and listening to Ella Fitzgerald. We alternated between singing along and talking about our favorite jazz standards like "They Can't Take That Away from Me" and "At Last." After we finished up, we brought the food to the table, and Anita smiled at me. "You're ok, Dani. Thanks for helping me this morning."

As she walked out of the room, I stood and gazed at the table set for breakfast. Just like for a big family, at least what I thought a big family table should look like. Sitting at a table with my sister, parents, and our extended family seemed like a lifetime ago. Or maybe more like a dream. The sound of the residents coming down the stairs brought me back to the present, and I forced a smile back to my face.

It didn't take long for me to fall into a rhythm. My mornings were spent helping make breakfast and then going to the garden to help with any watering or weeding that needed to be done before it became too hot outside. My afternoons were spent helping to plan for the big fundraising event and getting to know everyone. My evenings stayed mostly free to do whatever I wanted, but I always made sure to make it for family dinner.

I started to get to know the kids better, and my second week, I was invited to their group meeting to hear their stories in their own words. It was the residents' idea, and since she led the meetings, Mae asked me to come.

After we all sat down, Mae smiled at me.

"So, welcome Dani. Thanks for coming. I know everyone wanted some time to share a little more with you about why they are here." She turned toward the others in the circle. "Who wants to share first?"

Sebastian raised his hand just a little above his knee. I wasn't surprised. I had already started to connect with him over music and poetry.

He rubbed his knees as he spoke.

"Well, I've been here for a while. Longest of anyone to date. My folks kicked me out of the house when I came out as trans. They still refer to me with the wrong pronouns and my deadname. About eight months ago, I stopped trying to reach out. SASH is my true family now. They helped me find a doctor so I could start T, and I've almost finished college because of all their help. They really saved my life."

My stomach tightened at hearing just a taste of what he had been through. "Dang. Thanks for sharing with me, Sebastian."

Kyle cleared his throat and said, "I reckon I'm next." He pushed his long hair behind his ears and then crossed his arms. "I've been here about two months. I lived with my grandparents, and they couldn't handle the fact I'm gay. So here I am. Livin' the dream." He smirked when he finished speaking and looked down at the floor.

I kept my eyes on him for a moment, hoping he would make eye contact. He reminded me of my fifteen-year-old self, with his way of glossing over the most difficult moments with a shrug and a smirk. It's like believing it's possible to float just above the surface of a dark lake. No matter how hard you try, you'll eventually sink down. At least a little, even if it's just to swim out of it.

After adjusting her glasses on her round freckled face, Aimee spoke in a quiet voice. "My parents found a note I'd written to my girlfriend. They wanted to send me to a 'pray the gay away' type place, but I left home and came to SASH instead. I've been here about nine months. I still talk to some of my family, and I'm hoping that one of them will eventually take me in. I keep trying with one of my aunts. We used to be really close before ... well, you know. Anyway, that's me." She pressed her hands into the sides of her chair as she shrugged.

"I hope it works out for you." I tried to offer a smile through the feeling of nausea that had started to creep in.

Ja'Marcus spoke up in his quiet baritone voice. "I guess it's my turn.

My father is a minister, and so is my mother. They have their own church. They're real traditional. Like I mean—" Ja'Marcus stiffened himself up and straightened an imaginary tie, then shook his head and smiled. "Anyway, I started questioning if I was gay, and that was enough right there for them to lose it. But then I had to go and argue about what the Bible does and doesn't say, and well, it didn't end well. So I've been here ... How long have I been here?" He laughed.

"Seven months," Mae answered softly, smiling.

"Yeah, seven months. It's been real helpful. And I got some good counseling and some time to sort through everything to figure out who I really am. It's good."

I smiled at him and nodded.

Lastly, Sarah Beth, a young athletic girl with sandy hair shifted in her chair, looking down. "I was on the soccer team in high school, and I was going into my junior year, voted team captain. Then it all fell apart."

The room grew quiet, and Sarah Beth's face reddened as she swallowed hard and held her arm across her body. I held my breath.

"I fell for a girl in my art class."

Shit. The room felt too small.

"We went for a hike at some falls near our school, and we kissed at the overlook. It was the most amazing feeling—like the most me I had been. But, I didn't know a guy from school was nearby, and he took a picture and showed it to my parents." Sarah Beth clenched her fists.

"My dad said some really shitty things to me, things that still make me want to punch a wall. I was basically homeless for a few weeks before I came here. I've been here a year, and I'll be here 'til I go to college, I guess. I'm just glad I found out about this place when I did, cause I was starting to lose hope. But y'all really helped with that."

I swallowed hard. When I got kicked out of my house, it took a while to find my bearings. One night after waiting tables, I drove back to my old neighborhood by accident. It wasn't until I pulled onto the road where I once lived that I realized what I had done. Somehow I felt the same way just then. Sarah Beth's story hit close to home. Too close.

My eyes stayed on Sara Beth catching her breath and wiping a few tears away as the others looked on and Ja'Marcus held her hand. I had to focus on the people around me, not where I had been.

Mae reached for a tissue box to pass along, then glanced over at me. I looked down for a moment then back up at all the residents.

"Thanks for sharing with me everyone. I mean it. I know how hard it is to trust other people, especially when you've been hurt so deeply like this. It means a lot to me. So, thanks." I gave a half smile and felt my forehead burn.

"Let's call it a day, everybody. Thanks again for being so open. You all are incredible. See you at supper."

Everyone stood up, and I hugged the residents as they left and thanked them again for sharing their stories. Once they were gone, Mae walked over to me.

"Thanks for coming and for listening. I know how much it meant to them. They haven't exactly felt heard outside of SASH."

"Yeah, I got that," I shifted my feet and pushed back my hair.

Mae looked at me for a minute. "Hey, you want to go walk for a bit? We have about thirty minutes 'til supper time."

"Maybe some other time? I don't want to make us feel rushed."

"Well, how about later? I can stay a while longer than I usually do."

I looked back up to make eye contact. I thought about my conversation with my sister and my need to find something to help me not get stuck in my head. "Ok. Yeah, that sounds nice. I think I could use a walk."

"Ok, then. It's a plan."

MAE

Dani's eyes gave it all away. I knew the look well, after working with so many people with difficult stories. I knew that she was affected by what she heard in group. I also had a feeling that the next few weeks were going to be more challenging for her than she had probably imagined.

We headed out the back door just after supper. The sun had started to sink in the sky. After making our way past the garden, we stopped at the edge of an open field, and we rested at a wooden fence, tattered but still sturdy. The barn swallows swooped in wide circles overhead while dragonflies darted and danced nearby.

"So, are you ok?" I asked her. She looked off into the distance, biting her lower lip.

"Yeah, I think so." She leaned against the fence and continued to gaze across the field. "It's just a lot to hear at once. And it reminds me of where I've been. And why I chose to come to SASH this summer."

"Yeah." I sighed and leaned on the fence next to her. "It reminds me of why I'm here, too. Even though it's for different reasons than a lot of people, it's still a painful one. And that pain feels fresh sometimes. Like tonight."

I looked back over at Dani, a question continuing to bubble up to the surface of my mind. *What happened?* I wanted to know what was behind her withdrawing, the mystery behind her emerald eyes. Instead, I bit my lip. I knew better than to push. I also didn't want to say more. It had the power to send me spinning and add to what Dani was already carrying.

"How do you manage?" The lines in her forehead creased as she asked. "I mean the pain, when it feels fresh like this?"

I fixed my eyes on the trees across the pasture for a moment. "I walk. I write. Sometimes, I talk it over with Anita or Rachel. And sometimes I have to get away, go back home for a few days, or at least a weekend." I turned toward her again.

"That all sounds good," she said with a deep breath before she turned to face me. "I think I'm having a hard time figuring out what to do because it's kind of like being on the road for me right now, you know? I'm not home, and I can't retreat to my own space in the same way. But it's also lonelier than the road, 'cause I don't have my crew or my band. I could call my sister, Jen. She's great, actually. But ..."

"It's not the same," I offered. Dani nodded her head, and her hair fell forward, so I couldn't see her eyes for a moment.

She pushed her hair back from her face and held it there with one hand before blowing into the air. "I knew this was going to be hard on me. I just didn't expect it to be this soon or this much." She paused and then slid her hands into her pockets and looked at the ground. "I'm sorry, Mae. I don't mean to unload on you. You carry enough with working at a place like this."

"Hey, don't worry about that. I figured you needed to talk. That's why I asked you to walk with me. It was a hard afternoon." I looked at the sky and took in the changing light. That golden part at the end of a lingering day had always been my favorite time, and the days were starting to get long enough so I could catch it after work.

"Thanks for understanding," she looked at me with a half-smile. "I guess we should head back soon."

I realized I had lost track of time. "Yeah, it's probably a good idea. Follow me, and we'll go around to the other side of the field. It makes a big loop back to the house."

We made our way past a grove of oak trees decorated with Spanish moss, and the air became cooler in their shade. Then we walked along an old fence line, replete with blooming wild blackberries. We continued along for a few more moments before Dani stopped.

"What is it? Are you ok?" I asked her.

"Yeah, but what is that incredible smell?" she laughed.

I laughed, too, and took a few steps to get to the fence line. "Honey-suckle." I pointed out the vines with fragrant yellow and white blossoms. I plucked a couple clusters of flowers and walked back over to Dani. I handed one to her, and she inhaled the scent, closing her eyes.

"That's amazing," she said as she looked it over.

"Well, you should try it." I opened my hand, and she passed the flowers back to me. I stepped right next to her and held a flower up as she watched, her eyebrows sinched together. I pinched the green ball at the end of the flower and drew out the center stem, bringing a small drop of clear liquid to the base.

"What now?" she scratched her cheek and smiled.

"Just a Southern thing," I said as I held the base up to her mouth so she could taste the nectar. She paused a moment and then placed her lips on the blossom.

Her eyes lit up as she tasted it, and she relaxed her face. "That's nice. Thanks." Her breath fell on my hand, and I felt heat rise to my cheeks. I pulled my hand away and handed her more flowers before we stepped back on the path.

We both held honeysuckles to our mouths, enjoying those tiny droplets of sweetness as we strolled a little while longer in the fading evening light.

Soon we came close to the house, and we stopped at the back yard.

"Well, this has been the sweetest—pun intended—walk I have been on." Dani winked at me and then became quiet. "In all seriousness, thank you. I really needed that."

"Of course." I crossed my arms and shifted my feet. "You know? Maybe we can make a habit out of it. At least while you're still getting used to being here."

"Are you sure? I don't want to intrude or take away your time."

"It ain't no nevermind." I responded, and she threw her head back in laughter.

"That must be another Southern thing," she finally said.

"I mean don't worry about it. It's fine." I laughed as I touched her arm.

"Thanks, Mae. I really like that idea. I think it would help."

"Then, it's a plan." I patted her back, and we walked back up to the house.

As I rode my bike home that evening, I drove past a mess of honey-suckles, and when the scent hit my face, I pictured Dani, drinking the nectar from the flower. Her lips close enough to feel her breath on my hand, and me close enough to her to take in the scent of her hair, sandalwood.

I struggled to keep my mind on the road before me. My mind turned from Dani to the summer before with Heather, then back to Dani's warm smile.

When I got inside my house, I turned on some music, and Eva Cassidy's "Time After Time" played as I put pen to paper again, hoping that framing words around my thoughts would offer me some clarity.

FOUR

DANI

Walking with Mae soon became a normal part of my day—my favorite part, not just because it allowed me some time to sort through my thoughts, but more because it eased my loneliness. It had been a long time since anything had the power to break through that haze, and I looked forward to every evening as we made our way through the fields and beneath the trees, getting to know each other a little better.

Then one day, I woke up to a loud roar. I opened my eyes then walked to the window. A curtain across the field, the rain fell in a torrential downpour like I had rarely seen since leaving my home in the Midwest. Instead of going to the garden that morning, I stayed in my room for a bit to work on songwriting. I hummed out a few new lines and jotted them down, then looked out of the window again to see if the rain had eased. I needed it to.

By the afternoon, I looked to see no sign of the rain letting up. Damn.

Knowing I had to do something else to ease my mind, I took out my journal. Everything I had been running from started to creep back in. And that day, *she* had taken up space in my mind again. All of that alone time had opened the door. I wondered what she was doing. If she was in a better headspace. If she missed me like I missed her, or more accurately —I realized as I scratched my pencil across the paper—like I missed the idea of her and the space she once filled.

Late in the day, I moved through the motions of dinner and cleanup, pasting on a smile as I tried to stay present. After everyone had cleared out, I stood in the kitchen a moment alone. I stared out at the gray as it consumed everything in its path.

"You up for a little adventure?"

I turned to see Mae peeking around the corner of the doorway with a smirk and a sparkle of mischief in her eye.

"Sure?" The word slipped out slowly as I wondered what in the world she had in mind. I stood and looked at her a moment and couldn't help but smile and shake my head.

Mae laughed as she crossed the kitchen, took my hand, and led me out the screen door. We dashed through the downpour to the Ranger, and I shivered and gasped from the chill of the rain as I climbed into the passenger seat. Water dripped down Mae's cheek and off her hair as she started the engine and drove us into the monsoon.

We soon reached an old barn with a tin roof, and Mae parked near the doors. She dangled a key in front of her and flashed a sly smile. We made another rain-soaked run for it, and after she opened the padlock, we leaned all of our weight into the oversized door to get it open and then shut again behind us.

A sudden moment of darkness gave way to the light of a lantern Mae held in her hand. I looked up to see rustic beams and a loft area that was accessible by a wooden ladder. As we took a few steps and the light reached further in, I stopped walking and stood with my mouth open as I took it all in.

Where I had expected dust and cobwebs, tapestry rugs decorated a clean wooden floor. Stained glass lanterns dangled above plush vintage furniture, waiting to be lit. A wood-burning stove sat in the middle. *Just like the one I have at home*, I thought as I smiled and took a deep breath.

"This place is amazing," I half-whispered as I turned my head toward Mae.

"It's great, right?" She lit a couple of the colorful lanterns. "Go ahead and make yourself comfortable. I thought we could hide out in here for a while."

I settled down on one of the old armchairs close to the stove, and Mae followed.

"Coffee?" She pointed to a couple of clay mugs and a thermos on a nearby coffee table.

"Yeah, thanks. Seems you thought of everything." I leaned forward.

"I try." She wrinkled her nose as she poured coffee, and I watched her azure eyes, the grace and richness of them striking me as though I was looking into them for the first time. I got lost for a moment, then worried I was staring.

"So, what is this place?" I asked as I forced my eyes away.

"The family that owned the farm before used it for big get-togethers. We used to use it for retreats for other LGBTQ groups who do advocacy work. But it's been a while since we've done anything like that. Now we come out here and have a movie night sometimes. You can see the sheet over there that we use for the screen."

I looked behind me, then turned back around to Mae handing me a mug. My fingers brushed her hand as I took it, and we were quiet for a moment.

"But I come here to think sometimes. Especially if I hear a really heavy story or need some space." She leaned back into her chair.

"I can see it being really good for that." I made eye contact again and sat back, too. "Back in Missouri, where I grew up, I had a treehouse. When I was a kid, it was a place to go to get away from the rain but still be outside." I looked across at the barn wall, my voice becoming quiet. "Then as I got older and more aware of myself, it became a place I could go and be safe from any judgement. My treehouse didn't care if I was socially awkward, or a terrible runner, or if I secretly liked girls. I could go there and write and dream, feel free." I looked back up at Mae. "I know how much spaces like these mean."

"Somehow, I knew you would appreciate it." Her lips curled into a slight smile.

Before I put any thought into it, I reached over and touched her hand, and she caressed my thumb with hers before looking down.

She pulled her hand away. "I can't."

I looked down at the floor and slouched over my mug. "I'm sorry, I didn't mean ..."

"No, it's fine." She tucked her hair behind her ear with one hand and clung to her mug with the other. "I really enjoy talking with you, Dani, and maybe it sounds crazy from my end, but I already feel like maybe I can trust you, but then ..." She sighed and held her head down, pieces of her hair falling forward. "I can get distant and be slow to open up sometimes, more so lately." She took a sip of her coffee and a deep breath. "The end of last summer did a number on me. To be honest, I feel like I'm still coming out of it in some ways."

I still feel that resurfacing feeling, too, since Lauren and I ended things, I thought. I shifted so I could face her better. "Can I ask what happened?"

She leaned her head back against her chair and ran her fingers across the rim of her mug. "Her name was Heather. We were together for about two years. We both had a passion for working toward more justice and equity in the South, and that was exhilarating." She paused and pushed her hair back, resting her hand on her head. "But then things got pretty fucked up, and I eventually lost myself. I changed a lot, pushed everyone but her away, and I even stopped writing, which has always been a big part of me. I wanted things to work, so we kept trying, and we even moved in together. I thought it would be a turning point, but there was a lot of back and forth between things getting better and then becoming hurtful again."

It's amazing—the stories we tell ourselves to make us stay. I had told myself I could save Lauren, show her she was worthy of love, and that somehow that would make me worthy, too.

She bit her lip, and I kept my eyes on her, unable to look away.

"I came home early one day to pack a bag and surprise her with a little getaway. I noticed her car was there, which was strange since she was such a workaholic. Anyway, I walked in to find her kissing another woman." She rubbed the side of her face.

"Shit. That's terrible." The air hung heavy between us, and I didn't know what else to say.

She swallowed and peered down into her mug. "It's just ... I'm still trying to find my bearings, you know? I got really messed up. It broke a piece of me, but thankfully, I had Anita and Rachel to help me put those pieces back together again. I'm still working on it actually." She glanced up at me, and I breathed in.

"I'm glad you have them." My mouth twitched to a weak smile, and I looked into Mae's eyes. There was lead in my stomach as I realized how what she just said sat with me—how important it was for me to keep my distance, and how hard it would be to do. I reminded myself I would only be there a few more weeks. I needed to forget what I had felt.

"I'm sorry. I probably said too much. It's never in-between with me." She tucked her hair behind her ear.

I shook my head as I pulled my legs onto the chair. I didn't want her to see or hear the disappointment I felt. We barely knew each other. Why would I feel it that deeply? I looked up at Mae.

"No, not at all. Actually, it's been a rough year for me, too. I broke up with someone I had been with for about a year. Her name was Lauren. She never loved me as much as I loved her. She couldn't ..." I paused and took a drink of coffee. "Anyway, I pretty much stayed gone after we ended things. I haven't turned down a single booking or chance to be on the road this year, until now." I met her eyes. "Sometimes, it feels like music is the only thing that holds me."

I noticed how quiet it was. The storm had subsided, and we had lost track of time. "Anyway, it's late now. I'm supposed to head up to Birmingham tomorrow with Rachel." I rubbed my temples.

"Yeah, you're right—we should head back," she said as she stood up and stretched.

I stood up, too, and took a step forward to put my mug on the table, and Mae reached her arm around me. "Hey, thanks for listening to me, and for understanding."

"Of course, and thanks for bringing me out here." I put my arm around her, too, in a side hug.

By the time we got back, it was close to midnight. Mae got her helmet from the hallway as I whispered goodnight and crept up the stairs.

I went to my room and lay on the bed. My mind busy, I pulled up a song: Eva Cassidy's "True Colors." I thought of Mae, everything she said and had been through. I looked into the dark of the room, hoping it would help me forget the blue of her eyes and the feeling that had sparked in my heart. When it didn't work, I clicked on my lamp and picked up my guitar and journal. In the quietest of voices and softest of strumming, I wrote out how I felt through a song. It flowed from me as if I had learned it before, and afterward I put my guitar and journal away to look out across the darkness again until sleep had mercy and took over me.

MAE

The day after our late night in the barn, I got to work and Dani and Rachel were still gone from their trip to Birmingham to meet with the SASH Board of Directors.

I walked in and sat my helmet and bag down in the hall, and Anita waved to me from the kitchen counter, drinking a glass of sweet tea and looking over a calendar for the next couple of weeks. I opened the fridge and took out the water pitcher, and when I closed the door, Anita stood right beside me.

"Somebody had a late night," she smirked at me, arms crossed.

"It was nothing." My neck and ears burned.

She raised her eyebrow at me. "Mmmhmmm." We both burst into a fit of laughter.

"Ok, Mae." She shook her head, giggling. "What is going on? You better fill me in."

"Nothing, and that's honest," I shrugged my shoulders and took a sip of water. "I took Dani to the barn last night, and we talked awhile." I looked down and back up at Anita. "Well, actually, I told her a little about Heather."

"For real?" She leaned backward against the counter next to me.

"Yeah, I hadn't planned on it or anything—I just. There's something about her. Somehow I opened up a little more than I have in a long time." I bit my lip.

"Wow. I've noticed y'all getting closer, but you must really feel like you can trust her. It's only been a few months since ..."

"I know," I nearly whispered. I looked Anita in the eye then held my hands over my face. "I also told her because I'm really drawn to her, Anita. But it feels too soon, and she's only here for a few weeks, but more than that I just worry ..." I put my elbows on the counter and leaned onto them, looking down at my feet.

"I know," Anita said.

I clasped my hands together and gave her a small nod. "I basically told her that last night—that I can't let my heart go there. But then I couldn't shake the feeling all the way home that I wish I hadn't've." I paused and looked around the kitchen, then at the clock. "It's about group time."

As I walked away, Anita spoke up. "You know I'm here for you. Always."

"I know. Thanks, friend."

Group proved to be more intense than usual that day. Aimee had heard from an aunt back home that her grandfather had been diagnosed with cancer. We spent time with the grief of the cancer but also the grief of not knowing how to navigate her difficult relationships with her family. With the exception of Kyle, who stayed silent, everybody did a great job at being present and caring, but we found no sense of resolve by the end of our meeting. I spent some extra time with her after group was over, and we talked more about the logistics of her going home for a visit.

After Aimee left the room, I stepped out the door as Kyle hurried past me, pushing me to the side as he hustled down the hall.

"Kyle!" I called him out as I regained my balance.

He murmured a "sorry" and waved his arm as he continued out the front door.

He's still having a hard time adjusting, I thought. *Maybe I should try to talk with him in the next few days.*

My shoulders and chest felt heavy as I thought of the residents. I looked outside a front window.

"It's been too long since I've gotten out of Alabama," I murmured and looked at my phone. It was time to plan a trip back home, so I called my mom, and she answered right away.

"Hey, mom."

"Well, hey there, Mae. How are you?"

I smiled at hearing my mom's voice. "I'm good. You?" I didn't want to worry her, so I kept it simple.

"Well, that's good to hear. Things are good here, too. Just working on another painting. Your dad is out working on a project."

I smiled. "That's great, mom. I'm thinking about coming home in a few weeks, maybe stay about three days."

"Well, just let me know when, and I'll have the little cabin ready."

"That would be great. I'm thinking about the weekend after our benefit show. We still have quite a bit of work to do to be ready for it, and I've been helping Dani get adjusted. You remember I told you Dani Williams was coming for part of the summer?"

Mom laughed, "Of course I do. How could I forget? That's all you talked about for a good couple of weeks."

"Ok, Ok," I said through my own laughter.

"You know, if you wanted to, you could ask Dani to come up, too. There's a fair chance she's never been to the North Georgia mountains."

I responded with a quick nervous laugh. "I don't know. I'll think about it, and I'll let you know." *I do want her to come. But I don't want to send a mixed message, I thought.*

I heard tires on the gravel and glanced out of the window to see Rachel's car heading up the drive. "I have to go, but I'll call you again soon and keep you posted. Love you."

"Love you, Mae."

I hung up the phone and ran my fingers through my hair.

I stepped out onto the porch in time to meet Rachel and Dani at the front steps. They both looked up at me and smiled.

"I guess today went well?" I asked.

"For the most part," Rachel looked at me. "In good news, the board is pretty excited to have Dani here, and we have some new ideas for getting some more support and fundraising. Dani actually had some great ideas, and I think we will pursue one of them."

She looked over at Dani, and Dani shrugged her shoulders and looked down with a sheepish grin.

"Well?" I opened my hand and beckoned for more as I smiled at Dani.

"It's a surprise," Dani winked at me as she walked by.

I shook my head and stayed on the porch to talk with Rachel a few more minutes before she went home.

"So what didn't go well, Rachel?" I could have guessed it before she responded.

"It's The Way again. There were some letters sent to the board of directors. But this time they weren't just from Lenny." She stepped over to the banister.

"What kind of letters?" I took a step toward her, knowing to keep my voice quiet.

She glanced to make sure no one else was around. "They want us to leave the county. They are accusing us of being unsafe for the community and, of course, the residents. Our attorney says they have no reasoning or case, but that if something were to happen to give cause ..." She looked down and closed her eyes.

"Well, we will have to make sure nothing does," I answered. "Besides, maybe Dani being here will help us gain some more support in the community, and we can put The Way in the minority."

"Let's hope so." She gave me a half-smile. "I've got to get home. I'll see you tomorrow, and we'll all talk more about it then." She headed down the steps, and I walked back in the house.

Dani stood in the kitchen, pouring water into a glass. She looked up at me. "You up for going for a walk? I feel like I need to stretch my legs after all that time in the car."

I smiled at her, "Sure. I could use a walk, too, actually."

When we got outside, we noticed Kyle sitting under a tree next to the house.

"You ok?" Dani called to him.

He nodded and waved his hand.

"Hang on a sec, Dani." I walked over to Kyle to get a little closer and squatted down.

"You know, Kyle, there's a lot of us here if you need to talk. You don't have to go it alone." He looked downward as I spoke.

"I got it, Mae. Thanks." He closed his eyes and leaned back against the tree.

I stood back up, and Dani and I made our way toward the garden. We spent several minutes in silence as we got further from the house.

"So—" Dani said in a soft voice "—you think he's ok?"

"I hope so. He wouldn't tell us if he's not." I put my hands into my pockets. I knew better than anyone there that when someone is the most not ok, they probably won't say anything, and you'll still ask yourself over and over again how you managed to miss it.

"How was your day?" Dani asked, pulling me from my thought.

"It was good. Hard …" I sighed. "But still good. How about you? Sounds like it was a successful day at least."

"For sure, just tiring. I was glad to see that everybody on the board is so down-to-earth. But from what I've gotten to know about Rachel, that's not surprising." Dani smiled at me.

I let out a small laugh. "So true."

"The Way …" she looked down. "Sounds like things are getting worse from what I heard today."

"Yeah, that's what Rachel said. Don't let them get to you, Dani."

"I'm trying." She turned the corner of her mouth upward.

We reached the grove of trees and looked up at the hanging Spanish moss—one thing I loved about the Deep South, but in that moment, it made me miss the mountains.

"I talked with my parents today, and I'm thinking about going home for a weekend soon. Maybe the weekend after the benefit show, just to get away from everything." I looked toward Dani.

"That's great. I know you said that helps you." Dani smiled sideways at me, and I stopped walking.

"Well actually, this might sound kind of strange, but my mom wondered if you might like to come, too? She'd really like to meet you and thought you might like to see the mountains. It's about four hours from here. We would take my truck." It slipped out of my mouth before I could stop myself. "I mean, I would like it, too, if you're up for it."

Dani smiled and shook her head. "It's not that strange. And, yeah—I would love that. Count me in."

"It's a plan." I grinned at Dani and looked into her eyes.

We finished out our walk, then I got my helmet and headed back home.

All the way home, I imagined how it would be to bring Dani home to see where I came from, to meet my family, and to have more time to talk with each other. I tried to focus on the road, but I couldn't get the way she looked at me out of my head.

FIVE

DANI

Just as I was starting to feel settled, harsh reality smacked us all in the face.

On a stormy Thursday afternoon, Kyle didn't show up for group. Ja'Marcus checked the room they shared, but there was no sign of him or where he could be. Mae decided to cancel the meeting and look for Kyle around the house. They were still unable to find him, so Mae came to the office where I was talking with Rachel and Anita about the benefit show.

When Mae knocked on the door frame, I turned around and noticed her pale face.

"Hey, we ... um, we can't find Kyle. We've looked all over the house. He's seemed off lately, and I don't ..." Her voice cracked, and she bit her thumbnail.

"We'll help you look." Rachel got out of her chair, and we followed her to the family room. The look in Mae's eyes and the alarm in her voice brought a pulsing feeling of fear through my arms.

Lightning flashed, and Rachel looked out of the window a second then paced as she spoke. "Anita, call Jesse—I know he's off tonight, but we need him here. Mae, you and I will take the Ranger out and check around the property. Dani, you and Anita look closer to the house and near the garden. When Jesse gets here, he can stay with the residents. We meet back here in two hours, unless we find him before—and let's hope we do."

Anita stepped away to call Jesse, and Mae and Rachel hurried out the back door, into the rain.

I watched them disappear into the gray, and Anita touched my shoulder. "Jesse's on his way. Let's go."

The thunder and lightning soon stopped, but the downpour proved relentless.

I sprinted to the garden area with Anita, and we shouted Kyle's name while a stream of water ran down our rain jackets and our faces. I wondered if he could even hear us over the storm. With no sign of him, Anita's eyes widened, and we dashed toward the tree line.

About thirty minutes into our search, Anita's phone rang and her hands trembled as she looked. "It's Rachel."

Anita answered and brought her hand to her mouth as deep lines wrinkled across her forehead, raindrops on her cheeks falling like tears.

She hung up and took off toward the house without a word. I stumbled after, and the knifelike pain of a side stitch stole my breath away. I slipped on the wet grass, and pushed myself back up to run again.

Just as we reached the house, Mae pulled the Ranger near the back door. My ears rang as I looked closer. In the back, Rachel held on to Kyle's limp body, his t-shirt and jeans soaked through while rain dripped from his hair down his ashen face.

I stood and stared as Anita burst through the back door with a first aid kit and pulled out a small box and pressed it against Kyle's leg. Mae stepped away and called 911. "There was a bottle in his hand with a couple more pills inside. We just gave him Narcan. He is barely breathing. Please hurry."

Anita climbed into the back of the Ranger and draped a blanket around Kyle. "Hold on, Kyle. Please just keep breathing."

Mae came back, her voice shaking. "The ambulance is on the way."

Rachel nodded at Mae and clung on to Kyle. "Good, thank you."

She closed her eyes and put her head against Kyle's. "God, please don't let him die, please."

A shiver rattled my arms and shoulders, and I rubbed my eyes. It didn't feel real, yet here I was in the middle of it. The chill of the rain not letting me forget just how real it was.

"Hey," Mae said and touched my arm. I just shook my head to answer her unspoken question. *Are you ok?*

The wail of sirens on their way jolted me, and Mae looked toward the drive. "I'm going to run out and meet the ambulance, so they know where to pull around when they get here." She hurried around the house.

I stepped closer to the Ranger and looked at Kyle. I closed my eyes and silently wondered if I should pray. But the only prayer I knew to pray was with my guitar, and even that was answered with silence most of the time. Instead, I held my arm and watched.

"They're almost here. Hold on, Kyle." Anita touched his shoulder.

Within a few minutes, the ambulance arrived. I stood next to Anita and Mae as paramedics worked on Kyle and lifted him into the ambulance. Rachel climbed inside to ride with him to the hospital, then the three of us went back inside the house.

Anita and Mae talked with the other residents, doing their best to console them. Everyone was upset, but Sarah Beth was especially panicked, so Mae took her to another room to talk.

I walked into the kitchen and poured a glass of water. Jesse and the residents had made dinner and left some out for us, but my stomach turned at the sight and smell of food. I stepped back into the hallway and breathed in for two counts and out for three.

"Any word?" Jesse walked into the hall and asked me.

I just stood there and shook my head, unable to speak. He found Anita, and I tried to ignore the muffled sounds of them talking while I stared out across the darkening landscape. The rain and the coming of nighttime swallowed the gilded fields.

Over the next few hours, Jesse and Anita encouraged the residents to get some sleep while we paced the living room, standing by for more word from Rachel. Mae stayed silent as she stared out of the window. The rain eventually stopped sometime after 2AM, and I went outside to the porch to get some air and sat down at the wicker table. I held my hands over my face and heard someone walking over.

"Are you ok, honey?" Anita touched my shoulder as she walked by me and took a seat.

"I will be." I rubbed my eyes and looked over at Anita and whispered, "Thanks."

Within a few minutes, the screen door cracked open, and Jesse leaned out. "Hey, Anita. Rachel is on the phone. The doctor says Kyle's going to be ok. But you were right—overdose. She wants to talk with you about the plan for the next few days."

Anita sighed and wiped her eyes. "Oh thank goodness. I'm on my way." She got up to go inside.

I strained to push myself up from my seat at the table, and I shuffled over to the banister. The darkness around teemed with crickets and tree frogs, and the occasional hoot of an owl. A light breeze blew in the cooler air that came behind the rain, and I held my arms close to me.

I heard the screen door open and close gently, and I was too tired to turn around to see who was coming outside. A light blanket draped over my shoulders, and I turned my head to see Mae.

"You want to sit down a minute?" She put her hand on my back. I nodded, and we walked over to the porch swing and sat down.

We swung for a few minutes in silence, and I rubbed the space between my eyebrows.

"Dani, he's going to be ok."

"I know, but I just can't shake the feeling that ..." I started, unable to finish, and Mae put her hand on my knee. I looked at her. "Maybe I'm in the way or caused this somehow. Maybe cause I'm here, it made everyone miss it."

"What? You're not in the way, and this has nothing to do with your being here." Mae looked at me with a soft yet steady gaze.

I reached over and pulled one side of my blanket around her shoulders. We sat on the swing in silence for a few minutes, the sound of the chain rattling and groaning from time to time.

"Kyle reminds me of me. Of what happened ..." I held my head down.

Mae touched my hand.

"I used to get pills from people, when my parents kicked me out. I would stay with friends and eat their food, sleep on their couches, and raid their medicine cabinets at night." I shifted and focused on the boards of the porch floor.

Mae leaned her head over on my shoulder. We stayed that way for a while, and after a few minutes, her soft voice broke the silence. "I'm glad you're ok. And so sorry you had to live through that."

I reached for her hand and held on. We stayed in the swing a little longer, and then decided we had better head inside. Everyone had fallen asleep. Some in their rooms, some on the couches and chairs.

Mae walked toward the hall for her helmet.

"What are you doing?" I whispered. "Just stay. It's too late to go home—you have to be too tired to drive home safely."

She shrugged her shoulders. "I don't think there's any room, Dani. Besides, I'll be ok."

"There's one place. Come upstairs with me." I reached for her hand, and we walked upstairs to my room. I flicked on the desk lamp, and quietly shut the door behind us.

I let her borrow some of my clothes to sleep in, and she changed in the bathroom while I put on a sleep shirt and shorts.

As we lay next to each other, I scrolled for a song to help me relax, and I landed on Eva Cassidy's "Over the Rainbow."

Mae looked over at the screen. "Mind if I listen, too? I could use the help to shut off my brain, and I don't think anything could beat Eva's voice."

I pulled the earbuds from the jack and turned down the volume as low as I could so we could still hear, and we listened together.

After the song had ended, I turned off the light, and without a word, we held on to each other as we fell asleep in the deep watches of the night.

～

MAE

I woke up the next morning to Dani setting a mug of coffee on the night-stand next to where I was sleeping. I looked up and rolled on my back so I could see her better as my eyes came into focus. The shimmering light of the morning sun fell across her hair, bringing out the subtle auburns and coppers.

"Hey, good morning." She knelt down and smiled at me. "Most everyone is still asleep. Anita is up and getting some things out to make breakfast. I'm going to change and go help her."

I sat up and took my mug.

"What time is it?"

"It's about eight. Anita talked to Rachel, and she's going to stay at the hospital until Kyle is fully awake, and then Jesse is going to go sit with him a while so Rachel can go home and get some sleep."

I stared off into the distance. The haze from barely sleeping combined with the close call made it hard to think.

Dani touched my back. "Hey, why don't you lie back down? I just couldn't sleep, but if you can, you should. I'm sure you're tired." She reached across me and pushed my hair back behind my ear.

"Ok, I'll try." I rubbed my eyes.

I put my mug back on the nightstand and settled down on the pillow and closed my eyes. I heard Dani get clothes from the closet and go to the bathroom to change. She came back out and pulled the blanket up over my shoulder before she left.

I lay there with my eyes closed, and Dani's face stayed at the front of my mind. *Her closeness felt warm and reassuring,* I thought. *But it's too soon. I have to guard both of our hearts.* I lay there a few more minutes, trying to go back to sleep, but I soon realized it was pointless. I got up and changed back into my clothes from the day before, and picked up my coffee to head downstairs.

When I walked into the kitchen, Anita stood at the stove, frying bacon, and Dani was finishing up with mixing a batter in front of the waffle iron. I walked behind her to get to the coffee pot and put my hand on her back as I passed. I made eye contact with Anita and she raised her eyebrow at me.

I mouthed the words "stop it" and tried to stop smiling. *Thank God for Anita and her sense of humor.*

I emptied the coffee pot into the carafe and ground some fresh beans for the new brew.

"That's the best smell," Dani said.

"You ain't lyin'!" Anita answered, and we all chuckled a little.

Within an hour, the kids started coming downstairs, so we took the food to the big table in the dining room. All around the table, there were yawns and stretches in place of the normal morning hustle and bustle. After a quiet breakfast, we told the residents to take it easy that day and just get some more rest.

I helped clean up and said goodbye to Dani as she went upstairs to shower. Before I went home to freshen up, I talked with Anita to make a plan for processing what had happened. We decided to talk with the residents more at group and let everyone talk over dinner, too.

After we got our plan, Anita closed her notebook and peered at me.

"Ok, now let's talk about last night and where you were," she smirked.

"What? Ok, seriously?" I shook my head. She lifted her brow to give me "the look," and I knew from experience that she was never going to give up.

"Nothing happened. I slept in Dani's room …" My face got hot and stretched into an automatic smile. "I mean we slept in each other's arms. But there was nothing to it. I'm still keeping my distance, or trying to anyway." Trying was the word. I stared off as I thought more about it.

She belly laughed then looked at me with a big grin, but her smile faded and she looked to the side for a minute then back at me. "Are you ok? I mean with what happened with Kyle?"

My throat tightened as I pictured his limp body lying on the ground, being soaked by the rain. Picking him up and lifting him required all the strength Rachel and I could muster. But it wasn't just what happened to him. Memories of what had happened before caused my eyes to sting. Memories I had tried to bury with my work to help others.

I looked at Anita and nodded my head. *I don't have a choice. I have to be ok,* I said to myself.

Anita sighed and touched my hand. "I know it probably brings up …"

"I'll be ok," I whispered. "I know you know where it takes me."

"Of course, I do, and you know I'm right here."

"What about you, Anita? How're you holding up?"

"That was a close call. The closest we've ever had. I just can't shake that image of Kyle lying there soaking wet and breathless. I'm just glad we found him in time."

I touched Anita's hand. "Me, too."

We sat outside together a little while longer. Then, I went in to get my helmet so I could go home to shower and change. As I rode home, the sun peeked through the clouds, shooting little shafts of light down from the sky and across the field.

When I got back, it was time for group. All of the kids talked about their worries—not just for Kyle to get better, but also that they didn't see it coming. That they thought it had just been Kyle being Kyle.

"I know. We all did," was the best answer I could give them. *I missed it, too. Again.*

After group, we all gathered around the table for dinner. It wasn't as noisy as usual, as the residents talked to each other in quieter voices than normal. Dani took a seat next to me, and I scanned her face to gauge how she was. She smiled at me.

I leaned over and said into her ear, "Short walk after supper?"

She whispered back into my ear, "You bet."

Rachel came in soon, and the room got quiet as she sat at the end of the table. She looked at the residents and clasped her hands in front of her face, as if in prayer.

"Everyone in this room has had some time when we've felt alone or scared or helpless. And all of us know what it's like to be judged and to have someone look down their nose at you because of who you are or who you love."

She paused a moment to take a deep breath.

"But we also know what it's like to find family, and we have each other to thank for that. That's why we are here. That's why we will continue to be here. Come hell or high water or overdoses or whatever else." She swallowed then looked at everyone.

"When I started this home, it was because of people like you. People like me. People like Kyle. People who need a place to belong. And all of you are what make the family. Our family. And I'm thankful for all of you. I don't say it enough. And this is what will help Kyle the most right now, sticking together." She took Anita's hand on one side and Sara Beth's on the other, and we all followed, taking each other's hands for a moment.

I clung to Dani's hand, and I hoped she was ok. Her fingers lingered on my hand as we let go.

After dinner, Dani helped with cleanup and then met me outside on the porch to take a walk together.

"What a week. I bet you're glad it's Friday," she said to me with a half-smile.

"Yesss I am actually. How about you? Are you feeling a little better?" I glanced over at her.

"Yeah, I think so. I'm just still tired. I think I just need to breathe." She put her hands in her pockets.

I watched her walk with her head hanging down and pushed her hair behind one ear. The rosy light of the setting sun met the outline of her face, caressing the edge of her cheek with light and warmth. I could hardly bear to look away.

After we came back to the house, I picked up my helmet and toyed with the chin strap. "How would you like to go on a ride with me this weekend and get out of here for a little bit? Maybe tomorrow morning?"

"Um, on your motorcycle?" She scratched her head and wrinkled her nose. I nodded and laughed.

"Ok. Sure." Her eyes sparkled as her mouth turned upward in her sideways grin.

"I'll pick you up at eight," I said, winking as I walked out the door and headed home.

SIX

DANI

I tossed and turned much of the night, as I imagined going for a ride with Mae. My chest got light as I thought about holding on to her, but then my stomach wrenched at the idea of speeding down the road without the safety of being enclosed like in a car. When I woke up the next morning, I heard the steady drum of rain on the tin roof. I sighed and rolled over in the bed and grabbed my phone off the nightstand. I sent Mae a message, "Guess we will have to rethink that plan for today."

She answered right away. "Let's give it an hour to clear up. If it doesn't, then I can just drive my truck over. We can go park somewhere and listen to the sound of the rain. Cool?"

I smiled as I read the words, and sent back a simple "cool."

The rain kept its steady rhythm, so mid-morning, Mae came around the front of the house in her pickup, an old Ford that ran like it was brand new. The light green body bore only small areas of surface rust.

Mae leaned over and unlocked my door. I climbed inside onto the bench seat.

"Wow, this is nice." I touched the upholstery on the seat and noticed the new flooring.

"Thanks, I did a lot of the work with my mom and dad. It was definitely a labor of love." She smiled at me, and her damp hair brushed her bare shoulders, next to the wide straps of her tank.

I shook my head. "That's impressive."

"Thanks." She bit her lip and put her hands on the steering wheel. "You ready?"

"Yeah, where are you taking me?" I laughed.

"You'll see." She winked as she pulled out of the drive and onto the road as Joni Mitchell's groundbreaking album *Blue* played in the background.

We cruised down the main stretch of highway along tall pines as Mae's hands kept time on the steering wheel, and water droplets gathered and marched across the windshield. Soon Mae turned down a side road flanked with woods. As my eyes were drawn to the trees, I thought about the evergreens near my house back in Oregon. I missed the northwestern conifers, the droopy deodar branches and the varied cones of the atlas that all surrounded my home.

The fog from the rain filled the space between the trees and the road, and I couldn't make out what was up ahead until Mae steered the truck onto gravel and a vast lake came into view, surrounded by dense forest.

She parked near the shore, facing the lake so we could watch the rain fall upon the water.

The air had cooled down, and we cracked the windows to let it in. We sat like stones as we listened.

The water tapped on the roof and hood of the truck and scattered down the branches of nearby trees. I breathed in deep, watching the droplets dance across the lake, splashing as water met water. The rhythm reminded me of a folk song, peaceful and loving with ribbons of joy.

After a little while, the rain slowed down, and faint gray mist lifted off the lake as thousands of ripples blanketed the surface. The cycle of falling and rising again had become my sense of stability, especially when I felt myself falling like in the past year. In the distance an old bridge connected groves of pine trees, and I could make out small fishing docks and what I imagined was a small camping area.

I looked over at Mae. "It's so serene here."

The corner of her mouth twitched upward, and she leaned her head over against the back window as she turned toward me.

"Dani, I wanted to talk to you again. Alone for a while."

I shifted in the seat to face her. "Is everything ok?" Unable to hold my gaze, I looked down at my thumb nail and picked at the skin around it.

"Yeah—you seem nervous. Are you alright?" She reached over and touched my hand, her thumb grazing across the back of my fingers. I pulled my hand away and pushed my hair back behind my ears. The back of my neck burned, and I glanced up for just a second before looking down again.

"Yeah, I guess I am. I'm kind of worried. That maybe I told you too much?" I shot a look at her and lowered my eyes again. If there was one part of my past I was ashamed of, it's what I told her about the pills. Still, it was the easiest dark piece to share in some ways. It didn't have the power to pierce my heart like everything else.

"What do you mean?" She drew her legs up onto the seat.

"About my past. I haven't talked about any of it in a long time, and being here just a few weeks has already brought it all rushing back." I paused and looked at her eyes.

"I'm not afraid of where you've been. I think it just made me feel closer to you, you know?" She kept her eyes on mine.

"I don't know exactly why, because we haven't known each other long at all, but I trust you." I shrugged and looked out across the lake. "I know I'm deep and intense. More than once, that's frightened people away from me, and I just don't want that to happen again. Not now." I bit my thumbnail and looked at Mae.

"I know you said your heart was broken recently, and I know what you said about it being a while ... but I'm really drawn to you." My voice fell to a whisper, "It's getting harder to keep my distance."

"I know. That's why I wanted to talk to you." She paused and looked down and started playing with her wrist wrap. "If I'm honest, it's getting harder for me, too."

The rain picked up pace, and the chorus of its decent accentuated the quickening of my heart.

I swallowed and thought back to the song I had just written. For her. "Would you want to hear a new song I've been working on?" The words came out before I could stop them.

"Of course I would." Her eyes lit up, and warmth spread across my face.

I pulled out my phone and brought up the recording I had done in my room a few days before:

Please tell me you're lyin'
That what you say isn't true
Put my hand in your hands
And surround me in blue

Just let me down easy
And hold my heart above sea
Or let the love in between us
Plunge us deeper than deep

And I hate that I'm fragile
It makes me feel like a child
But you completely undo me
Can you please hold me for awhile?

Please tell me you need me
And that you want me too
Put your hand in my hands
And let me take care of you

Or let me down easy
Just show your true heart to me
And let the love in between us
Keep us closer than keep

And I see that you're fragile
You hate to feel like a child

There's pain behind your sapphires
Can I hold you for awhile?

Let the love in between us
Plunge us deeper than deep
Let the love in between us
Keep us closer than keep

Let us together
Tell of love in the quiet
And let us down softly
My darling

When the last note of my guitar had faded out, only the rain moved, and its thrum rose above the quiet to let me know that time had not stopped.

"Dani, that was gorgeous. I ..." She closed her eyes a second and drew in a slow breath. "I've felt so closed off the past few months, with everything that happened with Heather. But then I met you, and I'm opening up in ways that scare me and comfort me all at once. Sometimes I don't know what to do with how I feel, but you keep drawing me in somehow. Like I'm getting caught up in a whirlwind or wrapped up in a warm embrace, or maybe both at once." Her hair fell in front of her face.

I pushed her hair back behind her ear, and I looked into her eyes. "I don't know what's happening between us exactly, but I also don't want to push it away. I really like you. Southern accent and all." I smiled.

She snickered and shook her head. Then she lifted her hand to my cheek and took a deep breath. "I don't want to push it away either."

She held my face as her lips met mine, and I touched her hair. The scent of myrrh in her hair, the softness of her lips, and the taste of vanilla and chai on her mouth chorused connection I had longed for.

As we embraced each other, I disregarded the passage of time, and nothing else could fit into my mind. I don't know how much time went by before we stopped and rested our heads together for a moment, and I pressed my fingertips against hers. We held each other and watched the downpour for a while longer as Mae ran her fingers through my hair.

When the rain slowed to a near stop, we realized it was time to head back, and we held hands as Mae drove along the backroads. The sun pierced the cloud cover, and splatters of gold struck across the puddles and through dripping wet leaves.

Mae drove up to SASH, and she kissed my hand and gazed at me a moment. "See you soon."

"Yeah, soon." I winked at her as I opened my door.

I got out of her truck and waved goodbye, and I wondered if everything had really happened or if I was dreaming.

MAE

The next Monday, I was in the SASH kitchen, chopping vegetables for dinner when Anita came in and poured a glass of sweet tea.

"So what's new, honey?" She looked over at me.

My face flashed with heat, and I smiled at her. She laughed, "Lord have mercy. What are you grinning about?"

"Well, I took Dani out by the lake so we could listen to the rain and talk." I smiled at her then set my eyes on the cutting board. "I know I thought it might be too soon after the hell I had with Heather, but ... there's something special there."

"Go on."

I looked up again at her. "I've tried to hold myself back, but ever since we talked in the barn that night, I've had a harder and harder time keeping my distance. I kissed her, and it was so nice, Anita. I mean—not just the kissing. I don't know how to explain the connection I feel with her."

"I think that sounds pretty good." Anita smiled at me. "You deserve something nice for a change." She paused and took a drink of her tea. "Have you told Rachel yet? I think she'd be pretty happy for you, too, and she could use some good news."

I leaned my hands onto the counter. "I know. Not yet. I haven't gotten to talk to her much about anything since what went down with Kyle. But you're right. I'm sure she could use something lighter."

"Well, then go ahead. She's in her office. I'll take over here. And if you wanted to tell me more about that nice kissing, you know where to find me." She laughed as she picked up where I left off. I wiped off my hands and shook my head, chuckling under my breath as I left the kitchen.

I knocked on the door frame of Rachel's office, and she looked up from her desk. "Hey there, Mae."

"Do you have a minute? I was hoping to chat for a little bit if you have time." I stood with my hands in my back pockets.

"Of course. Come on in." I stepped inside and shut the door before sitting down across from her.

"Is everything ok?" She looked at me and leaned back in her chair.

"Yeah, it's great, actually." I shifted in my seat. "I just wanted to share something with you. I've been getting pretty close to Dani. You've probably noticed that with all the time we've been spending together."

"I have noticed." She tilted her head and smiled sideways at me.

I smiled in response then looked down. "I know it's only been a few months since Heather left. And I know how lost I was for a long time. But there's something really special there. Something I can't ignore or make go away. Believe me, I've tried."

I still didn't trust myself. I knew that. I hoped it didn't show to anyone else. But maybe if Rachel and Anita trusted me and if they trusted Dani, that could somehow help me trust again. I looked at Rachel, waiting for what she might say.

She leaned forward, her arms across her desk. "Mae, do you realize how far you've come since things ended with Heather?"

I looked down, not knowing what to say.

"Can I speak to you as a friend?"

I nodded and rested my elbows on my knees.

"I've known you for a while now. I've seen you high and low, and I've seen you thrive and be broken. The last two years, I saw you almost lose yourself, but now you're coming back into your own. I know it's seems recent, but if you think about it, that relationship was really over a long time ago. It just got drug out for a while."

"Yeah, that's the truth." And an understatement.

"You have to learn to trust yourself again, and maybe this is the step you need to get there."

She always sees it.

"Thank you, Rachel. You know that means the world to me." I stood up and hugged her before I left her office.

Later in the week, Kyle was released from the hospital. The day after he got back, Dani asked Kyle to take a walk with her. I stood in the kitchen, working on dinner, and I looked out of the window in time to see her touch the back of his shoulder. Then, Kyle hugged her.

After they came back inside, I waited for Dani as she came around the corner to start up the stairs.

She looked down as she shuffled across the floor. I stepped toward her and touched her hand. "Hey, I saw you talking with Kyle. I could imagine what you said. Thank you."

I hugged her, and her arms tightened around my back. "I don't know how you do this work every day."

I held her a little tighter and touched her hair. "I know. Sometimes I don't either." We held on for a few more seconds, and then we locked eyes.

"I think I just need a breather." She rubbed the back of her head.

"Well, how about a second attempt for a ride? Sunday morning is supposed to be nice. We might could go then if you're up for it."

She looked at me with her crooked smile. "Sure."

In the grey of early Sunday morning, I pulled in front of the house. Dani sat on the steps of the porch, bouncing her knees and fidgeting her hands. She stood up and walked toward me, looking around.

"Are you nervous?" I took a step toward her and handed her a helmet.

"Yeah, I've never been on a motorcycle before." She laughed.

"It's ok," I said as I pushed her hair out of the way and helped with her helmet. "Just hold on to me, and I'll take it really easy. I'm not into death defying antics."

We both laughed, and her shoulders relaxed. I put my helmet back on, and we got on the bike. Dani put her arms around me, and I started the engine. Her grip tightened, and I rested one of my hands over hers just for a second before we started off. As we neared the end of the driveway to turn on the main road, I felt Dani's body shift just a little closer to mine.

We drove through the countryside, making our way through stands of trees and farmland. We stopped at the lake for a while. We sat on the shore and watched the sky turn to rose, the lake reflecting the sun clearing over the trees.

Dani looked around. "This place is just … You know, I didn't expect to find so much beauty here." She hesitated and brushed her fingers on my hand.

I turned my head and looked at her, then Dani drew me in and kissed me.

Once the sun was up, we got back on the bike, and I took us along some of the newly sown fields of cotton. The cool morning breeze made the gentle ride even more pleasant. I turned us around and looped back toward SASH, but then pulled over on the side of the road and stopped the engine. I didn't want the morning to end.

"Would you want to go back to my place for a bit?"

"Are you sure?"

"I wouldn't ask if I wasn't." I laughed.

"Ok, let's go."

I started the bike back up and took off toward home.

Within a few minutes, we got to my small cottage, the black eyed Susans and Shasta daisies outlining the front perimeter in full bloom.

I shook out my hair and grinned at her. "Well? What did you think?"

"Well, it wasn't as scary as I thought it would be." Dani smirked at me and I raised my eyebrow at her.

"Ok, it was pretty nice," she conceded.

We headed inside, and I set my keys and helmet on the side table by my door and took Dani's helmet. "Well, this is home for me."

Dani looked around the room. "It's cozy. I like it."

"Would you like the grand tour?" My butler voice was terrible at best.

"Why yes ma'am." Dani's attempt at a southern accent was even worse, and we both laughed.

I showed her the kitchen, the living room, the guest room, my room, and the back porch—which I had turned into a sunroom with screened windows. We stood there a moment and looked across my back yard.

"Is that a brick oven?" Dani pointed.

"Yeah, it is."

"Let me guess. You made that." Her green eyes lit up as she waited for a response.

"Yeah, I did." I tucked my hair behind my ears, and Dani smiled at me.

We came back inside, and I turned on a Natalie Merchant album and lit some incense. I poured us some glasses of water, and we sat on the couch.

"You about ready for the benefit show?" I asked her.

"Yeah, I think so." She looked down into her water. "I'm glad things have calmed back down so I can focus on it better in the next week."

"Good." I smiled at her.

We sat in silence again for a couple of minutes, listening to the music. "Have you written anything lately?" Dani asked.

"Just some poems and some free writing. I try to get something down on paper every day."

"Can I hear something?"

I bit my lip and pulled out my poetry notebook.

"It was an early summer evening when
She took the nectar from my hand.
Her lips delicately close to my fingers,
As I breathed in and out again.
Didn't know just where we were walking with
My fingers close to her hand
While she continually filled my senses,
As I breathed in and out again."

I closed my notebook, and Dani smiled at me.

She touched my cheek, and our lips met as the incense burned and Natalie sang in the background.

I lost myself as my kisses traveled down to her neck and her breath felt hot on my ear. We paused, and I put my head against hers.

"I think we should slow down. Take it easy with both our hearts," I whispered.

"Of course," she said softly and ran her fingers through my hair. "Let's just take things slow."

We held each other a while and spent the afternoon together before I took her back to SASH. As I rode back home, I replayed the day in my mind, feeling light and easy for the first time since, well, I don't even know how long it had been.

SEVEN

DANI

A week before the benefit show, I found myself walking into a place I had carefully avoided for years: a church. It had been five years since I had been inside one, and even then, it was only for a wedding rehearsal. Rachel stood beside me and opened the great red wooden door of Open Hearts Church. I carried my guitar case in and took a deep breath as the last words I heard from my father threatened to surface again.

"Hey, Dani! I'm Lara." Lara smiled as she walked up to me with her hand outstretched. Normally, I wouldn't trust anyone in a clerical collar, but maybe because she was Rachel's fiancée, I shook her hand and smiled back.

"Well, seems like I don't need to introduce you," Rachel smiled at us then walked over and kissed Lara. I looked down the hallway, half-expecting someone to kick us all out or lightning to strike.

Lara led us into the sanctuary, where I could rehearse for the show.

"We'll be outside, but if it rains, we'll have to move everything in here." Rachel said as we stopped halfway down the aisle.

I worked hard to focus on what she said, willing my mind back to the present.

"Well, I need to go back to SASH for a bit. Dani, whatever you need, Lara should be able to help you get it. We seriously can't thank you enough."

I gave Rachel a half-smile. "It's nothing. I'm happy to help."

Lara walked Rachel out as I made my way to the stage and sat down on the steps to tune my guitar. The neck of my guitar in my hand and the vibration of the strings welcomed me like an old friend who showed up right after a big disaster. I played a few chords to a song I had planned to use for the show, and Lara walked back toward the stage, smiling.

"Want a cup of coffee?"

"I'd love one." I set my guitar down and followed her back out of the sanctuary and over to her office.

"So, I noticed you seem pretty uncomfortable." The corner of her mouth twitched upward as she handed me a mug. "Cream or sugar?"

"No, I like it black, thanks. Is it that obvious?" I stared into my mug. "I haven't been inside a church for a really long time. I've made sure I haven't." I sipped my coffee. "No offense."

She shook her head. "None taken. I'd honestly be surprised if you didn't feel that way. The Church hasn't exactly been a beacon of welcome and kindness for people like us."

"You can say that again." Those words started creeping back, the ones that were yelled just as I left.

"So, I guess you are probably wondering how someone like us would wind up here?" Lara's voice cut through the memory.

"I'm sorry, what?" I pinched my forehead just above the bridge of my nose.

"You want to sit down for a minute?" She held her hand toward a chair, and I sat down as she took the other seat.

I looked at the wall and surveyed the image of a serene mountain scene, a picture of Christ the Redeemer of Rio de Janeiro under renovation, and the last picture: a collage of many faces, which together made the face of Jesus.

"It can be disarming. Places like this when you've never been in one.

This church has always been a bit different. Back in the 60s, Open Hearts integrated before the rest of the South, and it didn't go over so well with everyone around here. The church got firebombed once, when no one was here, thankfully. But it did a lot of damage to the sanctuary, and took several years to get it into good shape again from what I understand. Then back in the 90s, the congregation became what's called open and affirming, meaning they welcomed folks like us to come, just as we are." She turned to face me better and leaned back in her chair.

"Disarming is right. That's hard to wrap my mind around. Pretty much the opposite of how it was for me." I took another sip of my coffee and looked at Lara. "My mom and dad were really involved in church. My mom did a lot of the music. That's what got me into singing, actually. My dad was a deacon, and he taught a Sunday school class." I fixed my eye on the image of Christ the Redeemer, surrounded by scaffolding that contrasted the natural wonder where the statue resides.

I went on. "I grew up believing, then I had a lot of questions starting in middle school. But no one seemed to want to give me space to ask. Anyway, when I was a senior in high school, I came out to my parents, and got kicked out of the house. My mom eventually came around a few years later, but my dad never has. He made sure to throw God in there when he berated me, so you can imagine ..."

Lara's forehead creased as she looked at me. "That's terrible, Dani. This book has held a lot of things." She lifted a Bible off her desk. "Stories, metaphor, hope, history. It's been held by a lot of people with a lot of different intentions. Some good, and some harmful. It's been used as a weapon to keep women in the shadows, people of color in literal chains, and people like us in the closet." She looked up at me, and I nodded at her silently.

"But they all miss what this book, or collection of writings, really is most about. It's mostly about love—that we were created to be loved and to love. When I read it, I see all kinds of problems, and humans showing up in the worst ways possible, but over and over God shows up somehow and speaks love and peace and reconciliation. I don't take this book literally, but I believe in the theme, this great love story between creator and humanity. And I believe that using this book to do harm, like what happened to you, is super fucked up." She chuckled, and I choked a little on my coffee.

"You're welcome here. Just as you are." Lara wrinkled her nose, and her eyes met mine.

I spent the day checking out the sound equipment the church had and testing a few different set ups. Once I found the right one, I ran through a few songs so I could hear what they would sound like amplified in the church space.

Hearing a song you wrote ring out in an echoing space feels surreal the first few times you experience it. During every sound check of my first tour, when my guitar and voice reverberated with the same words and chords I had hammered out alone in my room, it gave me the sense that even though I felt tiny in that moment, something bigger than me was coming from within. That's the only way I know how to describe it. Somewhere along the way in my career, that sense of awe faded like the end of a song when the chorus keeps going, but you cease to hear it as the sound gets quieter and quieter. But for whatever reason, standing in Open Hearts Church and hearing my songs ring out over the pews, I felt that way again.

That evening, Mae stayed quiet as we strolled along the grassy path and I recounted my conversation with Lara. I stopped walking for a moment and looked up at the sky taking on the color of peaches.

"What are you thinking about?" Mae looked up, too.

"That this whole experience has surprised me in all kinds of ways, including today. It makes me wonder what's next. And how it makes me feel—like I'm being stretched somehow and held at the same time."

Mae drew the side of her mouth upward and took my hand as we walked back toward the house.

When I went to bed that night, I had a hard time falling asleep as I ruminated on a few words. I pulled out my notebook and scratched out what I thought might be a line for a new song.

"It's love that holds us."

As I read back the words, I hoped they were true.

❦

MAE

Sometimes opportunity holds a tandem challenge meant to grow and stretch you. Like the opportunity to join a tennis team or to hold a leadership position for an organization you care about. The benefit show was that kind of opportunity. It held the chance for us to gain some more financial support for SASH, but it also challenged us to do what we could to garner more support in the hearts of the people who lived in our area—something we rarely had the platform to do.

We all sensed it, so we all worked our asses off to get ready for it. Anita and Sebastian practiced songs they planned to sing. Kyle, Aimee, Sara Beth, and Ja'Marcus worked on painting a backdrop and gathering props for decorating the stage while I worked with Jesse on getting the sound and lighting ready. Dani and Rachel teamed up to create the order for the program, and Rachel practiced a quick speech in front of Anita and me.

Midweek, I stood in the kitchen doing dinner prep and looked out of the window to see Dani playing badminton with the residents. Even Kyle looked happy. As I took in the grins and the laughter, I wished it could last.

Anita's raised voice startled me out of my thoughts. "What on God's green earth is this?!"

I hurried to the living room just as Anita turned up the volume on the TV so we could better hear the local news. The reporter read a letter from a concerned citizen of our community. I put my hand over my mouth as the list of concerns appeared on the screen: "neglect, overdose, near death, dangerous, promotes homosexuality and deviant lifestyles." The author wished to remain anonymous.

Dani walked in for some water just as the camera cut to a man with short spiky hair and tattoos, someone we all knew too well: Lenny Phillips, the lead pastor of the The Way.

"I've been saying for years that this South Alabama so called Safe Home is a danger to the public. Now here we have this perfect example of just how dangerous they are for those poor kids subject to their brainwashing and shameful promotion of a gay lifestyle." Lenny sneered as he spoke into the reporter's mic.

"Dammit," Rachel whispered behind me. "Nobody speak a word of this to Kyle. He's been through enough."

"We can't hide it from him forever, Rachel." I rubbed my temples.

"I know. Just not tonight, ok?"

I nodded my head.

As the story ended, Rachel paced the floor. "I don't know how they could have known.

Unless …"

"Unless it's somebody who works at the hospital. They know who you are." I put my hands on my forehead and sighed, "Shit."

Anita marched over to Rachel and pointed toward the tv. "You know that some of those anchors and reporters are part of The Way, too. They know we're having our benefit next week, and they saw an opportunity to sabotage it. To sabotage us. Just like they've wanted to for years."

"So that's The Way, and the pastor who leads it?" Dani asked the room.

"It's a hot mess is what it is." Anita's eyes blazed as she crossed her arms.

I sighed and answered Dani. "Unfortunately, yes."

Rachel sat down on the edge of a chair and rubbed her temples. "He's the one who wrote those letters to the board, heckles our events, and writes the long editorials in the paper about how what we really should offer is what he calls a 'reparative program to bring people out of the destructive homosexual lifestyle.'"

Anita walked over to the window and looked outside. "Their membership is large in the community, and their logo is all over town, on signs in front of people's yards and stickers on their cars."

Dani stared at the rug on the floor, and then looked at me, her face chalky white. "How do you fight that?"

"I'm going to call Lara," Rachel stood up and walked toward her office. "A reporter from another station is a member at her church. Maybe we can get another spin on things."

Dani shuffled her feet. "I'm going to go back outside, before any of the residents come in, too, and catch onto what's going on."

I nodded my head at Dani, and Anita gave her a weak smile. "That's the best thing you can do right now, Dani. Thank you."

A little while later, Rachel emerged from her office. "Ok, I'm going to Open Hearts tomorrow for a quick interview. What's out there is out there, but maybe we can do a little damage control."

The next night, Rachel's interview played on the tv sets across our community. She talked about why she started the home and shared some of the work we do to help the kids who come to stay with us. Lara also spoke with a very different angle as a minister to try to counter some of what Lenny had said.

As the story ended, Rachel looked outside the window at the residents sitting on the porch. "Now we wait. Is Kyle ok?"

"Yeah, I talked to him earlier. He's ok." I looked at Rachel and waited for her to make eye contact with me. "I think what you said was great, Rachel. For what it's worth."

She bit her lip and held her arms close. "I hope so. I just hope it was great enough."

That night, Dani and I took my truck out into one of the pastures at SASH so we could look at the stars and escape all of the chaos for a little while. As we lay in the bed of the truck, I touched her hand. "How are you holding up?"

"I'm scared shitless," Dani said through a small laugh. "I keep thinking about what Kyle has been going through, and all the hells so many of you have walked through. I think of me as a teenager, alone. Which makes me think of all those kids out there now who need hope. That helps to keep me going. Plus, I remember I'm only here for a few more weeks, just til the end of June."

My stomach dropped at the thought of her leaving soon, something we hadn't brought ourselves to talk about. I pushed it away again, needing to focus on the present.

"I get scared, too, Dani." I said softly. "We all do. I've lived in the South all of my life, and I still haven't built any immunity to the level of vitriol thrown our way."

"How do you stand it?" she asked, turning toward me.

"I don't know. I guess I've just had to." Then, we were silent for a while.

"Mae?" Her voice cut through the quiet.

"Yeah?" I turned toward her.

"Would you ever leave here? And go someplace that's a little kinder?"

I thought for a moment about how invested I was in helping other kids in the South who needed it most, just like *her*—my reason for doing the work, and how I wanted to stay somewhat close to my family. Then I thought of how much I wanted to build my own life with someone, maybe someone like Dani. "I don't know," I answered as honestly as I could.

"It's ok," Dani said quietly. "Let's not talk about that tonight."

She leaned over me and put her lips on my forehead, and softly kissed my eyes before landing on my lips.

We lay together there under the great expanse of beautiful and mysterious blackness dotted by white stars shining down, our hands together as we faced the night.

EIGHT

DANI

T hough the attacks from The Way frightened me and threatened to send me back to my hardest moments, I couldn't let Rachel or anyone else at SASH down. After all, I didn't think I was walking into a charmed land of acceptance when I signed up to help. I knew it would be hard, and I knew it would cost me something. I just hoped I had the strength to pay it.

I had left the Midwest for Oregon in my early twenties so I could build my life somewhere more open-minded, somewhere that would be the opposite of what my dad was, and seeing the closed-mindedness of The Way reminded me of why I made that decision in the first place. And it made me ready more than ever to go back home to Oregon. Well, almost ready. There was still Mae, and I knew a vast country would soon fill the space between us.

The night before the event, we all gathered at Open Hearts Church for a practice run and dinner. We worked out a few transition problems and changed the order of a couple things, but other than that, it went great.

Rachel stood and watched us for a while then asked us all to have a seat.

"I want to thank you all for the hard work you've done. Of course we hope this event will help us increase our support and our ability to grow and help more people. But I want to encourage you all to remember that this isn't just about getting more support for SASH—it's also about bringing some visibility and validation to other people who might feel alone, forgotten, or hated, like so many of us have. If anything has been made clear in the past week, it's just how much places like this are needed. So, thank you. Now please, eat and just relax the rest of the night. Tomorrow is going to be great."

She smiled at us all and motioned for us all to follow. We all moved to another room in the church with a small kitchen and a large area with tables and chairs set up for us. For a while, we ate and laughed together, resting in the moment, and it reminded me of the many greenrooms I had been in, waiting for one of my shows to start. Only this one didn't feel so lonely.

After dinner, Lara pulled me aside. "Hey, are you ok? A lot has happened in the past couple of weeks. I just wanted to make sure you're fine, especially after our talk in my office."

My eyes stayed focused on the carpet of the hallway. "Yeah, I'm ok. It's definitely not been easy, though. That's for sure."

The truth was too much. Lenny Phillips and my dad had a lot in common: from riding a Harley to disparaging people for being gay to keeping me awake at night and reminding me how hollow I could feel inside, like the empty church we were walking out of.

She put her hand on my shoulder. "I know there's a lot of hate and pain in the air, but I am praying that the gentle whispers of love will drown those out. Especially inside your heart, and in all of our hearts for that matter."

I stopped at the door and stared at Lara a minute. I didn't know how to respond to those words that seemed too easy. Words I needed a long time before that night, back when I was seventeen.

I nodded at Lara, and she stood in the doorway as I walked out.

When I came outside, I took a deep breath and found Mae writing in her journal, waiting to give me a ride back to SASH. The sky revealed the muted tones of dusk, and the fireflies glowed in a nearby field. A breeze whipped through and tousled our hair.

"You doing ok?"

"Yeah, I am. I think so anyway."

"Well I hope so," she leaned over and kissed me.

We walked to her bike, my hand in hers. My legs felt shaky underneath. It wasn't uncommon for her to still give me butterflies, but that night, the feeling swelled with more intensity than usual. I realized as I climbed onto the back of the bike and put my arms around her that there was more on my mind I needed to say.

I leaned in closer before she could get the bike started.

"Hey... can we go somewhere? Somewhere quiet so we can talk?" I asked.

"Of course," she said. "Want to go sit on my back porch?"

"Yeah, that would be perfect." I braced myself as she started the bike.

On our way to her house, we drove by the lake, and the shoreline stones reflected the glow of the moon next to black water. I turned my eyes toward the stars, the night sky holding the memory of where I had been.

When we got to her house, we went inside and put our helmets down. Mae opened her windows and made tea, then we stepped outside to the back porch.

She sat down beside me on the loveseat, and turned toward me. "So what's going on, Dani?"

"I've been feeling nervous, and I'm not sure why exactly," I began quietly. "But I was just thinking about how the event is already here, and that means I'll be going home with you soon. Don't get me wrong, I'm excited about it, but ..." I pushed my hair back out of my face. "I haven't said a whole lot about what happened with Lauren, the woman I mentioned to you before."

"Yeah, I remember." Mae's voice was soft.

"Things were going really great between us, and we were talking about moving in together. But she wanted me to meet her parents, something she had avoided for a long time. She didn't really accept herself. But she loved me, and I loved her, and I thought that was enough. Anyway, I went home with her, and that was the beginning of realizing it wasn't enough."

That my love wasn't enough either. *That I wasn't enough.*

"What went wrong?" Sincerity and softness flooded Mae's eyes.

"It's hard to say, to be honest. Her family was actually pretty accepting and welcoming of me. But Lauren still assumed the worst because they hadn't always been accepting of her." I shook my head and looked down. "Once we got back, all of her self-hatred for being gay got worse. She was so tortured that she would throw off all her covers from the bed every night with all her tossing and turning. Every day I came over, I put them back on her bed. I tried to convince her to find some help and talk to someone—like a therapist or something, but she wouldn't. I felt like she despised being with me, and like she hated this part of us that I had come to see as beautiful. We had to end it, even though I still loved her."

Mae touched my hand.

"I know you are nothing like her. And I know your family is great from what you've said, and I really want to meet them and to have this time alone together before I have to go back ... but I'm so afraid of what might happen. I'm afraid I've missed something, that this is too good to be true. I'm afraid of what the distance will do when I leave."

I gazed into her eyes. "I'm trying to take it slow, but I also feel like I'm falling in love with you, Mae."

She put down her mug and embraced me. She held me there for a few moments and then kissed me long and slow before wrapping her arms around me again as I put my head on her shoulder. We stayed that way deep into the night, falling asleep in each other's arms. We woke to feel the cool dampness in the air, then we moved inside and held each other until morning.

∾

MAE

As soon as we woke up, we headed to SASH so we could have breakfast with everyone and talk through our plan for the day and the benefit that night. Anita raised her eyebrow at me when we walked in the door. I bit my lip as heat rose to my face.

She pulled me aside after Dani headed upstairs. "Ok, Mae Tucker, what's going on?" She laughed and crossed her arms.

I couldn't help but smile back at her. "Are you my chaperone now?"

"Ha! If I need to be!" She lowered her voice, "Do I need to be?"

"Hell, no." I shook my head at her. "We went back to my place and talked last night, and it just got super late."

"So, if my math is correct, that's your second overnight. What happened to taking it easy? You do know she's leaving soon, right?"

"I know. I'm trying, and I know she's leaving." My throat tightened my voice into silence.

"I'm sorry. I didn't mean to upset you." Anita looked down at the floor.

"It's ok. I know. You're just trying to look out for me." I softened my gaze and looked across the room at the piano. "She's falling in love with me, Anita. She told me last night, and to be honest, I feel like I'm falling in love with her, too. But I don't trust myself, not after what happened last time."

Anita exhaled long and slow. "Look, friend. I know that the past year put you through the ringer. I know you've been building yourself back from the ground up. I know you, and I trust your heart. I'm just ready for you to get there, too."

"Thank you." If I couldn't fully trust in my own heart, at least I knew my closest friend did. And maybe that would be enough for a while.

We spent the rest of the day prepping and setting up the final pieces for the show. The stage sat at one end of the parking lot of Open Hearts Church, and we made a seating area in the grassy field adjacent to the lot. We had painted a backdrop of golden fields with a rainbow above, and people dancing in the grass and flowers below. Large canvases rested on stands around the perimeter symbolizing life, healing, sunlight, nature, harmony, and spirit. Though it was a far cry from a Pride parade, we did our best to use the event to create visibility, celebration, and connection.

A little while before the benefit, I headed to town to pick up some pizzas. On my way back in, I noticed some vehicles parked on the side of the road just before the Open Hearts property started. As I got closer, I could make out the shape of people with signs. I swallowed hard as I got close enough to recognize a man holding a megaphone: Lenny Phillips. Along with a dozen people from The Way, all holding signs claiming we were dangerous and warning of judgment. They had stationed themselves close to the road, enough to force passersby to slow down. Just as I passed the last sign, I saw a hooded figure with a skeleton mask stretch their arm out toward me and point.

"Shit," I whispered under my breath and turned toward the church, my eyes forward so I could avoid eye contact.

As I unloaded the boxes of pizza, Rachel and Lara hurried toward my truck. "How many of them are there?" Rachel's hands shook as she took boxes from me.

"About a dozen, I think. Including the reaper." I looked up toward the road, realizing their signs were too far away to read, but they were close enough that I could still hear Lenny over his megaphone. I looked back at Rachel and Lara. "What do we do?"

"They aren't on our property, so they aren't trespassing," Lara shook her head and crossed her arms. "I think we just get loud enough to drown them out and hope they don't deter people from coming." She rested her hand on Rachel's back as we all walked to the main group.

Cars slowed as they passed by the protest from The Way, but all of them still turned in. A total of two hundred thirty-six community members came, many with blankets and camping chairs. Some stood near the back and to the sides.

At 7:30 in the evening, it was time to begin. Rachel put her hands on Dani's shoulders. "With all sincerity, Dani, thank you for doing this. You're going to be great."

Lara walked out on the stage and led us all in an opening meditation of peace and hope. "We are grateful. For life. For grace. For mercy. For love. With gratitude, we come together. With peace let us speak our words. With love, we lift our songs. With hope, we act to inspire."

She looked out across the crowd and smiled. "Thank you all for being here, now please give a warm welcome to our special guest, Dani Williams."

I kissed Dani's cheek and wished her luck, knowing she didn't need it.

Dani smiled at everyone and waved as she walked out with her guitar. She took the mic and opened the night with a moving rendition of "People Get Ready" which was met with a chorus of cheers and applause.

Rachel came up on the stage and spoke for a few moments, her eyes glistening as she took in the size of the crowd. "Welcome to the Night of Hope. I can't tell you how much it means to us to see you all here."

I looked up the hill to see Lenny still shouting into his megaphone, but with the show started, he could no longer be heard.

Soon after, Anita brought the house down by singing "Ain't Too Proud to Beg" and "Wade in the Water." After singing, she shared what SASH had meant to her. "My family took a good ten years to come around and accept me. I was lucky enough to have an aunt who took me in until I went off to college and a good friend – Mae – who picked up where my aunt left off. But the kids I work with don't have that. I've seen some real hard things in my years working at SASH, but I've also seen what the power of love, family, and belonging can do. One of those moments has been working with a brilliant young guy who has stayed with us a while. He's going to share his story now and sing for you. Please welcome Sebastian."

Afterward, he shared his story of coming out as trans, being rejected by his family, and ultimately becoming a survivor of a suicide attempt before coming to SASH. He shared how much SASH had become his found family and talked about his success with college. When he sat at the keyboard and sang Leonard Cohen's "Hallelujah," his voice carried with it the pain he had been through, bringing us all to a moment of quiet and stillness.

I checked again to see The Way packing up and leaving, and I breathed a sigh of relief that they had given up.

The night was filled with more songs, stories shared, poems read, tears and laughs spread through the crowd, and even some moments when the crowd sang along.

Near the end, Dani came out to play her final song, "Holding" from her first album. While she played the opening guitar chords, she invited people to give what they could in buckets that would be passed around as she played. Then she started to sing. I looked out at the crowd again as she sang the lines:

"Though what I have in my hands is small
All I want is to give it all."

People gave generously, filling the buckets to the brim as we passed them around.

When the close of the evening came, everyone came back to the stage to sing "Imagine." The moment brimmed with beauty. The sun had set, the sky turned midnight blue, and the fireflies glowed throughout the field. The crowd sang along.

We never imagined it could be as successful as it was. We raised a good amount of money, and more than that, we felt incredibly proud to have brought the community together in a positive way.

Throughout the next week, all of us rode the high from all that success. Not only had we provided a night of hope and connection, but we also felt encouraged and supported from having so many attend and participate. Rachel even received a phone call from a prominent business-woman in a nearby town who was interested in joining the board.

Midweek, Dani said she had an announcement to make at dinner, and Rachel gave a knowing smile. I remembered then that there was some-thing Dani had up her sleeve but wanted to keep as a surprise.

Dani shared what she had been working on: a new song to raise money for SASH. She planned to come back for a visit at the end of the summer and then record the song along with the rest of her new album in Nashville.

Everyone was thrilled that Dani would be back and that she had so graciously offered to use her music to help SASH in another way. She looked at all of us, and rested her eyes on me.

The night before Dani and I left to go to my parents' home, we went to the lake and sat on the tailgate of my truck, looking out at the moon and stars reflected on the glassy surface. We held each other's hand as we talked about her coming back, and how happy I was to know she would be back soon.

"But I will be going soon, and then who knows how long it will be before ..." she whispered.

We were silent awhile, then I said, "Let's make the most of what time we do have."

She hugged me and leaned over and kissed me under the stars. I drew her in closer and held her as we looked at the sky mirrored below, and it seemed the stars were cheering us on, to continue in love.

NINE

DANI

The grey of the morning still prevailed when Mae and I left for Georgia. We packed a couple bags, and I brought my guitar in case inspiration struck. We loaded our things into her truck and headed northeast. It was a beautiful drive with major terrain changes as the flatness gave way to hills and then small mountains. They didn't compare to the mountains out west, but they were beautiful in their own right. Something about the gentle nature of the southernmost Appalachians felt familiar and reassuring.

After several hours, we finally made it to Mae's hometown. We stopped in town for a few things: some fruit to snack on, some fresh-made breads, and wine. I noticed a display of brightly colored zinnias, and I bought a bouquet to bring to Mae's parents.

After our quick stop, we headed out to the countryside again to her parent's home. We turned onto a gravel road which wound through a thicket of trees, eventually leading us to a beautiful cabin with tall windows, a spacious deck, a deep porch, a tin roof, and flowers everywhere. Handmade sculptures from natural items like logs, moss, sticks, and stones decorated the landscape. A homemade patchwork pride flag dangled from the overhang on the front. I couldn't wait to see how beautiful the inside was. I knew it had to be. Mae's dad, Todd, was a designer and builder of cabins and tiny homes. Her mom, Julie, was a local artist. Together, they had designed and built the cabin as well as the tiny home we were staying in.

Mae's parents stood on the porch waving to us as we parked and got out of the truck. Julie's graying brown hair was tied in a braid that rested on her shoulder. Todd's wavy silver hair was pushed behind his ears, and both of them wore wide smiles as they looked at Mae. Mae grinned at them, and it felt foreign to me, since I hadn't felt close to my parents since childhood. But Mae's excitement to be there made me feel more at ease.

"Hey! Mom, did you make that flag?! It's gorgeous." Mae ran up to the porch and hugged her parents.

"Of course! I had to do something for pride month! I'm glad you like it." Julie laughed then looked at me. "And welcome, Dani!" She hugged me as I reached the porch, and I handed her the bouquet of flowers. Todd shook my hand and patted my back. I couldn't help but smile at their warmth and welcome toward me.

We had some time before lunch, so Mae and I unpacked our things in the tiny home, and she showed me around the cabin.

Her parents' kindness was matched by their talent for aesthetics. Beauty engulfed me. Everywhere I looked, elements of handiwork, creativity, and inspiration met my eyes. From the branches used to line the staircase, to the upcycled lighting fixtures, something about it seemed familiar, like the feeling Mae had created in her house back in Alabama.

When we sat down to have lunch together, I connected with Mae's mother, Julie, especially. She smiled at me and spoke with a kind tone. Her eyes sparkled as she looked at Mae. After we finished eating, we talked about the Night of Hope and how things had been going at SASH so far, including the backlash we had endured recently with the people from The Way.

"Mae, be careful. I don't have a good feeling about all of this. I'll never understand how people can be so hateful," Julie said, then looked at me. "You be careful, too, Dani."

Todd spoke up, "And don't hesitate to call us if you need us. We'll be there in a heartbeat if we need to be." My eyes stung at how supportive Mae's parents were, a far cry from what I had experienced, and I looked away a moment.

"So, Mae tells me you are working on some new music," Julie grinned at me as she changed the subject. "How is it going?"

"Good. Actually, better in the past few weeks. I was starting to feel a little stuck creatively, but everything happening this summer has inspired me to write again," I answered.

She nodded her head. "Sometimes, I have to find a change in scenery to get past my creative blocks, too. I try to encourage Mae to do the same when she's trying to write."

"It's hard for me to get away most of the time, but you're right. It does help." Mae touched my hand, and I suddenly remembered we were in the same room as her parents. I looked to see Julie and Todd still smiling, and my shoulders and jaw line eased as I opened my hand to hold hers.

In the late afternoon, Mae took me to a hiking trail. The air in the mountains felt less hot and humid than the sweltering heat I experienced in Alabama. Eventually, we came to a clearing in the trees that revealed a scenic overlook. We stood there and took in the view before sitting on boulders and looking out. The trees looked like blue green brush strokes and the sky a palette knife backdrop of an oil painting. I breathed in deeply as I looked across the landscape.

Mae put her arm around me as I looked out over the valley and noticed a hawk soaring in the distance.

"Do you ever think about what it's like to fly?" I asked her. "I wonder, sometimes, what it must be like to have a view where you can always see what lies ahead. Where you can avoid the bad stuff and just move toward the good."

I looked back across the tops of the trees.

"But you know, I remember the beauty of wonder and the excitement of building trust, love, friendship. I guess we wouldn't really be living if we already knew what was going to happen."

I looked into Mae's eyes. "I get wonderstruck by you, Mae. It's the only way I can describe it. I don't know what the future holds. But I know that somehow I trust you, and I love every moment I spend with you."

Mae kissed me softly, then we took in the view some more before we headed back down the path, hand in hand.

We spent the evening in town with her parents before saying good-night and heading back to the tiny cabin.

We sat on the bed in the soft glow of lamplight as the dark of night cloaked the outside. I looked at Mae for a moment. Everything seemed right and good for the first time in a long time.

She smiled at me. "What are you thinking? You seem like you're deep inside your mind."

"I guess I was. I was thinking that I'm really glad you brought me here. It's cool to see where you came from. I see why you love it so much," I said as I brushed her arm with my hand.

"I'm glad you agreed to come," she smiled at me. "Do you mind if I play a song for you? It just captures how I have felt today. Maybe better than I can say it."

I nodded and smiled sideways.

She hit play, and I recognized it immediately: Eva Cassidy, "You Take My Breath Away."

Mae caressed my hair as the song played, and my eyes met hers as she spoke. "When we were at the overlook today, I knew I couldn't hold it back anymore. I'm falling in love with you, too, Dani. My heart feels full when I'm with you. Somehow, you reached into places I had closed up, and now I'm constantly working to find my breath."

I lifted my hand to Mae's cheek and held her face as I touched my lips to hers. She ran her fingers through my hair, holding the back of my head as she kissed me. It was as if the connection went beyond our mouths and deep into the valleys of our souls where the very essence of our beings resided.

Our hands traveled across each other's backs and arms as my breath mixed with hers. I brushed over the front of her shirt with my palms and lifted her shirt over her head. I took in her fragrance as I placed my mouth on her shoulders and then her chest. Her lips traveled up my neck, and her breath felt warm on my ear as she whispered.

Soon, our bodies were joined together in a full body embrace, nothing in between us except our skin and the love we shared. We held each other after, lying under the sheet. Arm in arm, breast to breast, our legs wrapped up together. My head rested against hers, and our hearts seemingly continued to dance as we fell asleep in each other's arms.

MAE

The morning after the first time we made love, I woke up first and watched the sunlight glimmer upon her hair. I felt as though I was living in a dream, a perfect dream, from which I never wanted to wake. I stroked the side of her face, and she cracked open her eyes and looked at me with her sweet smile.

That day, we spent more time with my parents, and I showed Dani around the area and took her to a favorite trail. Being at home always made me feel grounded, but having her with me made it feel new.

On our last evening in Georgia, before we had one more dinner with my parents, I took Dani to my favorite pub, and we shared flights so I could introduce her to some local brews before we headed back to Alabama and she made her way back to Oregon.

After we were there awhile, I looked into her eyes and realized there was more I needed to share with her that I had kept locked away. Not on purpose, but not by accident either. I knew I had been avoiding it. "So," I started, but trailed off.

Dani looked at me, knowing something was on my mind. She put her hand on the table, next to mine, touched my fingers with the tips of hers. "What's on your mind?"

"Well, I wanted to say ..."

"Mae? Mae Tucker?!" a familiar voice called out from behind. I turned around. "It *is* you!"

I saw a tall guy in his early thirties. He had an athletic build and sported a beard. He was heading back to our table from the counter he was sitting at, pint in hand. Alex Reynolds and I went way back, and I jumped up to give my old friend a hug. It had been at least a year since I had last seen him. I introduced him to Dani and invited him to sit with us for a bit.

"So, what are you doing back home?" he asked me.

"Introducing Dani to my family and showing her around. She's never been to this part of Georgia before," I replied.

Alex gave me a smirk and patted the side of my arm. "It really is so good to see you, Mae."

"It's great to see you, too, my friend." I paused. "How is Gregory? And your folks?" I touched his arm.

"They're doing ok," he said quietly, looking down a moment, his expression turning solemn. "Things have gotten a bit better," he said. "And I have some big news, actually." He grinned at both Dani and me.

"Wanna share?" I laughed.

"I'm getting married!"

"What?! You?" I smirked and used the most sarcastic tone I could muster, for good measure.

"Can you believe it?!" he asked, laughing. He always had the best sense of humor, and our love language for our friendship was sarcasm.

"Ok, for real, that's great," I said, touching his arm again. "I'm happy for you, and I'm glad your family is doing alright."

"Thanks, Mae. I'm happy to see you doing well, too. Listen, don't be such a stranger, ok? Let me hear from you now and then," he said as he started to get up from the table.

"Yeah, I can do that." I stood up and gave him a hug, "And you let me hear from you, too, ok? I want to meet this mysterious fiancé of yours. I bet she's great."

We embraced each other, and he hugged Dani, too, before heading back to the counter.

It was getting close to time to meet up with my parents again, so I looked at Dani and asked, "Are you ready? We need to leave soon to be on time."

"Yeah, but what were you about to say, before Alex came over?"

"Oh, it's nothing. Don't worry about it," I said, brushing it off. It was a lot. And there was no way I could say it all in a quick minute. We got up, paid at the counter, and headed to the truck.

As we pulled out of the parking space, I sighed, "I should tell you more about Alex. And how we know each other."

Her eyebrows cinched together, and she kept her eyes on me.

We drove in silence for a few minutes, then I pulled into an empty gravel lot.

"I'm sorry. I can't drive and tell you at the same time. It's a lot," I sighed. Dani turned toward me in her seat.

"Alex's younger sister, Rebecca, and I were the same age, and we became friends in elementary school. He was around when I would go over, and their younger brother, Gregory, too. As we got older, we all became friends. Alex graduated and went off to college, but we still saw him when he came home for visits.

"Rebecca and I got close, and when most of our friends were guy-crazy in middle school, we just preferred to spend time with each other. I already knew I was gay. I knew when I was ten and had a crush on an older girl at school. But when we were fourteen, Rebecca and I realized we loved each other. She was my first girlfriend." I smiled at remembering that simpler time.

"We kept it a secret for almost a year, but when we were fifteen, we decided to tell our parents so we could be more open. My mom and Dad weren't surprised, and they were happy for me and Rebecca. But Rebecca's family was different. They forced her to go to therapy with someone who tried to make her straight. She wasn't allowed to talk to me anymore. When Alex found out, he tried to talk some sense into his parents but couldn't, and he relayed messages between me and Rebecca."

Dani touched my hand as I paused.

"This went on till we were sixteen. Then I got a call from Alex, that Rebecca ran away. Gregory was distraught. Alex was beside himself and went looking for her. Their parents started waking up to how their actions were harming Rebecca rather than helping her. But the damage was deep. They didn't hear from Rebecca for a month. When they did, she had called Alex from Maryland. She had taken a bus with money she had saved from her part time job. Her parents tried to get her to come back, and they apologized and told her they accepted her, but she refused to come home. She told Alex to let me know she was ok, and for me to keep being me. And when he told me, I broke down. I knew something wasn't right." I breathed heavily, my chest tightened, and my eyes stung. I didn't want to think about it, but I had to tell her.

"She wasn't ok. And six months later, I got a call from Alex at 2 AM. Rebecca had died …" My voice had become a whisper. "Suicide." Even though it had been over a decade, the weight of it felt no less. I still wondered if something else could have been done, if I should have sent more messages or tried harder to find her. I still wondered if it was my fault for encouraging her to come out to her family.

Dani and I sat there in silence with the heaviness of it all, and she took my hand as if to remind me I wasn't alone.

I took a couple of deep breaths and started again. "It changed my life forever. Her parents were a basket case, and my folks tried to help them as best they could. Gregory withdrew for a long time, and then later came out of the closet, too. By then, they knew how to better respond, and they were pretty good with him, the best they could be."

"I wasn't ok for a while. It took me a good year of therapy, lots of hikes, and filling up four journals to reach some kind of normalcy. I was in college by then, and one day, I had a real breakthrough and realized I could work to help LGBTQ youth who had been rejected. I changed my major and did an internship at SASH. And well, I'm still here, trying to save as many Rebeccas as I can."

Dani put her arms around me and held me. "God, Mae. That's so much to bear." After a few minutes, she asked if I was ok, and I nodded then pulled my truck back onto the road, Dani's hand resting steadily on my knee.

After dinner that night, we went back to the tiny home and held each other a while, lying in the bed. I knew I would have to say more about what I didn't get to earlier, but it didn't feel like it was time. There was already too much heaviness, and it would have to wait. Right then, I only wanted to feel the safety of her arms around me.

TEN

DANI

When we left Mae's parents that Sunday to drive back to Alabama, I felt like I was leaving two new friends. Seeing that a family could be so open and loving gave me a sense of hope as I returned to SASH, where the worst experiences with family are the norm.

The entire trip felt rich, from seeing where Mae came from, to getting to know her more and taking our relationship to deeper levels. When Mae shared about how she got involved in the work she does, and the tragedy that she experienced, my heart broke for her. I couldn't imagine having that hard of a loss as a teenager. I admired her even more, for using her pain to help others.

The drive back to Alabama flew by, and I thought of how things would be different when we returned. I was going to miss her warmth beside me in the bed, and waking to her smiling face in the mornings. I would be heading back to Oregon soon, and it would be a while before I could come back.

"I'm going to miss having so much time with you," my voice sounded quieter than I had intended. I hoped it still sounded as strong as it did in my mind. The idea of leaving felt like creating a vacuum, but

I would have been lying if I said all of me wanted to stay. I was more than ready to get out of the South for a while.

She reached for my hand to hold it, and we rode in silent recognition of the goodbye to come.

The closer we got to SASH, the more I looked forward to seeing the kids again and making the most of my time left there. We had planned to have a small party for Pride month, and after all the work we had put into the Night of Hope, we all needed some time celebrate and relax together.

When we pulled into the drive at SASH, and made the bend where the house became visible, Mae let go of my hand and put both hands on the steering wheel and leaned forward. "That's odd."

I looked to see that Rachel's car wasn't there. Two of the board members who lived locally stood on the front porch, talking to Anita, holding newspapers in their hands and pacing. Mae got out of the truck with me, and we headed over.

"Rachel is on her way. Can I get you some coffee or a glass of sweet tea or something? Why don't you come inside?" Anita tried her best to keep calm while flashing a glance at Mae.

I carried my bag upstairs as quick as I could and came back, then Mae pulled me aside and handed me a newspaper. She bit her lip and looked from me to the living room where Anita and the board members were sitting, waiting. I unfolded the paper to see a front page story on the damage SASH was doing to the community and accusing Rachel of neglect. It went on to include salacious allegations made by members of the community, suggesting abuse of the residents at the hands of the staff members. My stomach sank and twisted.

I looked up at Mae, and she motioned for me to look again, her brows knitted together. There, below the main story, sat my picture, and a story on me and my ties to SASH. "Singer Dani Williams, Danger to Our Children." The room started to spin, and the paper quivered in my hand. I sat down on the steps to read, and Mae sat next to me. The article featured an interview with a local teacher who stated she was concerned about her students listening to my music, and what kind of influence I might have on young people in the community. There were even quotes from local parents expressing concern, and anyone who had any of my albums was encouraged to burn them at a service at The Way "along with any other music, movies, or books which promote the homosexual lifestyle."

I couldn't believe my eyes. This wasn't a religious paper, just the local news. I closed my eyes and rubbed the center of my forehead with my thumb and took a deep breath. *It's almost time to go back home to Oregon. I can do this for a few more days. It will be ok. I will be ok.*

The front door opened, and Rachel hurried inside, Lara by her side. I made eye contact with Rachel for a second before the board members paced over to her.

"We know this is all false," one board member reassured Rachel. "But we have to figure out how to fight back."

The other piped in, "We assume this is from The Way, but we're worried about what else is coming. We need to be prepared." Rachel nodded silently and led them to her office with Lara.

I sat down in the living room with Mae and Anita to wait. After a while, Sarah Beth walked into the room and looked at Anita. "Hey. What's going on? Everybody knows something's up."

Anita stood up and handed her the newspaper. Sarah Beth put her hand to her mouth and glanced at Anita then turned her attention back to the front page. She peered at it more closely, "Hey, wait a minute ... I knew it."

"What?" Mae stood up, and she and Anita looked as Sarah Beth pointed to the article about me.

"This teacher quoted in the article about Dani. She's the one we had all those issues with last year."

"The one who had your class read a memoir by a woman who went through that ex-gay ministry." Mae took the paper and scanned the article again.

"What the actual—" My voice was louder than I intended it to be, and I stood up and walked over to a window.

"Yep, see?" Sarah Beth pointed to the teacher's name. "I still think it's cause she knew Ja'Marcus and me were living here. She has The Way logo all over the place in her classroom, and she made announcements about events at her church all the time."

I stared outside the window. The sun bore down across the field, and I knew the heat would be unforgiving. All I wanted was to be back home, among the mountains and where a snowcapped peak or even just a cool breeze could be found. I needed air.

Soon, Mae's hand rested on my shoulder as she asked if I was ok. I didn't know how much of the conversation I had missed while I was lost inside my head.

Rachel opened her door, and the board members walked out of her office smiling and with shoulders at ease as she and Lara walked them outside. Lara stepped back in for just a minute with Rachel and held her for a minute before leaving.

When Rachel walked into the living room, Mae and Anita filled her in on the teacher quoted in the article about me while I looked out the window again, wishing I could will myself somewhere else. Anywhere but Alabama.

"Dani?" Rachel's voice cut through my absence, and she asked me to come to her office. I followed her in, and she closed the door and sat down next to me.

"I am *so* sorry, Dani. I didn't want to drag you into this mess. I never thought they would come after you. Are you ok?" Her eyes rested on me, waiting for a reply.

I nodded silently and turned my eyes to the floor, counting the wooden planks. *I could and should have guessed something like this would happen. Shame on me for thinking it could be different. And in the South of all places.*

"They obviously see you as a threat, and of course you are a threat to their limited thinking and their prejudice. But that means they are going to come at *you* full force, not just SASH this time." She paused a moment. "You need to contact your manager and a lawyer, just in case. This could get ugly. If you need to go ahead and leave now, I understand. And if you need to cancel the project for us, and not come back, I understand that, too. You've done so much for us already. I can't ask you to bear this."

I looked up at Rachel, her eyes still fixed on me and her body leaning forward. The grey streak in her hair framed the side of her cheek, and I noticed the tear stains. I swallowed a couple of times, trying to find my voice. I couldn't let her down. No matter the cost to me.

"Lara has that saying, that love will win in the end, and when I think about this summer and my time here, I think of all the love I have found and am still finding. I can't bear the thought of walking away from all of that love. I'm all in to stick with my plans. Besides, I'll be heading home for a bit soon, and that should help." *Surely that would be enough reprieve for coming back at the end of summer.*

Rachel hugged me and whispered, "Thank you."

Mae checked on me before she headed home. She offered to stay if I needed her to, but I needed some time alone to process. I needed to pick up my guitar and write. Gathering my thoughts had always been best when I could do it through music.

I worked late into the night, moving from playing guitar and writing melodies and chord progressions to writing lyrics and journal entries that held space for beauty and hope and also to mourn and be angry. I only stopped for dinner and quick breaks.

Close to 2 AM, I looked over what I had written and realized my art was reflecting the changes I was experiencing and the ways that I had grown so far. Fighting on the side of truth and love, and hope for deep connection stood out as the biggest themes. As I read through, something else stood out, too, a theme I never expected to see: struggle with belief and meaning. It was too late to contact her, but I needed to talk to Lara soon. I needed to sort through the questions in my heart.

My eyes too tired to continue, I put up my notebook, brushed my teeth, and washed my face. I went to bed, and as I lay on the pillow, I realized how exhausted—but determined—I was to follow through. I had new reasons to not cower under pressure: my new friends, my love for Mae, and something I couldn't quite put my finger on.

My mind still busy, I lay there wishing I was in Mae's arms, and I hoped she was getting better rest than I was. My thoughts stayed on her, and I remembered how she had started to tell me something before Alex came by. She said it was nothing when I brought it up again, but I still wondered about it and wondered how she felt about the weekend we had just shared together. As my thoughts turned there, my eyes gave away to their heaviness, and I drifted off into a deep and much needed sleep.

MAE

Sleep nearly eluded me the night after we got back. It sent shockwaves through me to have experienced such a beautiful weekend with Dani only to come back to trouble that had the power to wreck SASH. I worried how Dani might get impacted by the mess even with her leaving soon. I knew I couldn't let anything get in the way of the love that was growing between us. Thinking about the dark cloud hanging over our last couple of weeks together for a while was enough to keep me awake for most of the night.

At the beginning of the week, the staff all met together as we tried to gather more information on where the slander was coming from. We talked to more friends in the community and brainstormed responses beyond what Rachel and the board of directors had already done. The board and Rachel made statements and press releases that asserted the accusations were false. Dani had decided to lay low and not respond to the article about her, hoping she could leave without another direct attack. I asked Dani to stay with me her last weekends in Alabama, hoping it would give her a break from the backlash and allow a little more time to focus on us before she left for Oregon.

By the time the week was midway through, we had a plan in place for handling future articles in the paper and trouble with the residents' teachers. We knew there would be a chance the kids could face some negative attention in their schools, and we had to be prepared to respond. Our plans were simple, but they were enough to provide us with some sense of security and most importantly, confidence.

On Friday, after meeting with just Anita and me, Rachel asked if we had a few minutes to stay and talk.

"Anita are you holding up ok with all this?" Rachel turned toward her, waiting for a reply.

Anita scratched her head. "Yeah, I'm hanging in there. Trying to focus on the good, you know?" Anita looked at Rachel then over at me.

Rachel adjusted in her chair, "And you, Mae?"

"I'm tired," I sighed and leaned back into my chair. "It's a lot, and I'm trying to figure some things out that have nothing to do with SASH or The Way …"

"Want to talk about it?" When Rachel asked that question, I knew it was less prying and more inviting.

I looked at Anita and Rachel, and took a breath for a second. I tapped my foot on the floor as I sat forward in my chair again. "Y'all know I took Dani home with me this weekend. While we were there, I realized I needed to tell her more about what happened with Heather, about how it began with her. I actually started to tell Dani the whole story, but we got interrupted, because we saw Alex, and I told her about what happened with Rebecca instead."

"When are you going to tell her?" Anita prodded me gently. Anita never shied away from giving it to me straight, but when the situation called for a more delicate response, she always seemed to know somehow.

"I don't know, Anita. I know I need to." I looked away then back. "It's scary, you know? I just haven't gotten the courage to bring it back up. She's leaving so soon, and we're only getting deeper into this."

Anita put her hand on mine. "That's why you've got to talk with her."

"I think Anita's right, Mae. I'm glad to see you so happy lately, and knowing what I know of Dani, I think she would understand. You only deserve someone who would be understanding." Rachel kept her gaze on me as she spoke. She had never steered me wrong and always allowed me the space I needed to process and make my own choices, even when they were wrong, like with Heather.

"Maybe this weekend then, when she comes to stay with me. So we have plenty of time," I finally responded.

"It's going to be ok," Anita reassured me, and Rachel offered me a half smile.

I hoped so.

Once work was over, I helped Dani carry her backpack and her guitar to the truck. As I started down the drive to take us back to my place, I put my hand on her knee.

We made dinner together, shared a bottle of wine, and talked for hours. It was nearly 1 AM before we finally headed to bed. As we held each other, I drifted off to sleep thinking of how I could talk with her the next day.

I woke up to the smell of coffee and something sweet. I walked into the kitchen, and Dani was making breakfast for us: French toast, fruit, and coffee. As I looked at her standing there, I couldn't help but smile, and I walked over and stood behind her, put my arms around her, and kissed her on the cheek. A soft but steady rain dripped from my roof, making me glad we had planned to stay in anyway.

Throughout the day, Dani shared some of the new songs she was working on, and we watched *Breakfast at Tiffany's*. You can never go wrong with Audrey.

Late that afternoon, we listened to the rain together on my back porch. I lay down with my head on Dani's lap, and she stroked my hair.

"Dani?"

"Yeah, babe?"

"Do you remember when we were in the pub last weekend, and I started telling you something, but I stopped when Alex came up?"

"Of course. I was wondering when you would tell me." She laughed a little.

I looked up to see her smiling down at me. I turned my head away to look outside again, and she played with my hair again.

"I know I told you about Heather."

"Yeah, the woman who cheated on you."

"Yeah." I drew in a deep breath and exhaled. "There's more to the story that I haven't told you yet, because I've been afraid to. I've been afraid of messing things up." I bit my lip.

She touched my cheek. "Whatever it is, we will figure it out together."

I breathed in deeply again. "So, I met Heather through my work at SASH. She had been a pretty outspoken advocate over in Atlanta, and she came to SASH to help with some fundraising. She had this special power to get the more conservative types to actually listen and even change some of their minds. I was with someone at the time—Esther. We had been together a few months, but Heather's charisma drew me in, and I got closer to her through the work we did together ..." I paused. *No turning back.*

"I wasn't faithful to Esther." I had said it. I felt like I was going to be sick. "I'm so ashamed of myself for it. I look back now and see how far away I was from my true self, even in the beginning, but Heather had a way about her to get what she wanted, and anyway ..."

I looked at Dani, to check in, and she was quiet, "Go on."

"I broke things off with Esther and started seeing Heather openly. I know I told you before that things were good at first. A couple months in, she took me to Atlanta and introduced me to lots of her high-powered friends. When we were there, she encouraged me to change the way I dressed to help impress her friends. I didn't see it for what it was—trying to change me into this other person."

I sat up and faced Dani as I continued.

"By the time we moved in together, I had changed so much I didn't recognize myself. Her control became more about who I am and how I think. Part of me knew I was spiraling, but another part of me didn't care. Anita and Rachel tried to talk with me, but I insisted everything was fine. Before Heather, I had a tendency to shut myself down and withdraw when I felt like I was getting close to someone. I'm sure it was because of what happened to Rebecca. So, I convinced myself that everything wrong was just my own bad habit of wanting to withdraw."

"Sounds like she took advantage of that," Dani touched my arm.

"I withdrew more from my friends and retreated more into her, losing more of myself along the way. And you know how it ended up. There's part of me that's still afraid, and I still feel that tendency to pull away. And the most messed up part is I can't guarantee you that I won't. It's so deeply ingrained in me. But the way I feel toward you makes me want to be honest with you and have no secrets, even the things I'm ashamed of. When I feel shame, I still hear Heather's voice telling me that I'm too much. That's why I was afraid to tell you."

I finished talking and looked at Dani. She held my hand, and we sat in silence. I felt exposed and wanted to run.

"You're not too much," Dani finally said quietly. "I don't know what to say just yet, but I'm here, just processing."

"I need some air." I touched Dani's arm and walked out to the back-yard. I couldn't bear to look at her any longer.

I stared into my flowers; though the hot tears in my eyes blurred them, I could still make out the colors. My breath stuttered as I closed my eyes and inhaled. It overloaded my mind, thinking about Rebecca, then Heather, and now my love for Dani. I took a few minutes to calm myself down and walked back inside. When I got in, Dani stood in my room, and she had her guitar case in hand.

"Do you want me to take you back?" I asked her. Maybe Heather was right. Maybe I was too intense, and maybe Dani thought so, too.

"No, Mae," she said. "I actually wanted to sing a song for you. If that's ok. I thought it might help." The corner of her mouth drew up, and her green eyes beckoned me to relax a little.

I sat down on the bed. Dani sat in the armchair, took out her guitar, and started playing. She sang Eva Cassidy's "Songbird" to me, her eyes often meeting mine. When she was finished, she came over and kissed me then rested her forehead against mine, and we closed our eyes.

"I know you've been hurt. I still can't wrap my mind around why someone would treat you that way. I love you, and I'm not planning on going anywhere," she whispered, "and I hope you don't either."

ELEVEN

DANI

I wasn't the only one who could feel the change in the air. The SASH staff stayed on edge, and for good reason. The pressure of something always needing to be done remained a constant, replacing the ease we normally felt when we were all together. We worried over the reputation of SASH and hoped the new support we had gained through the Night of Hope would remain.

It only took a couple days before I received a call from the publicist at my record label. They were worried about how a continued fall out could happen, and they wanted me to leave SASH immediately and move my next recording project back home to the Pacific Northwest. My stomach wrenched into a tight ball as I hung up the phone. I knew I couldn't let Rachel down. I had already made a promise to stick with my plan, but I also couldn't lose the support of my record label.

I called my manager, Tee, and then we decided it was best for me to go to the top, so I contacted Jason, the label owner. It was a small label, and he had listened to me in the past, so I felt like it was my best shot for being heard. When he got my email that we needed to talk, Jason called me immediately. He had only been partially informed about what was going on. As we continued to talk, it became clear he was concerned for my safety, but he also understood my reasons for wanting to stay through the next couple of weeks and then return to record my album in Nashville. By the end of the call, he encouraged me to do what I felt in my heart was best. He reminded me that he started the label to let artists have more independence, and that I was always free to make my own choices. I had to keep my word to Rachel, Mae, and the others.

After a few more days of nervousness, it seemed we could breathe again, and I focused on making the most of my time left at SASH before heading back home. One evening, Mae, Anita, and I sat in the kitchen, breaking green beans to blanch and freeze. The residents played a board game in the living room while Anita cracked jokes, and the three of us sang "My Girl" as we broke beans and placed them in a large pot. Loose strands from Mae's ponytail formed a soft frame around her face, and the glow of the late-day sun gave her skin a golden luster. If we could have held onto that moment awhile longer, maybe things wouldn't have gotten so difficult to bear.

On Wednesday morning, Rachel came in a little early and helped with making breakfast. Some of the vegetables in the garden needed to be harvested before the next rain, so we turned on the local news to see the weather. As we worked in the kitchen, none of us were paying close attention until we heard the words "group home," "LGBTQ," and "petition to shut down." Rachel and I made eye contact as Anita walked over and turned up the tv volume. A petition had been created, signed, and delivered to local officials. One county commissioner decided to take on the issue, and submitted that the county act to remove SASH due to concerns over the safety of county residents.

Rachel sat down. Anita held her hand over mouth. I didn't know what to do, and I froze. The office phone and Rachel's cell startled me. The calls remained constant all morning: the board members and Lara checking in, the news stations asking for comments and interviews, an attorney from Lambda Legal, a few local community members who expressed support, and Lara checking in again.

Anita called Mae and the other staff. When Mae came in, she and Rachel faced the difficult task of talking with the residents during group before they found out some other way. I couldn't imagine being the one who had to break the news to them. They had already lost their homes once, and the possibility of them losing SASH nauseated me. When we sat down for dinner, everyone's faces bore the heaviness of grief. Where we usually filled the air with talking and laughter, silence lingered.

Mae and I took a walk after dinner, and we went into the barn where we had gone before. We climbed into the loft, and just lay together, talking about how anxious and afraid we both were. Mae wondered aloud about what would happen to everyone if SASH were shut down. I talked about how worried I was for the residents and what would happen after I left, then we fell silent for a while.

"Dani, I'm afraid," she whispered. "We have to be honest and face it head on. What's going to happen to us?"

I shifted uncomfortably, aware of the hard boards underneath my back. I searched for an answer. I had put it out of my mind for the most part, even though I knew we couldn't avoid it anymore. My first instinct was to tell her it would be ok and not to worry, but I knew that wouldn't ease her mind, or mine for that matter.

I tightened my arms around her and kissed the top of her head, noticing the scent of her hair as I breathed in.

"I'm scared, too, Mae, and I don't know what it's going to be like to be apart. But I do know that I don't want to lose you, and I will do everything I can to keep us together."

She put her forehead against mine, as we lay together in the quiet for a few moments. My mind rested on wanting to get out of Alabama and to somehow take her with me.

"Mae ... I know I asked you if you would be open to moving some-where else, somewhere that's safer and friendlier for people like us. I know it's still too early and too much to ask that. But with everything that's happened with The Way ..."

"I know," she managed to whisper, "I can't ask you to stay here. I know how unfair that is. But I don't know what to do. This is home for me, you know? And my work ... but, Dani, if I'm being honest you feel like home, too."

As I held her, I realized I had felt that familiarity and safety with her, but I worried it could disappear at any time. Home usually did.

As much as I wanted that moment to resound, I knew I had to be honest, or more accurately: as honest as I could be. I didn't want her to know my fear.

"I feel the same way, but you're right. I don't think I could ever live here. After everything happened with my parents and I moved out to Oregon, it made my life a little easier, just to be in a place where I didn't have to fight so hard to be me. I need that. I need to be in a place where I can hold my partner's hand without fear. I know you've never had that, but I know if you did, you would really love it, too. I just don't know what to do."

She nodded and pushed her hair behind her ear. I felt like I had run out of words, stuck at this crossroads neither of us could traverse.

The painful silence that followed echoed in my heart, reminding me that this wasn't going to be easy.

Mae stroked my hair and put her lips to mine as I felt a hot tear fall from her face onto mine.

"I trust the love we share." I whispered, my forehead on hers. "The love that exists between us has to be strong enough to handle this. If we can't do it ... how does anyone make it?"

She held me in her arms and forced a half smile as I wiped her tear away with my hand.

Time got away from us as it so often did, and we realized it was nearly 1 AM, so we headed back to the house.

As we walked outside, holding hands, I looked up through the darkness to see the stars peppering the expanse with tiny white dots, more noticeable with the waxing crescent moon. I stopped in awe of the beauty, and Mae gazed up at the sky, too.

"All of those tiny lights, shining in the darkness—they've guided people, inspired songs and poems and science," I spoke softly. "But the sun ..."

"It's a star, too. Somehow the distance makes the stars more beautiful." Mae finished my thought as she put her head on my shoulder.

I gave her hand a squeeze and we looked up a little longer before moving on. After saying goodbye, I went to my room, my heart heavy with longing, and listened to Eva Cassidy's "The Water Is Wide" before falling into an exhausted sleep.

MAE

The next morning, I took my journal to the lake to sort out my thoughts for a little while before going into work. Dani would be leaving soon, and as I looked across the water, I worried for what might lie ahead or more accurately, what might be below the surface in my own heart, threatening to sabotage me. Even when I could put that worry to rest, the thought of losing SASH loomed back in like the shadow cast by a storm cloud, ominous and threatening.

My plan that day would include meeting with each of the residents to make sure they were ok, and to try to help them identify any options they may have if we were forced to shut down the home. I winced even thinking about it. I looked down at the blank page in my journal and closed it before heading over to my bike to go to work.

When I got to SASH, Rachel asked me to come in her office to talk a little while. The pained expression on her face worried me. *What happened now?* She held her silence while she held the door open for me, and she looked at the floor. I sat in the chair across from her desk and watched her as she closed the door behind her, her eyes turned downward until she sat down next to me.

"Are you ok, Rachel?" I kept my eyes on her, waiting for a response. Rachel had always exuded strength, and to see her look so wary worried me.

"To be perfectly honest, Mae? No." She rubbed the side of her face. "I'm worried. Not just about the latest from The Way, but for the kids that sent that stack of letters on my desk. They need somewhere to go, and I don't know if we will still be here, and we have to put their requests to come stay here on hold. That terrifies me." Her voice quivered, and she shifted again as if she couldn't get comfortable. She alternated between clasping her hands together and resting them on the chair as her eyes resumed the downward gaze.

"I had a conference call this morning with all of the board and our attorneys. We brainstormed some ideas on how we can fight this and what might lie ahead in the form of a legal battle. What came up the most was the need to be proactive, and the need for us to cultivate strong local and regional support from the community. Everyone feels it's our best chance for surviving through this, so that's what we are going to throw our weight into."

"So what can I do?" I felt confused why she wanted to talk to me privately about this, but I also knew I was willing to do whatever was needed to save SASH.

She looked at me and swallowed hard and shifted again before leaning forward in her chair, putting her fingers together and bringing them to her mouth.

"Mae, we need to bring in a professional who has a proven track record for getting support in small towns and the region of the Southeast."

Nausea hit me as Rachel touched my shoulder.

"I know it's going to be hard for you. And you have to believe me when I say I wouldn't do this if there was any other option I could see working. But I talked with several people from several organizations, and she is who everyone recommended. We had to reach out to Heather, and she'll be here at the end of next week."

My mouth turned to sandpaper as I clinched my jaw and held my head down.

"Her work will mostly be in the community, but she will need to be here for meetings. I wanted to tell you so you can be as ready as possible. Mae, if there was any other way ..."

"No. I get it," I muttered. My hands gripped the chair below me, and I tensed my arms.

"Mae, are you ok?" Rachel asked me.

"Yeah, I mean ..." I tried shaking my head a little to find my bearings. "Yeah, I'm ok. It's just a lot. I won't have to see her that much?"

Rachel frowned. "Well, I don't know. I have to be honest with you. There's a strong chance you will have to work together, but we can try to avoid it if it's possible."

I ran my hand through my hair, pushing my locks to the top of my head, and I exhaled a long breath while closing my eyes. The last thing I wanted was to lose my cool in front of Rachel. I knew worry occupied her mind enough without adding concerns about me.

"I'm sorry Mae. I really am. I know what happened before, and I know how deeply hurt you have been. I was there then, and I'm here now. Please know that." She touched my hand.

"I know, Rachel," I said as I stood up. I couldn't take any more, and I felt dazed. "Thanks for the heads up." I opened the door and walked out without looking back.

I had asked Dani to come stay with me before she headed back to Oregon, so I tried to focus on that while operating on autopilot until it was time to go home. Dani gave me concerned glances from time to time throughout the afternoon when we would pass each other. I wondered if she knew about Heather and if so, was she worried I would betray her like I did Esther?

After dinner, I asked her if she was ready to head to my house, and she nodded and went upstairs to grab her bag. Anita walked by and put her hand on my back. I figured Rachel had filled her in right after me, but Anita knew I wouldn't be ready to talk about it right away. I was thankful for her silent reassurance.

Dani came down the stairs and took my hand. We walked outside together and got on my bike. When she put her arms around me, she gave me a little squeeze. All the way to the house, I thought of all the trust she had, holding on to me as I steered us down the road, in control of where we would go and whether we would get there safely or crash on the way.

When we got inside my house, we kept our silence. The days were long, and a couple hours of daylight remained, but I lit some candles anyway. I needed the calming effect they normally gave me. I wanted Dani to be there, but I also felt like I wanted to be alone. Somehow the flickering flames cut through that tension. I opened a bottle of chilled white wine while Dani put her bag in the bedroom. As I poured the wine, I felt Dani's arms gently surround me, her hands around my waist and her body leaning on my back. She leaned in and kissed my cheek. "What's going on? It feels like you're a hundred miles away."

I turned around and held her close to me, just standing there in silence for a bit.

"Let's go sit down," I whispered.

We sat on the couch, and Dani rested her hand on mine. She met my eyes and waited for me to begin.

"Rachel took me to her office when I came in today," I looked into my wine, only half believing what I was saying was true. *How could it be? Why is this happening now?* I looked into Dani's eyes. "She had a conference call today with the board and legal team. They talked about what needs to happen next, and they want to bring in someone to help with building more relationships within the community to try to build more support and prevent us from being shut down." I stopped and stared off a moment.

"So you're upset because it's come to this or worried it won't work?" Dani's voice sounded fuzzy as my heart pounded.

I shook my head and hesitated, taking a drink of my wine. I met Dani's eyes again, her forehead creased and her emerald eyes fixed on me.

"Dani, they're bringing in Heather." My voice faltered on her name, cracking much in the way I worried I would crack under the pressure of facing her.

"Shit." Dani whispered as she took me in her arms. We sat a moment with the weight of it. "What can I do for you?"

"I don't know. I don't even know what I need. I feel completely off guard." My throat tightened and I drew in a stuttered breath. "I worry about losing myself again, that I'll get lost in all of the pain. I worry that telling you all of this will make you worry about me too much, about us too much. That maybe you'll second guess us."

Dani shook her head. "I can't think of anything Heather or anyone else can do to change how I feel toward you, Mae. So, don't you worry about that. I won't let you forget who you are or how far you've come. And you know Anita will be there for you, and Rachel, too, for that matter."

I wiped my eyes. "I know. You're right."

Dani took my hand and held it to her heart. "You don't have to do this alone." I looked at her sheepishly and then leaned into her shoulder. "I've been thinking of something, since the story broke about the petition to close SASH. I've wanted to get back home as soon as possible, to get away from the hateful mentality here. But when I think about taking the flight in a couple of days, it feels wrong. I feel like I'm abandoning my friends when they need me most. I needed someone or something like SASH back when I was seventeen and my dad kicked me out. I don't know what I can do with my guitar and a song, but I know I'm willing to do it if it means standing up for love and what's right and fighting to save SASH."

I stared at her and bit my lip. "What does that mean?"

"It means I'm going to stay, just til the end of summer and then I have to go to Nashville for the album. I'm going to do whatever I'm asked to do, and I'm going to be here for you, too."

"Thank you," I whispered in her ear, and she placed her lips on mine. I intertwined my fingers with hers then stood and drew her up from the couch, leading her back to the bedroom.

I took in every sight, sound, touch, scent, and taste as we made love that evening so I could be as present as possible. I went slow, kissing her shoulders, her back, her hips, and thighs. I ran my fingers through the trusses of her hair and let her locks fall on my face when she was over me, inhaling the scent of her hair while we kissed. The way our bodies moved and connected was in rhythm with our spirits. We were together, in every way connected, and that was all that mattered or that I allowed to matter to me that night.

TWELVE

DANI

The next morning, I woke up first and looked over at Mae, her eyes closed softly, lying on her pillow. As I lay there, I longed for her to be able to hold on to any serenity as long as possible. My chest tightened as my thoughts turned to what the next week would hold. I had come to trust Rachel over the past few weeks, and I knew the fight to keep SASH was getting serious. Still, I worried what Heather's arrival could mean for Mae. Just as my mind began to dwell on my worries, Mae stirred and smiled at me.

"Hey," I smiled at her and brought her hand to my lips. "Good morning."

"Mmm. Good morning. You have that look. What have you been pondering over?" She smiled as she hugged her pillow.

"Just thinking about what all I could say to tell Heather off." *I wish it were that simple.* We both laughed then held each other for a while before getting up.

That morning, I called Rachel and told her I was staying, and I changed my flight to August. It surprised her that I was staying, but more than anything, she was thankful for my willingness to help. I just hoped I could muster the strength to follow through with it.

In the middle of the next week, we all went to a picnic and fireworks at the county fairgrounds. The county had observed the same tradition for Independence Day for decades, and a local school counselor encouraged Rachel to come with the residents just as they had for years, in spite of all the backlash that had come up.

We packed two large coolers and some blankets into Mae's truck, and we piled into four different cars to make the twenty minute ride to the fairgrounds. Once we were there, we found a shady spot where we could eat, play games, and relax while we waited for the fireworks.

As time passed, the crowd grew, and pretty soon, the grassy fields were swarmed with camping chairs, blankets, and all kinds of people. Young children, old men and women with leathery wrinkled faces, white folks, Black and Brown folks, small families, groups of teenagers, and everyone in between. All of them came together for this one night. I wondered, as I looked among them, how each of them would define freedom, and what they would think about SASH and the kids who had found refuge there. Time would tell, but my mind wandered down the possibilities.

"Dani?" Mae touched my arm, and I realized I had drifted away into my thoughts. "You ok?"

As I was about to answer, we heard some yelling behind us and turned around.

Anita had gone back to her jeep, and on her way back had been stopped by a man who was standing in her way. Even from behind, I recognized Lenny.

Rachel and Lara sprinted over, and Mae and I followed.

By the time I got there, Rachel and Lara had pulled Anita over to them and were encouraging her to come back. Lenny stood with a sneer on his face.

"What happened?" Mae moved closer to Anita. "Are you ok? Did he hurt you?"

"He told me he knew who I was and where I worked and that I best be planning to find somewhere else to work and live. All I was doing was walking. I mean ... What the hell? I told him to get out of my way, and when he wouldn't, I lost it. I know I shouldn't have yelled back. But damn, I can't even stand to look at that fool."

"I know," Rachel's forehead creased as she held her gaze to the ground and patted Anita's back. "Are you sure you're ok?"

Anita shook her head, and Mae put her arm around Anita's shoulder. The two of them walked away together, Mae's hand steady on Anita's back. Later, they made their way back to the rest of us, their hands clasped together and smiles on their faces.

The rest of the evening stayed uneventful, but a true sense of calm never returned. As the fireworks burst with color and the smell of embers and burned paper filled the air, I fought back tears: not over the beauty or from a feeling of patriotism, but for the unfair reality of celebrating the idea of being free while hatred and prejudice imprisoned us. I put my hand on Mae's, hoping it would ground me as my body tensed in response to the booms and pops in the air.

That moment stayed with me through the next morning and into the afternoon as I spent much of the day with Lara. I had asked her if we could talk, and I hoped time with her would help me sort through the thoughts that kept me awake at night.

"So, things seem to be getting serious between you and Mae." Lara looked at me with a smile on her face as we sat at her kitchen table.

"Yeah, you could say that." I smiled back. "I've never ... she's special, you know? Obviously, I can't even seem to find the words." I looked down, my smile fading.

"But?"

"But I don't know what's going to happen. I know she is committed to staying in the South—her work and her family are here, and making a difference is integral for her. But I ... I don't know that I could ever be ok here. Last night at the fairgrounds was just another blow. I don't know what to choose or even what choice we have."

"What if you don't have to decide?"

I didn't know what to do with that question. I stared at her, waiting for more explanation.

"What I mean is, maybe there's another option, maybe something you aren't seeing yet. You know, I'm not from here, which I'm sure you guessed by now, since I don't exactly sound like a local."

I laughed and nodded.

"I'm actually from Vermont. I came to Alabama several years ago to do some work in Birmingham, and that's when I met Rachel. Even though we barely knew each other, I immediately thought she seemed special, and I didn't want to risk losing a chance to get to know her better. So, I started applying at other churches and ministries in Alabama and Georgia. Over the next couple of years, I started getting to know Rachel more through some projects we worked on together. Once I got to know her, I knew I couldn't leave, because of her work in the safe home, and I didn't want to take her away from that, even though I wanted to go somewhere that was more open-minded."

"Do you ever regret it? Or ever feel like you're missing out on something?" I asked, trusting she would be honest.

"No—" she paused a moment to breathe "—not regret exactly, but I do wonder sometimes if we would be happier somewhere else. It's still on the table, Dani. That's one thing I hope you get out of what I'm telling you. Just because you two might decide one thing now, it doesn't have to be forever. You may decide to leave and then come back one day, or you may decide to stay and then leave ten years from now. Life is so full of twists and turns, we just never know what opportunities we may have, or even what we may have the bravery to make happen."

I certainly had learned about those unknown twists and turns in my own life. I thought about my career in music and then all the changes that happened with my family and how transient my life became for a season. My thoughts turned to the painful memories and the questions which still lingered.

"Lara? Can I tell you something? It's the main reason I asked to talk with you."

She nodded.

"Even with everything going on, between SASH and my relationship with Mae, I feel more connected and like I'm held by love and trust. Something about it has made me want to reconnect with some sense of spirituality, but with all this shit going on with The Way ..." I trailed off.

"It's reminding you of why you stopped trying before?" Lara offered.

"Yes, exactly. But, I also want it even more just so I can prove them wrong, and maybe even prove others wrong who made me feel like I couldn't belong, including my dad, even though we don't even speak anymore. I find myself wanting to fight for what I believe, and even hearing myself saying that feels foreign and uncomfortable." I paused a second and took a breath. "And yet it's familiar, taking me back to my childhood when I used to come home from Sunday school, excited for what I thought was true then."

"I think it makes perfect sense, Dani. But what do you want to do about it? I think you know what I would say about The Way and the other groups like them, but this is your journey. You have to decide what you believe to be most authentic, most true—and then decide what you have to do."

I knew she was right. What I wanted was to just push it away from my awareness, but that wasn't possible anymore. I had come too far to let anyone from past or present dictate my life to me in any way. What had sparked within my heart felt like coming home, and it was mine.

"I think I have a lot to keep sorting through and write about," I replied as Lara smiled at me.

We spent the rest of the afternoon talking about Lara and Rachel's upcoming wedding in Autumn. I wanted to write a song for them as a gift, and that evening gave me an idea of where to start. Heading back to SASH, I thought more about Lara's words, and how I wanted to stay open to possibilities with Mae. Maybe it wasn't up to us to figure it all out right away, and maybe that would be ok. The idea frightened and intrigued me and felt somewhat freeing, reminding me I could weather the unknowns.

~

MAE

I did my best to stay uninvolved as Rachel prepared for Heather's arrival. I focused more on the residents and what I could do to help them hold on to the hope we could beat the latest attack. Anita could sense my worry, so when I wasn't with the residents, she kept me busy with mundane tasks. By the time Thursday rolled around, just a day before Heather was to arrive, I sat down alone with Anita.

"I know this is what Rachel and the board think will be the best chance for SASH, but I hate it." I admitted to her. *Was I betraying SASH for saying that aloud?*

"I don't like it either," she shook her head and tapped her foot on the floor. "I get why they asked her—girl is damn good at what she does, but I know it's going to be hellish for you. I mean you haven't even talked to her since … right?"

"No!" I shifted and put my hands on my head and breathed out, exasperated at the idea of being in the same room as Heather. "And I hoped I never would."

"I know," Anita whispered as she clasped her hands in front of her face. "It's going to be ok. And you let me know if you feel like it isn't or like there's something you can't handle. Ok? I mean that. Don't shut me out like last time. You got it?"

I knew she was right; I had shut her and everyone else out when I was with Heather. The isolation fueled the shame and loneliness and allowed the manipulation and emotional control that diminished me. I couldn't let that happen again.

"Ok, I promise. And thank you."

"Good." Anita put her head in hands "I have so much on my mind with trying to keep everything running well and getting ready for Heather."

"What can I do?"

Anita handed me some of her administrative work and asked me to take over some more of the daily routines. I also offered to help her out with a couple of projects around her place.

When I pulled my bike in on Friday afternoon, I noticed Heather hadn't gotten there yet. She was supposed to drive in that morning to get to work, but when I went inside, Rachel told me Heather had some last minute wrap-up work to do in Atlanta and that she would be coming later and stay for dinner. Of course she would. I knew good and well that there was no wrap-up work. She was coming later to make a grand entrance and most likely to make sure she saw me, too.

Dani pulled me aside to check on me and ask if she could do anything. We came up with a plan for me to silently let her know if I needed to get away. If I squeezed her hand, Dani would ask me to go help her with a song she was working on. I felt a little better knowing I could escape if I needed to. The last thing I needed was to feel trapped.

A little before dinner time, I looked out the kitchen window and saw Heather's silver Audi pulling up the drive. Nausea crept from inside my stomach and into my throat, watching her drive up in the same car I watched her drive up in when we were together, and that same car I rode in when she was driving us to wherever she had decided we would go. Trying to push my feelings down, I realized how much harder this was going to be than I had thought. Anita rested her hand on my shoulder, and Dani broke the silence.

"Guess that's her. Should I put salt in her tea?" She tried make me laugh. I cracked a little smile and squeezed Dani's hand, and she kissed my cheek and reminded me to just let her know if I needed to get away.

I went back to work on helping get dinner on the table as Rachel opened the door and welcomed Heather in. I couldn't make out what was being said, but I could hear Heather's deep and silky voice. It had been months since I had heard it. I tried to tune her out as I put the bread on the table and helped Sebastian fill glasses with ice.

Rachel called Dani into the hallway to introduce her to Heather, and Dani gave me a reassuring wink as she left the kitchen and dining area. She came back a couple minutes later and raised her eyebrows. As everyone gathered around the table for dinner, I made sure to sandwich myself between Anita and Dani, and I took a deep breath as we waited.

Then Heather walked in, slender and athletic as always. *Guess she's still running.* Her tailored blue pantsuit fit her perfectly. Her dark hair came just to her shoulders, neat and in place, yet somehow natural and effort-less. Her smile was still as wide and charming as I remembered, and her blue eyes sparkled in the light.

She waved to everyone as Rachel introduced her to the residents who didn't know her. She said "hi" to Anita and then said "hello" to me. I nodded my head and waved, my throat on fire. I don't know how she made it seem so natural with no hint of awkwardness, but then again— that's Heather, and probably why she's so good at PR. She can smooth talk her way into anything with anyone, and you won't even know she's doing it until you've already agreed to whatever she wants. Even then, you might not realize what happened. I know that better than anyone.

Throughout dinner, I avoided Heather's eyes and held my silence. Rachel filled Heather in on the benefit show. Ja'Marcus, Sarah Beth, and Aimee jumped in to talk about the response we got from the community and shared their excitement for how well it seemed to go. After they had finished, Rachel asked Dani to share her perspective, too, and she echoed much of what had already been said. Heather sat silent as she listened, making eye contact with each person as they spoke. I wondered if she was tired, actually trying to genuinely listen for once in her life, or putting on a show. My bet was on the performance. Only, I couldn't determine who had the distinct pleasure of being her intended audience.

Before my cynicism crested, Rachel turned the subject to plans for the next week. Over the weekend, Heather would just settle in, and there would be a meeting with the board on Sunday. They would share their perspectives and then come up with a plan of action under Heather's direction.

"It sounds like you've done everything right, Rachel. I'll need to go out in the community and do some more assessment, too, just to find out what exactly we are up against and get a sense of who our true allies are. Then we can decide on the right course of action. I know we may need to adapt if anything else comes up, but I am confident we can beat this and do it in a way that will unite SASH with the community rather than create more division. That way you can have enough support to prevent any community action against you."

Heather displayed a unique combination of calm and power, like a jaguar assessing its prey. She made it clear she would be a force to be reckoned with, and as much as I hated it, I knew she was the best person to try to save SASH. She looked me in the eye, and I took a drink of my water, wishing it were whiskey instead.

After supper, I helped with the dishes and then stepped onto the porch to watch the residents play badminton. Dani had gone upstairs to get a bag to come home with me for the weekend. As I waited, I wondered if everything would be ok after all. My mind shifted to how I could make the most of the time Dani would still be at SASH and the murkiness of what would lie ahead once she left.

"You look like you are doing well." Heather's voice startled me. I didn't know she was still there, much less that she was on the porch. I turned my head to see her walk over and lean against the banister next to me.

Shit. She trapped me, just like always. I stared ahead and kept my mouth closed.

"I see you still have your bike. That's great. I always thought it suited you," she leaned a little closer as if she wanted to brush my shoulder with hers. I kept my eyes ahead and didn't respond.

"I know you're still upset with me, Mae. But maybe you can give me a chance to be your friend? At least while I'm here? It'll make it easier, at least, when we have to see each other so we can work together to save this place." She offered her hand, but I just looked over at her. I hoped she didn't notice that my legs were shaky. The corners of her mouth formed a slight smile as she patted me on the shoulder and walked over to a chair to sit down. Her touch sent a shiver across the back of my shoulders, and I breathed out as she moved further away, thankful for more distance.

"Dani seems great. I'm looking forward to getting to know her. Of course, it doesn't hurt that she's pretty, too. Do you know if she is seeing anyone?" Her forwardness unnerved me, and a slow burn rose from the center of my chest to the base of my chin.

"Actually, yes she is." My voice quivered, and I immediately regretted opening my mouth.

"Oh, you mean?" She let out a silent laugh. "Wow."

"What?" I looked at her a moment then crossed my arms. *Did she actually see me as small as she made me feel?*

"Nothing …" she responded and smirked as she looked across the yard. "I just didn't know you were with anyone, and I just didn't see that coming. That's all."

I heard the screen door open, and Dani came outside. *Just in time.*

"Ready, babe?" She looked at me with a half-smile, and Heather stood up again, hands in her pockets.

"Go on and enjoy your weekend, Mae. It was good to see you. And nice to meet you, Dani. I'll be seeing more of you next week," Heather winked in our direction and sauntered back inside.

I stood still for a minute, frozen in another moment in time. Dani touched my arm, and I felt as though I were waking up from a daze.

"You ok?"

"Yeah, of course." I smiled at her and took her hand. "Let's go."

We climbed on my bike and headed toward my house. As we rode in the dusk, I couldn't shake the feeling that something dark and stormy was brewing as the swirl of feelings I had experienced around Heather echoed like thunder in my mind.

THIRTEEN

DANI

Heather reminded me of record executives from major labels: polished, charming, take charge, and smooth talking ... the reason I chose to stay away from the big labels. Even if Mae hadn't warned me, I knew Heather's type all too well. However, I still had to work well with her to help save SASH's reputation in the community, and mine, too, after all the mess The Way had created. I just had to find a way to be able to be around her and not dwell on how she had hurt the woman I was growing more in love with.

Early the next week, I rode to Open Hearts Church with Rachel to meet with Lara and Heather. We walked into the church to see Lara and Heather standing in the sanctuary talking, and we joined them. Heather looked more relaxed that day, dressed in a nice sleeveless button down and khakis instead of a suit. It made her appear less intimidating.

"So, Heather has a great idea." Lara smiled and looked at Heather.

"Well, tell us about it," Rachel took a seat on a pew, and Lara and I sat nearby while Heather stood in front and turned to face us all.

"So, I know you had a pretty successful turnout for your Night of Hope here, and I've been thinking about building on that idea. What if we did a series of forums here and at a few other places throughout the county?"

"What did you have in mind?" Rachel leaned forward.

"I think it would be great to have Dani sing a couple of songs to get people engaged, and then we could have a panel of people to talk. You, Lara, maybe read some letters from residents or even former residents, like success stories. Give the people in the county the chance to hear firsthand about the good work you are doing. Let them see how normal we are instead of the monsters we are made out to be by The Way and others like them." Heather paused and raised her eyebrow, waiting for a response.

"What do you need from me?" Rachel's lips curled to one side, and seeing her hopeful did my heart a lot of good.

After we talked a little longer, Rachel looked at me and then Heather. "You know, SASH's reputation isn't the only casualty in all of this mess. Dani has caught a lot of flak for being here this summer. Maybe Heather can be helpful to you, too." Rachel patted my shoulder and stood up. "I'm thankful for all the work you've already started, Heather. Just keep me posted on anything you need. I need to get Dani back to SASH so Lara and I can go to an appointment about our wedding, but let's get the two of you together soon."

"I can drive Dani back, and you two just go on. It'll give us a chance to talk a little now," Heather flashed a smile, and I hoped the internal cringe I felt wasn't noticeable.

Heather and I walked out to her Audi, and I got inside. As I buckled up, she started the engine.

"Bet all this heat makes you miss Oregon. I know I miss it when it gets this hot outside." She looked at me and smiled sideways. "I went to Reed." She put her arm behind my headrest as she backed up the car.

"I didn't know that." I looked out the window and shifted in my seat. "Portland is nice. I don't make it over to the city much. I live on the outskirts of Eugene, and yeah, I do miss it."

"That's a beautiful area. I took my college girlfriend there a couple of times for a music festival. Oregon is a special place, and that coastline ..."

I looked out the window again, and she stopped the car just before she pulled out of the church parking lot. "Don't worry, Dani. I promise I don't bite." She chuckled a little and shook her head. "Tell me more about what Rachel said, about what's happened to you directly."

I filled her in on the article in the paper about me and how it was tied in with a teacher at one of the local high schools. I also shared my plans for the music project to raise more money and support for SASH. "I know it might sound kind of Pollyanna, but I believe music brings people together, across all kinds of differences and divides."

"Well, let's see how we can get you painted in a better light around here so you can have an audience to listen to you." She smiled, and I could see why Mae felt so captivated before; Heather sure knew how to lay on the charm and steer a conversation. She pulled in the driveway at SASH and parked her car at the front of the house. She told me she would be meeting with the board and other community members the rest of the week, but that she would be back on Friday to talk about what was next.

As I started to get out of the car, she touched my wrist. "I can't tell you how refreshing it's been to talk to you today, Dani. I've met quite a few people in the music industry, and it's rare to meet someone who is as down-to-earth and clever as you. I think we'll work well together."

"Thanks, Heather. I just want to help my friends, and what you see is what you get with me." I touched the door handle and paused, "For what it's worth, I think this whole forum thing is a great idea. I'm glad I get to help with it." I got out of the car and waved as I headed up to the porch.

When I walked inside and closed the front door, I heard Anita's voice.

"How did it go, darlin?" she called out and motioned for me to come to the office where she was working on a schedule, so I sat down in a chair across from the desk.

"Good. I think we have a pretty good plan for reaching out to the community. Heather has some more work to do to iron out the details, but Rachel and Lara are on board. They seem pretty excited about it."

She exhaled and nodded and then asked, "Well? How were things with Heather? I noticed she dropped you off. What do you think of her?"

"I don't know." I shook my head and looked around the room and back at Anita. "My first impression was that she was like others I've met like her, people in the music industry who are the wheelers and dealers, the types of people I've stayed away from for the most part. But ... it seemed like I saw a different side of her today, especially on the way back. On Friday, I didn't see what Mae ever saw in her, but today, I think I understood more."

Anita's eyebrows cinched inward, and she clicked her tongue as she shook her head and rested her arms on the desk. "I just don't like it, Dani. Heather is great at what she does, and we couldn't ask for a better person to help with saving this place from ruin, but ... she is dangerous. She nearly wrecked Mae. I've been friends with Mae for a long time. I've never seen her get so lost, and we've never had anyone drive a wedge between us, but Heather did."

"What happened? If you don't mind telling me. I mean, I know some from what Mae has told me."

"Well, Mae had been dating Esther, and I know she told you about what happened. I was shocked when Mae told me she had cheated, and with Heather of all people. It was so unlike Mae. I tried talking with her about it a few times, but she didn't want to listen to any voice but Heather's. Then she started changing her appearance and acting like someone else. No matter what I said, when I expressed concern, it only pushed her further away. Even Rachel tried to get through to her, but nothing worked. We could see how toxic Heather was for her, and we watched her self-worth disappear like a cloud coming undone in a storm."

I leaned forward and rubbed my temples and looked up at Anita. "What happened at the end? To Mae, I mean."

Anita looked at me a moment and sighed. "Right after Heather finished getting the rest of her things, Mae got on her bike and disappeared for a couple of days. We were sick with worry. I took my Jeep and looked everywhere for her, called her parents, and kept trying to reach Mae. I finally spotted her bike at a cabin she had gone to before to write. I'm just glad I thought of it."

Anita stared out of the window in the office as if she were watching a replay of the memory.

"She opened the door as I was getting out of my Jeep, and I could tell she wasn't ok. Her clothes were messy, eyes puffy and red, and she hadn't taken a shower in a couple days. There were emptied bottles of whiskey and pages ripped from her journal all over the cabin. She was too ashamed to reach out to me or Rachel. I just held her for a while, and she wept, like it was deep from her soul. I've never seen her that broken. I made coffee and got a shower running for her, and then while she got herself cleaned up, I cleaned up the cabin. We burned the journal pages while we drank coffee and let her sober up. She stayed with me for couple of weeks to make sure she was ok."

I pictured Mae in the depths of the pain and felt a keen awareness of how hard Heather's presence actually was for her. Mae hadn't wanted to talk about it over the weekend after Heather's arrival. I thought it was because she didn't want to focus on that when we had time together. But hearing more, I worried it might be more than that. "Do you think she is ok?"

"Dani, I'm going to level with you. I love Mae, and I mean it when I say you are so good together. She's being herself again, and you don't try to change who she is. I don't think she would ever go back to Heather, no matter what Heather pulled out of her ass, but I do worry about the pain coming back just by Heather's presence. I'm scared about how that pain might affect her. She's an over-thinker and a deep feeler. She will need us to check in even if she doesn't ask, especially if she doesn't ask."

I trusted what Anita said and the care she had for Mae. I nodded as I stood up.

As I went upstairs, Mae stayed heavy on my mind, and I couldn't shake thinking of her lost in all that sadness. I closed the notebook I was working in and lay on the bed and cued up Eva Cassidy, "Kathy's Song," while I closed my eyes, returning to her voice for solace and comfort.

MAE

When I got to work a little early on Monday afternoon, I wanted to see how the meeting with Heather went. Dani wasn't downstairs, and Anita said she had gone upstairs to work on some music. I went to check on her and tapped on her door. There was no answer, so I cracked open the door and called for her, "Dani?"

When she still didn't respond, I opened the door a little more and saw her lying on the bed, asleep with her earbuds in. I smiled and walked in, gently closing the door behind me. I leaned over Dani and touched my lips to hers, and she opened her eyes and smiled at me.

"Now, this seems familiar," I smiled before kissing her again.

"Except this time I didn't scare you away," Dani laughed as she touched my hair, then she turned and patted the space next to her, inviting me to lie down next to her. "How are you, love?"

"I'm fine. At least I think so. I'm just trying to focus on saving SASH. How did it go today?" I asked.

She paused a moment. "It was good. Rachel and I went over to the church and met with Lara and Heather. I think they have a really solid idea for getting more support from the community."

"That *is* good to hear." I did feel glad to hear that. I just wished it came from someone else.

"So, after that, Rachel and Lara had to go meet with someone about their wedding plans," she continued. "Which left me alone with Heather for a bit."

I felt my eyes avert away from Dani. "What was that like?" I imagined Dani alone with Heather and how Heather could say a thousand things to sabotage the connection Dani and I shared.

"She drove me back, and she asked me about the slander I received in the newspaper. Rachel had mentioned we should talk about it. She thinks the plan will help with my reputation, too. Before that, it was a little awkward, though. She tried to get a little more personal on the way, asking me if I missed home. She told me she went to school in Oregon— which I didn't know of course, and it caught me off guard a little. We talked a little bit about how beautiful the area is."

Dani must have known how I was feeling, because then she touched my hair. "I can't wait for you to see it and to share it with you."

I smiled at her and hugged her before I got up. "I'll see you in a little bit. I have to get to work."

"I love you. Let me know if you need me. I'll be here working on a song."

I went back downstairs and started making some lemonade for group. Anita walked in to check on me and rubbed the back of my shoulders.

"You doin ok?" she asked me.

"I think so," I replied and put my arm around her to give her a side hug while I stirred with my other arm. "Thank you. I think between you and Dani, I'll probably be ok."

At group time with the residents, there were a lot of questions about what would happen if our efforts to stay open failed. I tried to encourage everyone to think positively and talked about how Heather had helped SASH before, and how her efforts had helped other LGBTQ organizations thrive and find support across the Southeast. My stomach lurched to talk about her so positively, but what I said was true, and I knew I couldn't let my own feelings and the history I had with Heather cloud the residents' hopes.

Over the next week, more news came of the potential for an ordinance that would cause us to have shut down. There was talk that there may even be a vote for county residents to take on in August, to decide if SASH would be allowed to remain in the county. The prospect of a vote frightened me, but we had to stay focused on how we could win against whatever The Way and their allies might do. Heather didn't come to our staff meetings, which I was thankful for. She kept her word and focused on working behind the scenes and making connections within the area.

By the time Friday rolled around, we all felt anxious to hear what the report would be from Heather. Rachel planned for Jesse to take the residents out for an evening of pizza and bowling so that we could have a meeting with Heather over dinner, and so they could have a good distraction from all of their own worries. Lara came, and so did a few board members. About an hour before the meeting, a blue Subaru pulled into the drive, and Rachel looked out the window as her eyes filled with tears. A woman with salt and pepper hair walked in and embraced Rachel. It was Cynthia, a former school counselor who had taken Rachel in when she was a runaway. She had driven all the way from her home in Asheville, NC, to be there for Rachel. She was retired, but still very active in volunteer work and advocacy. She had served on the board of directors for

SASH from the beginning and then took a step back to participate on a lower level once she retired and moved out of state.

Cynthia had adopted Rachel as her own, and she had also come to help with wedding planning. Lara walked in from the living room and embraced Cynthia, too.

"I can't believe you are here." Rachel held onto her again.

"Well, I can't imagine being anywhere else." She looked at Rachel and Lara and then walked toward me. "Mae, how are you? Oh, it is so good to see you," she said as she hugged me.

"I'm doing great! You look fantastic," I replied.

"Thanks, honey." She smiled and then looked toward the dining room. "Who is this?"

I turned around to see Dani standing and smiling. I walked over and put my arm around her, and introduced Dani to Cynthia.

"Cynthia is the school counselor who took me in," Rachel said, smiling as she walked into the room.

Dani's mouth spread into a wide grin, and she took a step forward with her hand outstretched. "I have heard so much about you! I am so honored to meet you!"

Cynthia laughed warmly and took both of Dani's hands. "I'm honored to meet you, too."

We sat down at the table, and Heather soon arrived and flashed a grin. I hoped she was bringing good news. Anita and I poured glasses of wine and passed supper around the table. I sat next to Dani and held her hand. I noticed Heather glance over at us, but then turn to talk with the board members instead.

Over dinner, Heather shared what she had learned from talking with more people in the community. She had reached out to local officials who had a track record of wanting to help marginalized groups. There were only two of them, but it was a start. They both expressed unwavering support for the work of SASH and even suggested that some of their more conservative counterparts might come around if they formed a meaningful connection. That bit of information offered us all a more hopeful outlook as we looked ahead.

Lara shared that she had spoken with leaders of other congregations that had partnered with Open Hearts for other ministry and mission work, and they were supportive and ready to help with keeping SASH open.

Heather had a plan for continuing to reach out to the people she had already been in touch with, and she talked with us about the importance of reaching out to others, like people who work in the schools where the residents attend. She went over her idea for forums where Dani would sing, and a panel of people could share stories and talk about the positive impacts of support and love like SASH offered.

The board echoed their excitement for the plans moving forward, and the room felt as if we breathed a collective sigh of relief.

Then, Heather looked at me for a moment, silent, and continued, "There's one more thing. Something that I think may be a game-changer for us. I reached out to a family in Northeast Georgia, the Reynolds. Their daughter, Rebecca, was gay, and they rejected her when she came out. Unfortunately, the damage they caused went deep, and she died by suicide. I think their story can be powerful and serve as a warning. They aren't eager to talk about what happened, but at the same time, they want to help other families avoid their mistakes. They can't imagine speaking in front of a group, but they are willing to create a video, so we will get to work on that soon. It will be a way for them to share that will protect them from facing questions and conversations that may be too intense for them to handle."

I felt like a knife had stabbed me in the side, and my heart pounded in my chest. The room seemed to darken. I couldn't believe Heather had talked with them without even warning me. *She knew I was part of that story. I was the one who told her about what happened back when we ...* I wrapped my hand around Dani's and gripped it as tightly as I could.

Dani leaned in closer to me and cleared her throat and then said something about needing to get her things and head with me to my house so she could work on her music for the upcoming shows. Anita looked at me and then looked at Heather, and her eyes flashed with anger. I knew she would not let this go.

I got up with Dani and left the room just as Heather called my name.

As we went upstairs, I could hear Anita's raised voice. "Are you shittin me right now? Oh, hell no! Don't you dare. I'm fixin to tell you everything I been holding up for months."

We got Dani's guitar and bag and headed downstairs to find Heather outside on the porch, as if she were waiting.

"I'm sorry, Mae. I should have warned you." Heather took a step toward me.

"Yes, you should have," Dani answered her and pulled my hand along as we walked down to my truck and left Heather alone on the porch.

FOURTEEN

DANI

I understood why Heather thought the Reynolds story could help save SASH, but her recklessness and insensitivity toward Mae infuriated me. I had only known Mae for a couple of months, and even I knew how deeply it would affect her. Heather had to know, too. Over the weekend, Mae told me she was worried about what Heather might be up to. To be honest, so was I.

On Monday, Rachel asked Mae to sit down to talk with her and Heather. Mae agreed to meet with them but asked if I could be there, too.

Before we went into Rachel's office, Mae looked at me. "I'm sorry for asking you to do this Dani. I just need another person in my corner, and I know Anita would have a hard time staying calm."

"Maybe that's why you *should* have asked Anita," I smiled at her, but she didn't smile back and bit her lip. "I'm sorry. I was just trying to make you smile. I'm glad you asked me." I took her hand as we walked in.

After an awkward silence in the beginning, Rachel spoke with a firm tone toward Heather. "I had some hesitations about bringing you here to help. When you were here before, you did good work, but you also did some serious damage. I feel protective of Mae, and all of our SASH family. I need you to promise me you will show a little more sensitivity and kindness for everyone involved. And I do mean everyone."

"I understand, and I promise." Heather looked at Rachel and then turned to Mae. "I know you probably won't believe me, but I am sorry, Mae. I never forgot about the Reynolds family after you told me what happened with Rebecca, and I just wanted to do something meaningful, to help the other Rebeccas in the world, as you used to say." Heather looked down for a moment, and her hair fell beside her face, so I couldn't read her expression. Mae swallowed hard, and I squeezed her hand.

"I know I should have told you earlier. I thought I would surprise you with their video, because I didn't think you would feel comfortable talking with me alone." She looked up and met Mae's eyes. "Obviously, I'm right since you needed Dani here in addition to Rachel." She sighed and looked down again.

My face burned, and my jaw tightened. I wanted to say something, but I didn't know what words to use or even what point I wanted to get across. Before I could figure out something to say, I noticed Heather's shoulders soften, and she rubbed her eyes.

"I'm sorry," she leaned forward in her chair, hands together. "This is hard for me, too. I didn't mean to hurt you, Mae, not now or before, for what it's worth. I was just trying to do something good. I'm sorry, Dani, for dragging you into my own stuff, and Rachel, I promise I can put everything aside and do the work you asked me to do." She looked down again, silent.

Mae's face reddened, and I noticed tears in her eyes which she refused to let fall.

I looked up as Rachel spoke softly, "I know this is hard. I don't think anyone expected it to be easy. But I do hope you can do your best to just focus on our common goal and for you to keep the lines of communication open. I am here. I know Lara would be willing to listen, too, and we can all meet together more if that's what it takes to get through the next month or so. But nobody has to go it alone, ok?"

Mae's voice cracked as it broke through, soft yet resolute, "We can make it work. This is important, and—" she paused and looked up "—I'm sorry, too, Heather. I will try to be more open, and I'll try not to assume the worst of you. You're right that the Reynolds using their story will have an amazing impact. You all know how I've made it my life mission to help other people like Rebecca. But mostly, her story deserves to be told. So, thank you, Heather, for remembering and making sure that happens."

I held Mae's hand with both of mine. I knew it had to be difficult and confusing for her to have so much from her past brought up at once in the middle of trying to save the future of SASH.

After the meeting, Mae seemed more herself. She focused on her work, and in the evenings she helped me go through ideas for songs I could use in the forums. We talked about going back to Northeast Georgia and made a plan to go visit her parents again the following weekend. I hoped it would be a helpful getaway from The Way and all we faced, but more than that, I wanted her to have space away from Heather.

My own working closely with Heather felt like working on an album with a producer who might not understand my vision for a project. I knew we had to work well together, but I didn't trust her intentions. She asked me to come to the apartment where she was staying so we could map out a plan together for my role in the community events.

I walked into Heather's living room and sat down on her couch. She got glasses of water for us, and sat down in the floor across from me, the coffee table in between us. She pulled out a portfolio with a notepad filled with notes. Her organization and focus made me feel a little more at ease.

We talked about the areas we would visit. She had a map of the area and placed stickers on the towns we would need to visit within the county, and she had planned a meeting with the board and a few prominent citizens of Alabama. It seemed like she had everything covered. In all, we would have seven forums over a period of nine days. It seemed like a lot, but I knew it gave us a good chance at building lasting support.

She went over her notes for what she was planning to talk about, her plan for working in the Reynolds video, and success stories from former residents.

Heather liked the list of songs I was considering, and I played a couple of the new songs I was working on. She smiled at me. "This is going to be great. Your voice is incredibly warm and inviting, and your lyrics are inspiring, as always. I think you'll do just fine."

There was a slightly awkward silence, which she broke. "I don't know about you, but I'm hungry. Ready for lunch?"

I nodded, and she winked at me as she got up and went to the kitchen and made salads for us. We worked into early that afternoon, and by the time we left, we had an outline. All that was left was for Lara to finalize our venues.

On the way back to SASH, I thought about the importance of our work and my hopefulness that it would help save the home.

When she pulled in front of the house, Heather looked at me and offered a smile.

"I see why Mae loves you, Dani. You really are a wonderful person. Thank you for helping with this.... I know we got off to a rough start, but I hope you know I really am sorry, and I'm not out to hurt anyone. I know it hasn't been long, but that whole experience with Mae is not who I am. I'm enjoying working with you, and I hope we can become good friends by the time all of this is over."

I paused with my hand on the door as I searched for what to say. "I enjoy working with you, too. Thank you." I opened the car door and stepped out, not knowing what to believe.

~

MAE

Rachel's intervention of sorts reminded me I needed to focus on the real crisis at hand: saving SASH. I still felt like Heather should have known how the mention of Rebecca would trigger me, but I also believed her when she said she was just trying to do the work she was brought in to do. Thinking about her apology to me sent my mental chatter to a dizzying pace.

I needed to write more to ground myself. So, I pulled out my journal in the mornings and wrote out my thoughts. Sometimes, the intensity of them frightened me, reliving moments of pain and wondering if the fires of my own torment would be reignited by Heather's proximity.

I didn't want to scare Dani with how dark I was feeling, but I knew I couldn't hold it in either. So, I let her read some of my entries one evening. She touched my hand and asked me to walk outside with her.

It was late, so the unbearable heat had given away to a residing warmth. We walked along the fields as the sounds of crickets and tree frogs swelled into a chorus. The lonesome song of the whippoorwill broke through here and there. Dani held my hand, and we soaked in the beauty of the night, the stars shining down and the fireflies echoing glows back and forth through the dark.

"Mae," Dani said softly, "I know everything happening with Heather has to be hard for you. I would imagine it makes you want to retreat, but I'm glad you aren't shutting people out this time."

I turned and kissed her, then lay my head over on her shoulder as we walked along.

"There's something else, too, that I want to share with you. From a long time ago."

I raised my head, "What is it?"

She tucked her hair behind her ear. "I had a really rough period when my parents rejected me, and I know I've told you a little about that. But I had another time, too. One I don't really share with a lot of people. When I was in college, I had a really big crush on this girl, and things got complicated pretty quickly." Dani exhaled slowly then took a breath in. "She was engaged to someone. We never crossed any lines physically, but emotionally, we got pretty tangled up, and our feelings for each other were intense. Anyway, I carried a lot of shame and rejection from that experience, and I kept it inside because I didn't want anyone to know I had been involved with someone who was already committed to someone else. That shame nearly killed me. I sunk low into my grief, and I was so paralyzed with fear and shame that I didn't reach out."

I paused in my steps, and so did Dani. I looked into her eyes, barely lit by the light of the evening. "What happened?" I asked.

"Jen called me one day just to catch up, but being the great sister she is, she picked up on my tone and got me to open up to her. She listened and helped me feel not so alone." She paused and looked at me a moment. "I went to therapy for a few months, and having someone affirm me and listen to me without judgment helped me to rethink the way I think about myself. I reached a point of more peace with everything—the broken relationship, the problems with my parents, the spiritual distance I felt. I still hated it all, but I didn't let it destroy me anymore."

She took my hand. "Mae, I know that you said what happened before nearly destroyed you. I just want you to know whatever you need, I'll help. I'm here. I'm always here."

I nodded and looked into her eyes. "Dani?" I asked. "Can you tell me more? About what happened with your family?"

We walked along some more, and Dani looked up at the sky, "I used to walk in the field across from our house with my dad and Jen. We threw a frisbee in the fall and spring, and in the winter, it was the prime location for the best snowball fights. Sometimes on a clear night, we would look up at the stars and name the constellations."

The corner of her mouth curled upward.

"One year, for my tenth birthday, we went outside to go look at the stars. Mom came, too. It was a bit chilly, so we all had on our jackets. Jen grinned from ear to ear, and I couldn't figure out why. She just skipped along, hands in her pockets, while dad and mom walked with their arms around each other, smiling too. We walked into the field, and I could see that there was something ahead, but couldn't make it out until I got about ten feet away. Then I jumped up and down from excitement, and Jen giggled. In unison, there under the stars, Dad, Mom, and Jen sang "Happy Birthday" to me as I ran up to my brand new telescope.

"It wasn't super fancy, but it was mine, and a way for me to see the stars even better. We stayed outside at least another hour, looking at Saturn, Orion, and the dippers. As we looked deeper into the sky, I felt like I was being held. Like my family really understood and loved me. And like we all belonged together and belonged to the stars somehow. It's my favorite memory from when I was a kid."

She held her head down.

"When I was a senior in high school, I fell super hard for a girl, Kendria, in my art class. She painted these really amazing landscapes, that when you really looked, were full of patterns and abstract shapes. I'd never really allowed myself to even flirt with another girl, but something about Kendria, was different. Maybe more importantly, something about me was different. I was still going to church with my parents, but I had some major questions—enough that I didn't believe being gay was a sin. I had started to accept my feelings weren't just feelings, and they weren't going away."

"Anyway, Kendria invited me to a party, and of course I said yes. At some point, we went outside and sat on the hood of her car and looked at the stars. She kissed me, and it was incredible. I realized in that moment how crazy it was to not be me, and how natural this was for me, despite what I had been hearing in church. I decided I couldn't hide it anymore."

"So then you told your parents?" I asked.

"I told Jen first," Dani sighed. "She was accepting and happy for me from the get-go, but she was also a couple hours away at college. She didn't think mom and dad would be so happy for me, but she also didn't think I had to worry about them reacting in any sort of hateful way. I thought that, too, but we were wrong. I told mom and dad the next week-end, and mom cried. She asked what she had done wrong to make me this way. Dad paced around and yelled a lot. Not just raising his voice, but yelling at me. He had never done that before. He shouted at me that if I wanted to defile our house, our family name, and the Lord, that I needed to do it somewhere else and get out. He was still shouting when I ran out the door."

My chest tightened, and I took in a stuttered breath. I reached over to push Dani's hair back behind her ear, and I rested my hand on the back of her shoulders as we walked on.

"So, I stayed with a couple of friends whose parents didn't really care. I finished out the last few weeks of high school that way and then gradu-ated. Only Jen came to the ceremony. I went to the same college as her, and then I moved out West. I'd already lost home, so it didn't matter where I lived."

"God, Dani," was all I could say. She stopped walking and put her hands in her pockets.

"Mom came to hate dad for what he did, and by my sophomore year of college they divorced. After that, mom and I started talking again, but it's never been the same. I tried to reach out to Dad a few times. He still talks to Jen, and she tries to get through to him for me. But he's never been open to welcoming me again. I stopped trying a couple of years ago."

My throat strained in the moments of silence that followed. I watched Dani look up at the sky, blinking and breathing deeply.

Dani's voice rose through the quiet. "When the kids share their stories, it takes me back to that night and those months after, trying to find home. I can't bear the thought of them losing SASH."

I took her hand in mine and brought it to my lips before embracing her. We stood that way for a while, holding each other in the field underneath the night sky.

FIFTEEN

DANI

A s Heather continued to make meaningful connections and work on our plan for the forums, we all kept a close watch for signs of what might happen next and how The Way might attack again. After a brief respite, our answer came as Rachel got the mail.

She stepped in and scrutinized a postcard-sized piece of mail.

"What is it?" I took a step closer to her.

Mae came in the door before she could answer. "Have you seen this?" Her hand shook as she held the same glossy paper.

Mae handed her copy over to me, and I saw a picture of Heather with large letters above her name: "Warning." The mailing went on to discourage residents of the county from speaking with her, labeling her as a "self-proclaimed homosexual" before listing some of her work in the South as if it infringed upon the rights of others.

"They don't waste any time, do they?" I handed the mailing back to Mae, then looked over at Rachel.

"They also have money and resources." Rachel sighed and looked out the screen door.

"Oh my God," Mae whispered. She held her hand over her mouth as she read over the back.

Rachel looked at Mae and then turned over her flier. She gasped.

"Do you think she is safe?" Mae asked, and I stepped closer to look for myself.

There was another picture of Heather on the back along with some verses, including a verse from Leviticus, the last few words in red: "their blood is upon them."

Rachel's voice startled me. "Hey, Heather, it's Rachel." She paced around with her phone pressed to her ear. "Yeah, I was calling about the mailing ..." She listened for a couple of minutes. "Are you sure? Ok. See you soon."

Rachel hung up the phone and grabbed her car keys off her desk. "I'm going to meet Heather at her apartment. She already knew and called her attorney and a friend who is an officer in Atlanta. She thinks it's just a fear tactic to make us worry for our safety and to make the people in the county worry about what she could be up to. I just hope she isn't underestimating all of this."

Mae put her hand on my back as we watched Rachel leave. I breathed heavily, hoping she would be ok, hoping we all would.

"Heather has done a lot of hurtful things, but she doesn't deserve this." Mae spoke with a quiet voice as she looked ahead. She looked down again and then ran her fingers through her own hair, sighing. "Group is in a little over an hour. Are you still ok to come?"

"Of course," I nodded and walked around a moment with my hands in my pockets, looking at the floor. "I don't want to let them down."

Mae had asked if I would talk with the residents about what happened with my family. I wasn't so sure at first, but I wanted them to know that even when families don't come around, you can still have a meaningful and fulfilling life and be surrounded by people who love and support you. Most of all, I wanted to give them a reason to hope.

I shared my story during group time, and the residents leaned in as they listened to me, remaining quiet until I had finished.

"Sounds a lot like the way my parents have been," Sarah Beth looked at me then down at the floor and half-smiled. "It's good to know you're still doing ok in spite of it."

Ja'Marcus cleared his throat a little. "Did your sister take heat for standing beside you? I ask cause I worry about my cousins and my little sister getting treated different cause of how they support me."

A memory flooded my mind: of when dad stopped sending money for Jen's tuition because she supported me. Jen was sharp and a brilliant student, so she had scholarships that covered most of her school costs, but she worked long hours to help us both with basic expenses.

"Yeah, she did," I said, my voice soft and breaking as I remembered the sacrifices my sister had made for me. "She helped me through the darkest times in my life, and sometimes that meant she joined me in the darkness."

"That's awesome you have somebody like that." Kyle looked directly at me and then around the room. "That's kind of how I feel about this group. Y'all were really there for me when I couldn't see anything but pain, and I know it hurt you, too. But, anyway. I guess I'm saying thanks."

"You're welcome, Kyle," Mae answered then paused a moment. "You know, there's this whole idea in our community—I mean the LGBTQ community as a whole, of *found family*. It's basically the idea that if and when we are rejected by the families who raised us, we make our own family."

"For sure," I piped in. "Some of my family includes people I'm related to, like my sister and my mom, but I feel like SASH is part of my family now. All of you."

Mae smiled at me as we made eye contact.

After group, I needed some time alone, and I slipped upstairs to my room and looked out the window for a few minutes, taking in the picture perfect blue sky.

I took out my phone to call Jen. She answered on the second ring. "Hey, Dani. How are you doing? How is the extended stay going?"

"Hey, I'm okay. And it's going ok so far. Hopefully, we'll be able to save the home. But how about you?" Jen had always taken care of me. Even though I had more on my mind than I let on, I didn't want to put anything else on her and cloud my real reason for calling her.

"Things are good. I've been painting again, and work has been good.

Josh and I hiked a new trail last week. When you come visit, we'll take you, too. You'd love it."

My shoulders eased up at hearing the happiness in her voice. "That's so great. I can't wait." I was overdue on visiting my sister and brother-in-law. The heartache over the past year had cornered me into isolation, and I hung my head and grew silent while I tried to remind myself their door was still open.

"What's wrong, Dani?" Jen asked.

"Nothing. I just ... I've been thinking about all you did for me—back when I came out and got kicked out of the house, and how you've been there for me when I got my heart broken. I just want you to know how much I love you and how thankful I am that you're my sister."

"Oh Dani, listen, I feel grateful that I get to be your sister. I love you, and ever since you were a baby, I've been protective of you. I'm more than happy to always be here for you. Don't you ever forget that."

My throat burned as I swallowed. "Ok, Jen. I'm here for you, too. Always."

"How are things with Mae?"

I told her a little about Heather's arrival and the confusion and sadness it was causing Mae for Heather to be around again. Jen's wince was audible over the phone.

"Be careful with your heart, Dani."

I nodded and then whispered, "Yeah. I'm trying."

I decided to ask her one more thing, since it was in my mind.

"Jen, how's Dad? I was telling Mae about how we would look at the stars in the field across the house, and that year I got the telescope, and it just made me think about him." We hadn't talked about dad or that night in so long, it felt like I was telling her about an actor and movie we had watched together years ago. Yet, I knew she would know it was my favorite memory of dad, the dad I knew when I was a kid.

"He's doing ok. He retired a couple months ago, and he's been going on a lot of rides on his bike." She hesitated. "He asked about you recently. Somehow, he heard about the negative press you were getting. He didn't say much after I updated him."

The silence that followed contrasted the swirling feeling in my heart and mind. The room grew small, and I wished I was outside.

"I'm sorry, Dani. I still try to get through to him for you."

I forced myself to speak while I closed my eyes. "I know. I have to go, Jen. I love you."

"I love you too, Dani."

I opened my eyes and rested my head against the window frame and stared outside over the fields for a while before heading down to dinner.

Later that night, I went home with Mae. We had plans to head over to her parents' house for the weekend, and we needed to leave early. As we lay in each other's arms, I had a lot on my mind. She fell asleep within a few minutes, but I couldn't slow down the thoughts. I eased myself away and stepped out to her back porch. Bits of moonlight peeked through cloud cover, and I replayed the memories I had recently shared and my conversation with Jen. I wondered, for the first time in a while, what might lie beyond the stars and if even through the clouds, I could find the way home, if home even existed.

MAE

Even though it had only been a few weeks since I had last visited home, the need to go back overwhelmed me. I knew some of that feeling came from wanting to get away from the conflict with The Way, but more than that, I needed to put more distance between myself and Heather. Another reason stayed on my heart, one I didn't want to talk about with Dani. I knew she loved coming home with me before, and I hoped it would entice her to be open to moving to the South if things between us kept growing.

The first night back home, we had dinner with my parents and sat on the back porch sipping chilled white wine after the sun went down. We walked to the tiny home, hand in hand, while the moon shone bright through the trees.

The next morning, Dani stayed in the cabin to work on some music while I went to talk with mom for a while. We sat together in the living room, drinking coffee.

"So what's going on, Mae? I can tell something is troubling you."

"How do you always know?" I shook my head then my smile faded as

I looked at the wooden floor and wrung my hands across my mug. "They had to bring someone in to help with SASH's reputation in the community." I hesitated and looked up. "Heather's back."

"Oh, Mae. No ..." Mom looked me in the eyes before she sighed. "How is it going so far?"

I nodded. "Not too good, to be honest. I swear half the time it feels like she is trying to push my buttons and get me to react, and the other half she's coming up with great ideas and working hard to save SASH. I don't know what she is up to or what to think."

Mom looked into her mug and then at me, her eyes an unspoken request for more, so she could know I was ok. I wasn't, of course, but I had to make myself be.

"Rachel is on my side, well as much as she can be. She has to walk a fine line since Heather has been hired by the board. Of course, I've got Anita. She's definitely let it be known where she stands." I couldn't help but chuckle at Anita's boldness. "I've been open with Dani, too, and she helps me get away when I need to. I don't think any of them will let me sink down where I was before," I answered. "But, I don't think I'll let myself go there, either. I know better now, you know? But something *is* bothering me."

"What is it honey?"

"I don't know exactly. Something awful happened right before we left. There was a mailing sent out all over the county with Heather's picture on it and passages from the Old Testament about stoning and judgment. I'm worried for all of us, but especially for her safety right now. It's just confusing to me."

My mom leaned in closer.

"Mae, I don't think I could ask for a more compassionate and grace-giving daughter. You see the good in people when others can't or won't. I know you loved Heather before she broke your heart. Love doesn't just disappear. It only changes its form. Of course it's confusing. Be careful with your heart."

We sat in silence, and mom touched my hand.

"You and Dani seem really good together."

I smiled at mom, and my thoughts turned toward the love I felt for

Dani and the steadiness she gave me when I felt blindsided by Heather's actions.

"We are. I just worry about it. If it's too good to be true, or what will happen when she leaves Alabama to go back home."

"You've been through a lot the past couple of years, honey, and it only makes sense to be afraid, but let love be."

Let love be.

That was a phrase my family had used for years, and it took on some different meanings over time. Sometimes it meant rest. Sometimes it served as a reminder that love would win. Sometimes it provided solace and comfort to know that we are held by love, by the love in our family, our friends, and all who love us. I knew my mom held all of those meanings in her mind this time, and maybe even more.

"Thanks, Momma." I hugged her and hoped she was right.

Dani and I spent the rest of the weekend resting, hiking, and spending time with my parents. On our last night there, we headed back to the tiny home in the orange light of the late setting sun.

"Mae?" Dani asked me. "What are you thinking about? I can tell something is on your mind."

"I don't know, Dani. I'm just confused. Maybe Heather really has changed, but I don't want to trust her just yet. That mailing scared me for all of us, not just her. But feeling worried for her feels odd and familiar at the same time. I don't think I'm making any sense."

"You don't have to have it all figured out," she said back to me. "It is messy, and it's hard, and that's ok."

I knew Dani was right. We got back and spent some time just holding each other and talking about how good it was for me to be home. Then Dani talked about how she couldn't wait to take me to Oregon to see her home, and the heaviness returned.

"It won't be too much longer until summer is over," I said to her. I knew we had to start talking about what would happen when it was time for her to head home. Even though she would be staying in the South to record, I knew that was only delaying the inevitable. She would leave and go home eventually, all the way on the other side of the country.

"Yeah, I know. It's going by so fast," she said quietly. "I'll be in Nashville for a bit, working on the album. But after that, I'll have to get back to Oregon to be home before I go back out on tour."

"But what happens after that?" I asked her.

"I don't know, Mae," she said in a quiet voice. "But I do know that I am going to start thinking about it some more. And maybe you could think about leaving, too? I mean, we have to figure it out at some point."

I didn't want to think about leaving my family and friends behind. I didn't want to think about leaving home, but I also didn't want to think about losing Dani.

"I do know one thing." She wrapped her fingers around mine. "More and more, my heart is somehow tied with yours. Like the roots of two trees, growing together. I can't explain it any other way."

I snuggled closer, her arms wrapped around me offering security as I worried over what might be coming down the road.

Sixteen

DANI

I knew I needed to focus on Mae and figuring out what would lie ahead for us, but the work before me to help save SASH hovered over my mind like a coming storm. When I signed up to go to the safe house for the summer, I had no idea I would be thrown into the fires of prejudice and injustice while finding love all at the same time. Most mornings when I woke up, I felt unsure of how I should feel overall. On the morning we left, I felt the same confusion.

As I packed to head to Alabama, I thought back to the night before, when we were with Julie and Todd on their back deck, listening to the sounds of the summer night. I brought my guitar and played a few songs, and then we sat and talked together. Todd asked me about the new music I was working on and shared some of his own creative process when he is making something new. Julie talked about wanting to have me come back in autumn for the changing leaves. She promised to make soups and homemade breads, and it sounded comforting and inviting. Unlike with my own parents, I felt so at ease with Mae's family, and leaving felt sad and heavy with not knowing what fall would hold.

As we loaded up Mae's truck, Julie pulled me aside and hugged me tightly. "Dani, we really love you. You take care of yourself, and please be careful with all the work you are about to do. People can be so hateful, but know yourself, and remember love, and let it be." She looked me in the eyes and said, "And please make sure Mae does the same."

I met her eyes with mine and promised I would.

On our way back to Alabama, Mae and I stayed mostly quiet, and I knew I would have to work hard to keep my promise. The evening after we got back, I met with Heather again to plan the forums. I started to become more hopeful of the impact we could make together, not just to save SASH, but to help families be more accepting and loving. I also wondered if we might be able to give hope to others like us, who had faced rejection for who they are and who they love.

On Monday, Heather went to Georgia to help make the Reynolds' video, and on Wednesday, she came back to show the video in a meeting with some members of the board, including Cynthia, the SASH staff, Lara, and me. Before she started it, Heather asked Mae to come to the hallway for a moment. Anita and I made eye contact as we waited, and I wondered if her stomach was as tight as mine. Within a few minutes, they came back in the room, Mae looking at the floor. Before I could lean over and ask her if she was ok, Heather turned down the lights, and we all watched together.

The video began with the Reynolds talking about Rebecca as a child and what she was like growing up. They shared a couple of funny and heartwarming stories. Then, they talked about Rebecca having a wonderful friend in Mae, and pictures of them together as kids, then in middle and high school, came across the screen as soft music played in the background. I reached for Mae's hand as Rebecca's parents talked about how they made terrible mistakes when they found out Mae and Rebecca were dating. They regretted their response and the way it affected Rebecca negatively, ultimately resulting in her death. They shared their wish that they could go back in time, and about the way that they responded better when their youngest son came out to them. The video ended with their hope for more parents to be more affirming and to love their children better. They even sent a message to LGBTQ+ youth and asked folks to open their hearts and save places like SASH.

When the video was over, there was a hush in the room for a moment as many of us were moved to tears.

Rachel spoke up first. "Wow, Heather. This is incredibly impactful."

"Yeah—I gotta hand it to you, Heather. I think this will do more good than what I had imagined," Anita echoed.

Mae kept her silence a moment as tears fell down her face. She stood up and walked over to Heather and thanked her, and then she embraced her in a long hug while she continued to cry. I shifted in my seat and looked over at Anita as she looked down to the floor.

The rest of the evening, I stayed close to Mae, yet quiet. I wanted her to know I was there for her, but also give her the space I imagined she needed to process and be with her thoughts. I kissed her goodbye when she left that night, and I lay in bed looking up at the ceiling, replaying the story of Mae and Rebecca as I fell asleep, my chest heavy as I thought of what Mae had been through. I worried over how it would impact her now.

The next morning, I drank a cup of coffee with Anita as we worked in the kitchen together to prep breakfast. I wanted to talk with her about what was going on with Mae and Heather and to hear what she would say, but before I could ask, the office phone rang, and Rachel walked over and answered. I watched through the kitchen door as her face paled and her hand covered her mouth as she started to pace.

"Are you ok? Is anyone hurt?" She blurted her words out in a shaken cadence. "I'll be right there." She hung up the phone and looked at me. "Someone attacked Open Hearts Church!" She choked on her words, then took a stuttering breath. "They heard the glass breaking and took cover. Lara is ok, and so are the others. They're waiting on the police. I have to go."

The second she finished telling me, she sprinted out the door. I ran after her and got in the car, too.

When we got to the church, Rachel ran to Lara and took her into her arms. The police were already there, taping off the scene and gathering photographic evidence and collecting shards of glass into bags. I walked over so I could see the side of the church better. I gasped as I read the lime green spray painted words.

Church of the Dyke.

My heart raced as I stared at the remains of the stained glass windows, gaping from bricks hurled through them. On one in particular, the face of a shepherd was missing, while the sheep below looked up for a master who was no longer there. The graffitied words "repent fools" in large capital letters marred the parking lot near where I stood. I stayed there a moment, taking it all in through burning eyes. My jaw tightened as I clenched my fists. For once in my life, I didn't want to run away. I wanted to fight whoever was responsible, no matter what it might cost me.

I walked over to Rachel and Lara and put my arms around both of them, not knowing what I could do or say, but determined to do what I could.

I heard the crunch of tires and looked up to see a silver Audi heading into the lot. Heather. She parked and sprinted over to us and checked to make sure everyone was ok. She asked if she could speak with Lara for a moment alone, so they stepped to the side for a moment. As Heather talked and gestured toward the church, Lara looked at the ground and pressed her thumb just above her nose and beneath her wrinkled forehead. After a long pause, she looked at Heather then nodded and put her hand on Heather's shoulder.

"I wonder what's going on," Rachel put her hands in her pockets and kept her gaze forward. Then, Lara shuffled back over, while Heather made a call.

Cynthia showed up soon after and had brought some bottles of water. It was a much-welcomed small comfort as we stood in the sweltering sun. Lara took a drink of water, and then squinted up at the sky. She looked over in Heather's direction and watched her hang up and make another call.

"Heather is calling some of her friends for legal advice," Lara said. "She's also called the news stations. She's got an idea, and I think it could work."

Rachel raised an eyebrow and looked over at Heather. We watched as she finished her last phone call and then walked over to where we were standing. Sweat framed her hairline as she pushed her hair back with her hand and puffed out her cheeks in an exhale. Cynthia handed her a bottle of water which she pressed to her head before taking a drink.

Two news crews soon arrived, and Heather took the lead in communicating with the reporters. She and Lara spoke to the stations on camera. Near the end of the interview, one reporter said their station had received a call from Lenny Phillips from The Way. He issued a statement that the vandalism was a much deserved warning sign from God, and he challenged Lara to meet him for a public debate. Before Lara could answer, Heather spoke up as she pointed into the camera, "We accept, and we will win."

I looked at Rachel, and she shrugged her shoulders. The interview ended, and Lara smirked as she walked over to us again while Heather talked some more, off air, with one of the reporters.

"Well, I guess I have some prepping to do," Lara laughed.

"Did that not catch you off guard?" I asked her.

"No, Heather had a heads up from that news station. That's one of the things she asked me about when she pulled me to the side. She thinks it's a good chance to use this for good—' she gazed at the broken stained glass, and her eyes brimmed with tears "—and I agree."

"What else did she say?" Rachel asked.

"Of course we don't know for sure, but I feel pretty certain that there are members of The Way behind this. Especially since Lenny already knew about it. Of course, he could have been tipped off by an officer or heard something over the scanner. But if they are responsible, then Heather is putting together a legal team so we can take them to court. And by we, I mean Heather and her high-powered attorney friends. This is big. They really crossed a line this time, and I don't think they can get out of it." She looked back at Heather marching toward us. Somehow, this singular woman was turning the tide, and she was making a bigger impact than we had imagined. In that moment, I wanted nothing more than to be part of it.

~

MAE

Over the weekend after the attack, Dani and I scrubbed the outer wall of the church and painted over the graffiti in the parking lot. We went back to my house afterward, and Anita called to update us on the latest. An arrest had been made, and just as our intuition had told us, it was a member of The Way. The news was confirmation that we were still up against a great deal of hatred and ignorance. To add salt to our wounds, we also received word that SASH's fate would, indeed, be on the ballot for a special election near the end of August. That meant that the forums and the debate would be our only chances to connect to the community before the vote happened.

Dani and I lay in my bed on Sunday afternoon, and she touched my hand and asked me how I was feeling with all that was going on.

"I think I'm ok," I answered. "I'm definitely afraid, but at the same time, I still have hope that things will work out for SASH. It just has to, you know? I'd hate to think of what would happen to the kids if ..." I stopped, unable to finish, breathing a moment. "There's something else. I think I am starting to have some sense of closure, with what happened with Rebecca. I didn't expect that from the video Heather made, but somehow it helped."

Dani put her arms around me and held me. We were silent for a little while. I touched Dani's face. "How about you? How are you?"

"The attack on the church really shook me up. I just don't know. I'm scared and hopeful like you, but I feel angry, too, and it makes me want to do even more. I just don't know what yet. Lara is one of the nicest people I've ever met, and I keep thinking she didn't deserve that. Nobody has deserved any of this."

I watched Dani as she lay on her back and stared up at the ceiling before speaking again. "I keep thinking that this isn't what I signed up for this summer, but then I remember that this is exactly why I am here. Because the work you are doing is so needed, and I of all people should know that, with everything I've been through."

She touched my hand and put her fingers through mine. After a few minutes of silence, she spoke in a soft voice. "I am obviously staying and fighting for now, but it also reminds me of why I moved to Oregon. I just don't know, Mae. I miss home."

I touched her arm with my other hand and drew in a long breath.

"I know, Dani," I whispered back. It was all I could manage to say.

What had happened to Open Hearts had only made me more firm in needing to stay, to make a difference and honor the memory of Rebecca. I silently wished Dani could understand that, but I knew better than saying it out loud.

A few nights later, Dani and I rode with Anita to the debate. Jesse stayed with the residents back at SASH. We walked into the auditorium of a local school which was already filling up, and the news stations had set up their cameras. Heather appeared in her element: wearing a dark pantsuit that displayed her ferocity. She saw us and flashed a smile as she looked at me. As we got closer, she stepped into the aisle and hugged all of us. Lara wore her usual slacks and button down, with a clerical collar. Her meek appearance contrasted her natural courage. I felt confident that Lara's gift for bringing people together would illuminate the truth. I just hoped it would be enough.

We sat near the front, and I turned to scan the room, taking in where the exits were and formulating a plan to escape if we needed to. My mind flashed to their violent words and the damage to property they had already inflicted. Who knew what else they might be capable of? As I did this, I saw many friendly and familiar faces: SASH board members, folks from Open Hearts church, and people I recognized from the benefit show. Some local and regional legislators entered the room, and I hoped the night made a good impression on them. We needed their influence.

I spotted many people I didn't recognize at all, but who looked curious and eager to listen. Local law officers flanked the back and front of the room, just in case.

As I scanned the room, I also spotted a long line of people walking in, all wearing t-shirts with the logo of The Way. I recognized Lenny Phillips as he walked in front, dressed in jeans and a trendy button down shirt, his hair spiked with gel. Their entrance demonstrated their desire to intimidate and make a statement. I looked over to see Lara watching them, a slight look of concern on her face. Heather, glared at them without looking away —her face straight, jaw set, eyes piercing. I couldn't help but smile, because I knew what that look meant. It signaled she was ready for whatever they would throw her way, and she was not in the mood to back down.

Before we knew it, it was time to start. A local teacher introduced both sides and announced each would have ten minutes to speak, and then the remainder of the hour would be spent answering questions the moderator had prepared.

Lenny went first, of course, and stood behind the podium in the middle of the stage while Lara sat in a chair just outside of the brightest stage lights.

"Friends, we are here to decide if we want to house sin and perversion in our community. Now, I know that some people in this room would say otherwise, but let's remember what Jesus said when the pharisees brought the adulteress before him. 'Go and sin no more.'"

He flexed his arms on the podium, looking down and then back up again at the audience. "If SASH wanted to be a place to help people do just that, then we wouldn't have a problem, now would we? But instead they choose to wallow in their sin, and Scripture tells us that they will receive their due penalty for that. We already know one poor kid there succumbed to the homosexual lifestyle of drug abuse, and he barely escaped with his life."

I cringed that Lenny would bring Kyle up in such a public way.

"I can only imagine what other perversions go on in a place that promotes a deviant lifestyle, and I worry for the kids who stay there. But I worry for our own children, the children of this town and our families. I can't stand for the breaking down of the family or for how sin will lead to more sin. We have to recognize the God-given roles we have in life as male and female and where a man's place is and where a woman should and shouldn't be." He looked back at Lara.

I saw Lara shake her head and let out a brief chuckle. Her ability to laugh off people like Lenny eased my tension from the moment.

"And God help us if we don't, and calamity comes upon us," Lenny ended and looked out at the crowd as The Way's section of the auditorium stood and applauded, while a few others scattered about also showed enthusiastic support.

Lara walked up and took the microphone in her hand. She stood with a relaxed posture, one hand in her pocket and began with quiet reflection.

"I keep thinking about the woman in the Bible who Lenny brought up and how if the religious leaders had done it their way, she would have been stoned, and that would have been the end of the story. But that's not how God chose to write that story. Instead, she was given a second chance. I want to ask you—what if she didn't deserve that second chance? Who here has been given a second chance before? Or been shown grace when the cards have been stacked against you? I'm not going to get deep into the argument of whether being gay is a sin or not—there isn't enough time for that tonight. Obviously, I don't believe it is, and if you want to talk about that more, we will have some forums where we will go deeper, and you can always contact me if you want to have a conversation. Instead, I want to focus on a word that was painted on our church parking lot—'repent.'" Lara paused and looked around the room.

"The word repent was used as a weapon against us, but I wonder what it is that we should be in true repentance for. Repentance is an interesting word, because it implies some remorse, some decision to change something from wrong to right. For a long time, folks have tried to use the Bible to justify hatred toward people like us. Yet, in Ezekiel, a book in the Old Testament, a story that has been used against gay people to try to make us afraid or feel sinful is revisited for a moment. Sodom and Gomorrah. It's here we learn the true sin of the two cities destroyed by fire. And you know what it was? Inhospitality. Refusal to welcome a stranger who was in need—and instead, exploiting and shaming them."

Lara's eyes sparkled as she held the mic close, her voice steady.

"We have a chance to provide a home for some young people, kids really, who are hurting, broken, and without a safe place to go. Do we give them shelter? Or do we commit the sin of Sodom and show we are no better than Gomorrah? May God have mercy, indeed."

After a moment of stillness and breath, many in the crowd clapped. Heather stood in the front beaming with pride, and the corner of Dani's mouth turned upward as she applauded. I looked around the room to see many folks with thoughtful expressions and even some tears.

The teacher who was moderating seemed to fumble on her words a bit as she returned to the microphone to ask her prepared questions. She asked Lara to address what a typical day looks like in the home and then asked Lenny to explain how such a day would be dangerous for the community. The remaining questions focused on questions from the community about where money comes from for SASH and how each side would answer how SASH's presence in the community would be dangerous or not.

Lenny's attempt to disparage SASH seemed to be failing, despite his blatant lies and hateful rhetoric. He gritted his teeth as he answered questions and barely looked at Lara. At the end of the hour, Lenny invited people who wanted to know "the truth" to come to his church on Sunday. When Lara gave her closing remarks, she asked people to reflect on what they had heard and invited people to come ask questions if they wanted to.

With that, the debate ended, and we met Lara, Rachel, and Heather at the front of the stage. As people were filing out, a news reporter asked Lara and Rachel if they would be willing to speak on camera for a few moments. They agreed, and Heather stood close by. Dani, Anita, and I kept a few feet away as we waited to congratulate Lara. As the interview went on, a young man in his early twenties came up and stood nearby, holding his arm.

Lara continued talking to the reporter about her role as pastor, and the guy paced around a little then said, "excuse me, Lara?"

Lara stopped talking to the reporter, and looked at him. "Yes?"

Before anyone knew what was happening, he lunged at Lara, swinging his arm to punch her. Heather stepped in front just in time for his fist to catch the side of her face, knocking her backward and onto the ground. An off duty police officer grabbed the attacker while two officers in uniform rushed over and placed him in handcuffs. I looked over to see Lenny leering at us from across the room.

Rachel and Lara helped Heather get up and take a seat. The reporter repeatedly asked if she was ok. Heather held a cold bottle of water against her red swollen face and nodded. "Yeah, I think so."

"Good," the reporter answered. "We got that on camera, and I think that'll be a pretty effective clip. Don't you?" She winked at Heather.

Heather laughed and nodded again. Dani and Anita hugged Lara, and I sat next to Heather and took a look at her face. "You ok? That must've been a hard punch to knock you down like that."

"Yeah, Mae. I'm alright." She offered a weak smile to me, and I touched her shoulder as I stood back up.

I hugged Lara and thanked her for speaking up and being brave, and Anita and Dani walked ahead as I said goodbye to Rachel. I ran to catch up and looked back one more time to see Heather watching me leave. She gave me a little wave, and I turned back around to walk into the night air.

SEVENTEEN

DANI

I clung to every word Lara said, desperate for her to halt Lenny in his
tracks. I needed for her to say something that would turn everyone
in the room around. I longed for the wrongs to be made right, and
somehow, to feel vindicated. By the end of the night, disappointment
set in when it didn't happen that way, and then my deepest fears about
our safety became a reality when the man lunged at Lara and struck
Heather.

Feeling unsettled, I needed to talk with Lara, so I borrowed Anita's
Jeep and drove over to the church the next day. I pulled in just as
Heather was leaving, and she waved to me as she drove out of the
parking lot. I wondered how she was feeling after being attacked the
night before. When I walked in the church, Lara filled me in on the
updates. They had filed a police report for the assault the night before,
and lawsuits were being filed against The Way and Lenny Phillips for the
vandalism to the church. Heather hoped it would pressure them enough
to stop the escalation of attacks.

I walked back with Lara to the sanctuary, and we sat on the steps of
the stage, facing the rows of pews and stained glass windows. Plastic

stretched across the window frames where bricks had shattered the colorful images. The glass had been cleaned up, and other than the plastic over the windows, and some painted areas of the parking lot, the church looked almost like it once did. As I looked out upon the damage, I couldn't help but think of how my soul felt much like the church. Harmful words had been hurled in my direction, from members of the church I grew up in, from locals back home in Missouri and right there in Alabama, and most painfully: from my dad. I had worked hard to repair the damage, and on the outside I appeared ok most of the time, but like the stained glass, I would never be the same.

Lara waited for me to speak first.

"I feel tattered, Lara. Last night shook me up. That man could have really hurt you."

"I know, Dani. To be honest, it shook me up, too."

"When I saw the damage to the church, it made me want to fight back with all that I am. I still want to fight this while I'm here." I paused and held my head in my hands. "But all of this shit that keeps happening is making me realize there is no way I could live here. I would live in constant fear. I can't imagine ever being ok with living somewhere like this, but I am terrified of what that could mean for me and Mae."

"That sounds incredibly heavy to bear alone," Lara offered.

"What choice do I have?" I asked. "I can't say anything right now. Not while Heather is here. It would push Mae away when that's the last thing she needs."

Lara looked at me as she put her hand on my shoulder, and I brought my knees closer to my body and wrapped my arms around them.

"That's not the heaviest worry on my mind, though. I came here to talk with you about something else. I've been thinking about what you said last night and what you didn't say that I wish you would have." I looked up at her.

"Go on."

"I wanted you to put Lenny in his place. I wanted you to give all those examples that I've heard you say before, about how LGBTQ people aren't fundamentally flawed, that our relationships aren't harmful or wrong, and how those scriptures people use against us are taken out of context and don't mean what people try to say they mean."

I paused a moment, feeling my face becoming hot.

"I wanted you to say it—right there in front of everyone in that damn auditorium, that the things Lenny says aren't just lies, but that they harm people in a deeper way than is imaginable."

Lara looked at me in silence for a moment.

"What do you think is so important to you about that, Dani?"

I looked out at the remaining stained glass windows, and studied the images. One was a dove, descending from the heavens, and it sparked a painful memory in me. Something my dad had said to me.

"On the day I moved out, my dad told me that I was so defiled that I would one day need to be baptized again to wash away the sin, and that if I didn't repent, I would be baptized in fire." I took a deep breath, hoping it would release the heaviness in my chest. "It's important because I want all the people like my dad to know how wrong they are before they hurt someone else."

"God, Dani. That's terrible he said that to you." She pinched the space of forehead above her nose and looked at me. "Is there more?"

I nodded and looked at her. "I also want people like me to know that they can hold on to their spirit, no matter what anyone else says. That they aren't evil or disgusting or broken. That they don't have to feel lost or thrown away. Like I have." I looked down at my hands to see they were trembling, and I put them down to anchor myself to the floor.

Lara put her arm around me.

"I've just shoved this part of myself down for so long, and I didn't expect it to resurface this summer. It feels so raw and tender."

"Of course it does," she said quietly. "It never healed. It just got pushed aside for a long time."

"I hope all of this pain is part of the healing." I rubbed my eyes, and she nodded. "This summer, any time I have come to this church, I have silently thought of a scripture I remember from a long time ago. *I want to believe. Help my unbelief.* But now, I keep thinking, *I do believe. I believe in Love, and I want to believe there's a place to belong.*" I looked up at Lara.

"That sounds like part of healing, too." She smiled at me.

As I drove Anita's jeep back to SASH, I thought about the feeling of belonging and the lyrics I was working on. My mind turned to the memories I had recently shared about Dad, and I thought over what Jen had said the last time we spoke: that he asked about me. I wondered if I could ever forgive him for everything he had done and was still doing, but I didn't feel ready or willing. Still, I wondered if doing it would free me somehow, but I didn't know where to start.

I got back to SASH and walked inside. It was almost time for dinner. I walked into the kitchen and thanked Anita for letting me borrow her Jeep. I stood silent for a moment and asked if I could help with anything. Mae stopped stirring the pitcher of tea she was working on and walked over to me, put her arms around me and kissed me on the lips and told me "welcome back."

I held her tightly after kissing her back. The weight of all I had to consider started to feel heavy throughout my body. I knew I needed to talk to Mae about how I was feeling, but I just couldn't bring myself to do it.

I meant what I said to Lara, about feeling that Mae had been having a hard time dealing with Heather's return, but what I was most afraid of was losing her. I just could not shake the feeling that if I told her I couldn't move to Alabama that she would not only withdraw from me, but that she would end our relationship, and that was not a risk I could take until I was absolutely sure. I still had a few weeks left before I would head to Nashville, and even then I wouldn't have to go home to Oregon until my recording project was done in mid-late fall. I wanted to wait as long as I could so we could relish in being together and focus on saving SASH. I had to hold on to the hope that if we did belong with each other, our love would find a way.

∼

MAE

If it had happened a few months before, seeing Heather take a punch would have caused me to laugh and feel vindicated, but that felt like a life-time ago. I didn't realize it until I saw her get hurt by the man who tried to attack Lara. Heather deserved a lot of things after what she did to me when we were together, but she didn't deserve that. I always thought it would be difficult to find someone as selfish as Heather, but when she jumped in front of Lara to protect her, she put herself in harm's way and put someone else before her. *Did that signify a true change in her? Had she become a better version of herself since she wounded me?*

Between the assault and the vandalism at the church, we all stayed on edge but tried to carry on with as much normalcy as we could. One night, I had lost time talking with Dani again, and I forgot I needed to stop for gas on the way back. It was close to midnight when I pulled my bike into the station, and there was a large SUV at the pump across from me. The man who was driving it looked at me while he closed his tank and got in his vehicle, but he didn't drive away. I stiffened as I continued to fill my tank, and a prickly chill crept across the back of my shoulders and up my neck. I stopped pumping before my tank was filled and yanked my receipt out of the printer as soon as it spat out.

I put my helmet on and looked out of the corner of my eye to see the man in the driver's seat watching me. I recognized his face from the group of The Way members at the debate. I started my bike and pulled out of the station and drove towards town. The lights of the SUV blared into my rearview mirror with every turn I made. I thought of the only place I knew was open, a Walgreens on the corner next to the grocery store. I pulled into the lot and hurried off my bike and went inside. I stepped between aisles and checked the time on my phone, 12:17 AM. I knew Anita and Rachel would be asleep, and Dani too, for that matter. I didn't want to alarm any of them any more than they were, but I also knew I couldn't get back on my bike and head home alone. That left one option.

Heather picked up after the first ring, and for a second I didn't know what to say. "Heather? You're up?"

"Yeah, I've been working on some analytics for our messaging. Are—are you ok? I just saw what time it is. Is something wrong?"

I bit my lip and craned to look out the window without walking toward it. "Can you come to town? The Walgreens? I think I'm being followed, and I hate to ask, but if you wouldn't mind following me home?"

"Are you inside?"

"Yeah." My heart pounded in my ears.

"Stay inside, ok? I'm on my way."

I hung up the phone and paced around while I waited. I knew the place Heather was staying wasn't too far away, and she walked in the store within seven minutes of hanging up with me.

I waved at the cashier as I walked toward Heather.

"Are you ok?" She rubbed the side of my shoulder.

"Yeah. Is there an SUV out there? A big one, like an Expedition or something? I think it was blue? I tried not to stare."

"No, they must have already left." She motioned toward the lot.

I pushed my hair back and walked outside, "I'm sorry."

Heather stepped out beside me. "Don't be, Mae. People do some pretty shitty things. Come on, and I'll follow you home."

I nodded then walked over to my bike and noticed the rear tire was low, then I heard the distinct hiss of air leaving my tire. I knelt down and noticed the long thin scrape of a key across the side of the body and a screw sticking out of the tire. "What the hell?"

I stood up and looked around. *Where did he go? What would he have done if I hadn't stopped?* Heather closed her car door back and walked over.

"Do you want me to call the police?" She sighed and shook her head then pushed her hair behind her ears. The bruise on her cheek became more visible, reminding me of what we faced.

"It can wait til morning." I touched the seat of my bike, and Heather walked over to her car and opened the passenger door.

"Ok, fair enough. Let's get you home." She stood with the door open and then closed it behind me after I got inside.

As we started on the way to my house, the house that we used to share, my insides twisted at the memories of coming home late together from concerts, fundraising events, and trips to Atlanta. I watched Heather from the corner of my eye, her hair hiding the wound on her face, and the silence between us exposing the wound in my heart.

"You should probably drive your truck, even after you get your bike fixed, just to be safe." She spoke in a quiet voice and leaned on one arm against her door, her eyes fixed ahead.

She pulled into the driveway, put the car in park and turned off the ignition. She got out and walked with me to the front of the house. I unlocked my door and set my helmet down on the table just inside and turned around to face her again.

"Thank you."

"Of course, it was nothing. You feel ok to stay here alone? I mean I can take you to SASH or Rachel's if you need me to." Heather rarely stumbled on her words or had to rephrase herself, unless she was upset.

"I'll be ok." I looked at her and noticed the swelling in her cheek, and I eased my hand toward her hair to push it behind her ear. "How is your face? It looks really tender." I pulled my hand away and stood with my arms close to my body.

She brought her hand to her face and half-smiled. "It's healing up. Just some bad bruising. I'll be alright. Are you sure you're ok?"

"Yeah, I'm ok, but—." I looked down. "I am worried, just to be really honest. Between the attack on the church and the mailing about you and then the guy trying to punch Lara, and then this tonight … it scares me. I hope you are being careful." I looked her in the eyes. "I'm also really proud of you for taking that hit for Lara." *I said too much.* I looked down again.

"Don't worry about me," Heather stepped closer and pushed my hair behind my ear, and I looked up at her. "And thank you, that means a lot to me." She put her hands in her pockets and took a step back. "Get some rest. I'll see you soon." She smiled at me and then headed back to her car as I closed the door and locked it. I watched her headlights head down the street, and I bit my lip.

The next day when I went in to work, I sat at the table and filled Anita in on what had happened. After I finished telling her, Anita stared at me for a good minute. "So, what was that?"

"What was what?" I asked her, shrugging.

"Mae, what is up with you and Heather?" she asked me, her eyebrow raised. "What happened to keeping your distance? You could have called me, or Rachel and Lara. You know we would've been there."

I looked at Anita, not knowing what to say. "I just didn't want to worry any of you. That's all. Nothing is happening."

"Mae, I know you. You are too nice sometimes, and you give people second, third, and twentieth chances. But you can't do that this time. She is that same woman who manipulated you, isolated you, made you believe you weren't worthy, and then cheated on and left you," she looked at me, waiting for me to give an answer.

I knew she was right. My guard wasn't up in the past couple of weeks, and maybe it should have been.

"I'm not interested in building a friendship with Heather," I said honestly. "But I am trying to give her a second chance that she probably doesn't deserve. I'm just trying to be open-minded so that my feelings don't get in the way of the work to save SASH."

Anita sighed and scratched the back of her head. "I know this has to be really hard for you. I just don't want you to get hurt again. That's all. I can't forget what happened before."

"I know," I said quietly. "Thank you. It's on my mind, too, even though there isn't much room for it to be there with what's eating at me the most."

"Lay it on me." She propped her elbow on the table and leaned her head over on her arm.

I picked at the cuticles on my left hand. "I'm still thinking about what Dani asked me—if I could move away from here. I don't know. It scares me to think of living somewhere else and being away from the people I love, but more than that—this is where my life work is, you know? I really care about the work we do to provide a safe place in the South. If we all move away, then who will fight for those left here?" I looked up at Anita.

"Yeah," she sighed, "I don't think I could leave this work, either."

"I am going to keep thinking about it, of course, but what if we can't come to an agreement?" I asked her, and she shook her head.

"I don't know, Mae, but surely to goodness the two of you can come up with something that works," she tried to encourage me.

"I hope so." I looked at the clock and realized it was nearly time for group. She grabbed my hand and squeezed it as I stood up and walked away.

When Dani got back that night for supper, we sat next to each other as always. I held her hand, and we walked as the sun was going down. We avoided talking about the inevitable. We were coming to an impasse, and neither of us wanted to face it. For the time, we just tried to be in the moment, and to stay with love.

EIGHTEEN

DANI

Two weeks before the forums in the area, I went to Heather's apartment to run through my finalized set list and go over a plan for what to do if someone heckled us or worse, like they did at the debate. I wondered what had to be running through her mind after being hit and why someone who seemed as powerful as Heather would ever subject themselves to living in a place where she had to fight to be respected.

We sat and talked about her ideas for what she would say at the forums and about letters from former and current residents she planned to read aloud. She pulled some ideas from similar events she had hosted and talked to me about how successful they were. I started to feel more hopeful as we planned out the order for the evening including the video, the letters, and my music.

After a couple of hours of working, we took a break for a bit and talked a little about her college days in Oregon and laughed together at a couple of stories she shared from that time in her life.

"So, what's next for you?" I asked. "Once you leave here, I mean."

"I'll head back over to Atlanta, at least for a while. But there's a chance I'll be back in Alabama sooner than I thought." She looked down and then back up at me. "I haven't told anyone this, but I've actually been offered a pretty great opportunity at one of the universities—forming and leading the LGBTQ resource center for students." She smiled.

"Wow! That's a great opportunity and a really good fit for you! I think you would be great in that role." I smiled, picturing her in that type of work, her boldness making waves in the world of higher ed.

"You think so?" she wondered aloud, smirking. "It's different from what I'm used to doing, but similar enough. I like the idea of a new challenge, and I think I'd enjoy doing more direct work with helping people for a while. It seems like a good blend of working behind the scenes and working at the forefront."

I nodded at her and smiled. "I think it's great." I picked up my guitar.

"Thanks, Dani." She smiled and looked down.

"Ready to hear the last two songs I have to close out each night?" I asked.

"You bet." She put her hair behind her ears. "Go for it."

I started playing the intro on my guitar when my phone lit up on the coffee table. I saw it was Jen, so I answered.

Before I could say hello, I could hear her crying.

"Jen, what's going on?" My heart pounded. "Are you hurt? Are you ok?"

"It's dad." In the silence that followed those two words, I ran through scenarios of what it could be. *Had he done something to her? Was he hurt? Did I care if he was?*

"There's been an accident." Her voice sounded strained.

"What kind of accident?" I forced myself to ask, but I knew the answer. "His motorcycle?"

"Yes." She wept for a minute, as I waited for her to be able to speak again.

"He's in really bad shape. I was the emergency contact in his phone. He isn't conscious. The doctor I spoke with said to come now, so I'm getting ready to leave." The rustling of her packing a bag filled the space after she spoke. I knew I had to be there with her.

"I'm going to come, too." My throat tightened, and I took a breath.

"I think that's a good idea, Dani. Hurry. I'll see you as soon as you can get there. He's in St. Louis. I'll call with the hospital info later." Her voice shook as she spoke.

"Ok, I love you Jen."

"I love you, too." Her staggered breathing calmed a little. "Be safe."

We hung up, and I stared, feeling dizzy and unable to breathe. Heather took my guitar from my hands and put it on the floor.

"It's my dad. He was in an accident. It's really bad." I stood up. "I have to go and get there as soon as I can. I don't know if I'll make it in time," my voice cracked, and tears formed in my eyes, but I refused to let them fall.

"Oh, God, Dani," she said as she put her arm around me. "Come on, I'll take you to get a bag and drive you to the airport."

Heather drove me back to SASH, and I called Mae on the way there to tell her what was going on. Heather parked out front, and I ran in to get a few things from my room. I packed my small backpack with a few essentials. I went as quick as I could, and as I came downstairs, Mae sprinted in the door. She embraced me and asked if she could do anything. I told her I didn't think so, and I hugged and kissed her good-bye, promising to call with updates.

As Heather started to drive away, I pulled out my phone to call and book a flight.

"I already booked you a flight," Heather said. "I have tons of miles from traveling for work, more than I'll ever use. You're taken care of."

"Thank you." I couldn't manage to say anything else as I stared out of the window, afraid that if I made eye contact with anyone I would cry.

The drive seemed agonizingly long, even though she drove fast, and we made better time than I thought we would. I still had the feeling I was running in place when I wanted to cover distance. Heather dropped me off at the airport entrance, and I hugged her and told her thank you before heading inside.

All the way to St. Louis, the memories of dad I had recently shared replayed in my mind, the good moments and the heart wrenching reality of what he had done. I wondered what forgiving him might look like at this point, and I mulled over what I might want to say, if it wasn't too late when I got there.

By the time I got to the hospital, Jen had been there for a while and had a better idea of what was going on. He was unconscious, and barely hanging on with a weak pulse and fluctuating blood pressure. His external injuries were bad enough, but the internal ones were worse. There was nothing they could do. They had him on a morphine drip for pain, and he wouldn't last much longer.

"They said he can hear. I've been talking to him. Do you want to go in with me?" Jen asked as she wiped tears off her cheeks and touched my shoulder.

I shook my head. "I don't want to." I took a step back and looked at her. "But I need to."

We walked arm in arm to his hospital room. I immediately felt like I was going to throw up. The light was low. Machine sounds, beeping monitors, tubes, blinking lights, the smells of hospital and blood cumulated into a sensory overload. The room felt cold and dry, and my eyes burned from the saltiness of my tears.

I walked closer to his bed, Jen's arm around me. She looked at me and I nodded.

"Dad, I'm here. And I have someone with me. Dani's here. She rushed here from Alabama. She ..." Jen trailed off, unable to speak anymore.

I swallowed hard, but the lump in my throat remained. His face was swollen, arms covered in road rash, and hands bloodied and bruised.

I took a step closer and touched his hand. I hadn't held his hand since before he disowned me. The roughness felt foreign while at the same time calling back memories of being a little girl, walking in the field with my father, looking at the stars.

I had so much I wanted to ask him, so much I wanted him to answer to, so many words I wanted to yell and put together in a way that would simultaneously vindicate me and repair the relationship we once had.

Instead, I could only say, "Hey, Dad. It's been a long time." My breathing stuttered.

Jen stood next to me and rubbed my shoulder. "Go ahead," she said to me. "Now's the time. There won't be any other."

I took a deep breath and exhaled slowly while closing my eyes. I pictured the stars and a quiet field below with honeysuckle in bloom. With my composure a little more gathered, I started to speak again.

"I'm doing well. My career is going great, and I took some time off. I'm spending the summer volunteering in Alabama. I met someone really special there. Her name is Mae."

My voice became a little stronger as I continued to speak.

"I've made some friends this summer, with all the work I'm involved with. One of them is a minister. She's like me. She's gay, too. Anyway, I don't expect you to understand. But I've been talking with her a lot the past few months, and I've been revisiting what I was taught about God and what I believe. It's brought up so many memories, and I've been thinking about some of the things you said to me the last time we talked, when I left the house."

I paused, and thought a moment, not wanting to say those things out loud. Especially not as the last words I would say to him. He deserved it, but I knew it would wreck me. I needed to be free.

"I had other memories this summer, too, walking under the stars with Mae." I smiled and let out a small laugh. "You remember all the snowball fights in the field across the yard? Like that time you and I built a snow fort and we pelted mom and Jen when they came to look at it, or when you put snow in my seat on the four-wheeler so it would shock me with cold when I sat down? Or when you all surprised me with the telescope for my birthday?"

Jen let out a combination of laughter and crying.

"Dad, I'm ok. I don't understand you. I never will. I don't understand why you shut me out of your life. I don't know what forgiveness looks like for something like this. What you did to me was terrible, and I felt alone and scared for a long time because of it. But I am ok now. I'm finding my way, and you don't owe me anything. Even though sometimes I feel like you do."

I paused and breathed in. "I never stopped loving you, Dad, the you I used to know."

Tears blurred my eyes, and I tried to squint through them to see. The sound of beeping, monitoring his weak and slowing pulse, the air in his oxygen mask, and the click of medicine being fed through the IV were the only response I received.

I felt Jen's arm around my shoulder as I stepped back. She embraced me, and we stood there and cried together for a few minutes.

The weight and exhaustion from rushing to get there caught up with me, and Jen noticed me stumble as we stepped back from holding each other.

"Are you ok, Dani?"

"Yeah, I just need some air. I'm going to step out for a bit."

I went to the hospital cafeteria and got a cup of coffee and went outside. I had a voicemail from Mae, telling me she loved me and was thinking of me. I called her and talked to her for a few minutes to update her. I couldn't talk much. I needed some solitude and a bit of quiet for a few minutes to process.

After I hung up the phone, I put in my ear buds and pulled up Eva Cassidy to help clear my tangled mind: "Bridge Over Troubled Water." After the song was over, I sat in silence for a few moments then went back inside and fell asleep in a chair in the ICU waiting area.

Dad died that night, and the sorrow of every missed opportunity and the weight of wondering if he heard me landed in my chest, but soon after, I noticed the lightness of not carrying it all alone anymore.

MAE

At 4 AM, I woke up to a phone call from Dani. Her voice sounded hoarse and broken, and I knew what she would say.

"Are you ok? Is there anything I can do?" I wished I was there with her, and being so far away rendered me helpless.

"No, I mean—yes, I'm ok. I just needed to hear your voice." She sighed into the phone. "I was able to say some things to him before ... and that helped give me some closure, I think. It's just so heavy, you know?"

I thought of everything Dani had shared with me about her dad and the pain in her eyes every time she brought him up. "I'm sure it is, Dani.

Listen, I want to come out there and just be there with you. Would that be ok?" I waited as she started crying.

"Yeah. I think that would help me a lot. I'm trying to be there for Jen, but we are just in such different places with him. I think I need someone else here with me, so I'm not alone when she is doing what she needs to do you know?"

"Ok, love. I'll update you once I know more. I'll be there as soon as I can. Why don't you try to get some rest?"

"Ok, babe. That's probably a good idea. I need to try to sleep. I love you."

"I love you, too."

By the time we hung up, it was a little after five. I couldn't go back to sleep, so I made some coffee and took a shower then started packing. I ate a small breakfast and then called Anita once I knew she was awake. I told her I planned to go to Missouri to be with Dani, and she asked if there was anything Dani or I needed.

When I called Rachel, she told me to take as much time as I needed, and that she would ask Jesse to cover my shifts. Lara said she could take me to the airport, and to just let her know what time to pick me up.

I was almost done packing when my phone rang. It was Heather. *Not now.*

I stared at my phone for a moment before I answered, "Hello?"

"Hey, Mae. I know I'm probably the last person you want a call from right now, well except for maybe Lenny Phillips."

I chuckled, and guilt for laughing washed over me.

"Anyway, Rachel told me about Dani's dad passing and that you're heading out to Missouri. I want to help—can I take care of your flight?"

My mouth was dry as I tried to answer. I needed to keep up my boundaries. I didn't want the help from her, but I also knew I needed it. "Actually, that would help out a lot. Thank you, Heather. Oh and thanks for helping Dani get out there so fast." I closed my eyes and bit my lip in the awkward quiet that followed.

"Of course. I'll book your flight and send you the details. Stay safe."

"Ok. Thanks again. You too."

I hung up the phone and tossed it on the bed and stared at it for a second. I shook my head, and refocused on getting ready to leave.

Lara picked me up at eight, and I was in Missouri by the afternoon. Dani met me at the airport, and I sprinted to her as soon as I spotted her looking at me with red watery eyes. I held her for a long time, and she thanked me for coming before we went outside to the parking lot. She had driven her dad's truck, an early 90s Ford with a bench seat. As we left the airport parking lot, she held my hand.

"I'm so glad you are here." She gazed ahead at the road as she drove in silence for a few moments. "We're staying at Dad's house." She winced. "It's weird and uncomfortable, even without him there, but it makes sense with all we need to figure out and go through."

I squeezed her hand, not knowing what to say that could bring comfort. I hoped being there was enough.

Dani drove us to the house, and her sister met us outside. Jennifer hugged me as I walked up, and her warm and welcoming nature helped me feel more at ease. I hated that we were meeting under such sad circumstances. I liked her right away.

Jen had their father's will, and the three of us sat down with a bottle of wine that night while she went over his final wishes. I held Dani's hand while Jen read it out loud.

He wanted a memorial service at his church and to be cremated, his ashes scattered along his favorite riding route for his motorcycle.

He asked that one quarter of his money be donated to his church. He left the rest of his finances to be split between Jen and Dani. He also indicated there was something for Dani in his shed along with a letter. Everything would be in a box with Dani's name on it.

Both Jen and Dani stared at the will. "I can't believe ..." was all Dani could say before looking away.

Jen went to the laundry room and came back with a flashlight and the key to the shed dangling from her other hand. Dani looked up and paused a moment before she stood up and took the flashlight. I followed them out the back door.

Despite a nearly full moon, the darkness of the night gave away how late it was. Missouri felt much cooler than Alabama, and I took a deep breath of the night air as we walked across the backyard to the shed. Jen unlocked the door and held it open while Dani held the flashlight and looked around.

It didn't take long for her to find it. She handed the flashlight to Jen
and took out the box. Dani placed it on the ground outside, then she
crouched over it and opened the lid. There was an envelope at the top,
crumpled newspaper below it. Dani opened the envelope, and Jen
handed her the flashlight so she could see better. As she read the letter,
she swallowed hard and handed the letter to Jen. Jen looked at it then
handed it to me as she put her arm around Dani, and Dani buried her face
into her sister's shoulder.

I held it up to the moonlight to read it.

Dani,

Never stop reaching for the stars, kiddo.

Dad

Dani wiped her face with her forearm and then moved away the newspaper. She gasped, and then she reached down and pulled out a small
telescope.

"Is that ...?" I asked.

She nodded, her gentle laugh mingled with her tears.

"Oh, Dani ..." was all I could say while I hugged her.

Jen reached down and pulled a small stand from the box, and she set
it down on the ground. Dani put the telescope on and stood and looked at
it for a few minutes, breathing slowly.

Jen went back inside and came out with the wine bottle. Dani pointed
the telescope toward the moon, and we all took turns looking through it.
We spent a couple of hours out there looking through that little telescope
and drinking wine from the bottle. Watching Dani and Jen, my heart
expanded as I took comfort in the beauty of the bond they shared.

The next day, their mom came into town. She hugged me when she
met me and thanked me for being there for Dani. Dani didn't want to go to
the service. She hated funerals and didn't feel comfortable with the idea
of being in the church her dad attended. While Jen and their mom went to
the service, Dani and I drove out to a lake and talked.

"It's so surreal," she said to me. "But at the same time, it is real, and
there's nothing I can do. I did what I could. There's no more trying."

Finality has a strangeness to it. The things you still wish you could
say, could do, or could try. *No more trying.*

I put my arm around her and put my head on her shoulder while we looked out across the lake.

"I'm not ready to come back to Alabama, Mae. I need to go further west, and go back home for a few days. I need to see the mountains and sleep in my own bed. I need a little respite before heading back to what we face." She paused. "I want you to come with me. I need you to. Will you?"

"Of course, I will." I held her and kissed her head. We stayed at the lake until we knew the service was over.

Late that afternoon, I went with Dani, Jen, and their mom to scatter the ashes along a road popular for motorcycle rides. I stood back a little out of respect and felt slightly out of place as I watched Jen, Dani, and their mom walk back with their arms around each other.

The next morning, Jen and Dani came up with a plan for coming back to St. Louis after Dani was finished with the forums in Alabama. Then they would go through the house and settle the estate. Jen encouraged Dani to go ahead and keep the truck and take it home to Oregon.

Late morning, Dani packed up the truck with her things and mine. Jen walked us to the truck and handed Dani the telescope.

"Be careful, Dani. I love you, and I'll see you soon," she said. She hugged me, too. "Mae, I hope I get to see you again sooner before later. It's been great to get to know you a little. You take care, too."

Dani and I got in the truck and headed out of town and westward, to Oregon, hoping to find something kinder before returning to the throes of hate.

NINETEEN

T he drive back to Oregon took three days. I was relieved to have
Mae along so I wouldn't feel so alone after all I had just been
through, and it didn't hurt that she helped with the drive. We stopped
to rest in a couple of towns along the way, and for the first day and a half
or so, we swapped stories about some of the other travels we had each
been on. I told her about my first time playing in New York: I got a
craving for Chinese food after sound check and almost missed my own
show because I got lost trying to get back to the small theater. Mae
shared funny stories about family vacations with her parents. I cracked
up the most at her dad going the wrong direction one year and taking
them to the wrong state.

We listened to music, and we talked about our past favorite concerts
and what shows we'd attend if we could go see anyone living or dead.
Mae's top choice was Joni Mitchell. Mine was Eva Cassidy. I savored
those couple of days with nothing to do but talk about the lighter things
in life while we drove across the changing landscapes.

As we made our way into Idaho, my mind turned back to Alabama
and all of the turmoil we would soon return to.

"So, how are you feeling about SASH's chances?" I glanced at Mae before setting my eyes back on the roadway.

"I'm hopeful. But I'd be lying if I said I wasn't worried, too." She shifted a little in her seat. I reached over and touched her hand a moment.

"What about Heather?" I asked. "I've actually been surprised by her in some ways, but how are you doing with it all? I know it's really different for you."

"To be honest, it's been confusing. At first, I only saw the same manipulation and control I've been used to, you know especially with how she handled the video situation. But, after she took that hit for Lara and after all she has done to help tell Rebecca's story, and then her coming to make sure I got home safe that night I was followed ..." Mae paused a moment, then stared out of her window again.

"Do you think she has changed?" I asked.

"I don't know," Mae looked over at me. "In some ways, yes, and in others, I just don't know. I'd like to think so." Mae returned her gaze outside. "Just thirty more miles to Oregon."

She kept her head turned, watching the fields go by, and we rode together in silence for a little while.

As we made our way into Oregon, Mae commented about how beautiful it was. I couldn't help but smile at her enjoying the beauty of it as we got closer and closer to my home. I loved it, too, and as the mountains came into view, my shoulders eased, and I breathed in deeply.

Once we got into town, we stopped by a grocery store for a few things and pulled into my driveway a couple hours before sundown. As the small rustic A-frame came into view, I sighed and looked at Mae. "This is it. Home at last."

When we walked in, the tongue and groove walls and cast-iron wood stove grounded me. The skylights and large windows allowed in sunlight filtered through the conifer trees surrounding my home. I grinned as Mae stood and looked around, taking in the beauty I had missed.

I walked into the kitchen and noticed my mail on the stone counter-top, placed there by my neighbor. She had also left a kind note with a bag of homemade biscotti and a box of jasmine green tea. I opened the fridge to put the groceries away and saw a pot of homemade soup, her usual way of welcoming me back home when I had been away for a while.

Mae and I warmed up the soup and then went outside to sit awhile. When darkness fell, I brought out the telescope, and we looked at the stars. We stayed mostly quiet that evening, exhausted from all of our driving, and we drifted off to sleep in each other's arms.

I had dreamed of Mae coming to stay with me in Oregon since we'd gone to visit her parents. I hated that we would be on a short timeline and that the reason I was home was to have some respite from all the heaviness. I wanted, so desperately, for Mae to fall in love with Oregon so much that she would say she could move there one day. Even though I couldn't say that out loud to her, I had to hold on to that hope.

We spent the mornings at my house, just resting, playing board games, and spending time together with nothing else to worry about while we had the chance. Still, we both knew the storm was ever present, looming in our minds and raging over two thousand miles away.

In the afternoons, we went hiking. I took her to some of my favorite trails, and one afternoon, we ventured closer to some of the bigger mountains in the area.

While we were trekking through the forest, I stopped at a majestic Douglas fir and admired the way the tree stretched so high, I could barely see the top. The branches spread in a glorious display, and I took in the aroma of rich earth and evergreen.

Mae came beside me, and I took her hand. We stood in silence and shared the moment together, and I drew in a deep breath, letting the sacred nature of the tree permeate my body and mind.

"What are you thinking, Dani?" she spoke in a near whisper.

I looked at her and back out at the forest.

"This is one of my favorite trails. I haven't been here in almost a year, but I still know it. I still know where it's heading, and what to expect when we get to the overlook. But I also don't know what to expect—what trees may have fallen, what new plants have sprouted, what trees have grown and created new lines on the horizon. In some ways, it feels like where I am now in life. I don't know what lies ahead exactly, but I feel comfort in that it feels familiar somehow, and I trust that I'm going in the right direction. At least I hope so."

We resumed our walk down the trail, hand in hand, and in my heart, I wondered if that sense of knowing paired with hope would be enough to sustain me, to sustain us for what was to come.

On our last night in Oregon, I pulled out some vinyl records, and put on Ella Fitzgerald and Louis Armstrong. I took Mae's hand, and we danced in my living room as we listened to "They Can't Take that Away from Me." Her cheek brushed across mine, warm and soft, her chestnut hair close enough for me to take in its scent as we moved to the music. I had often longed to dance to those songs with someone special. Then there we were—with the glow of candlelight, the crackle of the needle on old vinyl, the taste of wine on our lips, and the stars peeking down through the sky lights. I wished I could stay there, holding on to that moment, and holding to love that would be for no one to take away.

∾

MAE

The beauty of Oregon blew me away. The natural wonders around us rejuvenated me. I had never been anywhere quite like it, and Dani's home somehow gave me a feeling close to the serenity I felt at my parents' house.

While I was with Dani in Oregon, I tried to imagine what it could be like to live there. We held hands as we walked in public, and every time, I felt grateful for the ability to do that without the worry that we would be attacked. It seemed simple yet foreign from what I was used to in the South. Still, I couldn't shake the feeling of how hard it would be to be that far away from my family and to leave SASH and the work I had dedicated my life to.

As our flight took off to take us back to Alabama, I watched the mountain ranges disappear into the clouds, uncertain of when I might see them again. It was a long trip back, and the jet lag depleted all of my energy. By the time we landed in Alabama, it was after dark.

Rachel and Lara picked us up at the airport to drive us back. As the four of us rode southward, Rachel and Lara checked in on Dani.

Rachel turned her head to the side. "Dani, listen. I know that you've been through a lot, and we've asked a lot more than what you originally agreed to help with. If you need to sit out of any or all of these forums ..."

"No way, Rachel." Dani chuckled. "Are you kidding me? They are in four days. That's not enough time to plan something else."

Lara and Rachel glanced at each other.

"You know I'm right. Besides, I wouldn't dream of backing out even if I could. This is important to me, and I think it will help me to have this, ok? I'm ok."

Dani reached for my hand, and Lara smiled as Rachel nodded her head.

"So what have we missed?" I leaned forward a little in my seat.

Lara spoke up. "Well, we haven't had any other major attacks. Just the normal rhetoric and protests we've been seeing from The Way. But, Heather sure hasn't let up. She's been working her magic with a couple of radio spots and a guest appearance on the Birmingham morning show for Rachel. She's raised some awareness beyond the county and into parts of the state that have more money, and we've had some folks reach out wanting to help."

"It's pretty amazing actually. Heather's a rock star." Rachel's voice trailed off and she looked out of the window.

I pictured Heather orchestrating it all and beaming at the impact she had made, her ferocity paying off. It made me think of when she was at SASH the first time, and then most recently when she came to make sure I got home safely. The back of my neck burned, and I pulled gently at my shirt to keep it away from my neck, hoping no-one would notice in the dark.

It was nearly 2 AM on Saturday morning when we got back, and Dani stayed with me at my house so she wouldn't wake anyone at SASH. I got up early and made breakfast for the two of us and woke Dani up with a kiss and mug of coffee. We spent the early morning together, then I took her back to SASH so she could have plenty of time to rehearse her songs and reconnect with everyone before she would meet up with Heather that night to review and time their parts for the forums.

After I dropped Dani off, I drove back home, and heaviness stretched across my chest as I thought over the trip with Dani. I called Anita and asked her to come over. I knew I needed to talk to someone who could get it, and we sat down that evening on my back porch.

"How's Dani?" Anita asked. "I didn't get to see her much today."

"I think she's ok. I can tell she is tired, but I think going to Oregon for a couple of days helped to ground her a bit. At least, I hope so. Once the forums are over, she'll go back to Missouri to help her sister with settling their dad's estate."

"It just seems like a lot to deal with all at once," Anita sighed as she looked at me.

"Definitely," I looked into my wine glass then stared off the back porch into the fading light.

"What is it, Mae?"

I nearly whispered. "I really *really* love her, Anita. I can't imagine ... I hated seeing her in that much pain."

Anita drew up the corner of her mouth. "Sounds like you do really love her."

I smiled thinking of our drive. "Going out West, it was a long drive with nothing really to do but talk and listen to music, and we shared some stories with each other. It never got old, just being with her."

Anita gave a sideways smile and took a sip of her wine.

"You should see Dani's home, and the trees there look like they are from another world. We looked at the stars, and we danced together in her living room to old jazz records by candlelight."

Anita stared at me over her wine. "Damn, girl. If Lexy and me ever get back together she better step up her game" she said, and we both cracked up. Then she touched my hand. "Ok, so that seriously sounds amazing. What's keeping you from just basking in all that goodness?"

"I don't know, Anita. I thought it was amazing while I was there. I liked the idea of being somewhere where we could just be us without the stares or the fear, but it's just so far away. I don't want to be that far away from my family or my closest friends, and I just don't think I could leave SASH or doing this kind of work, like I've said before. It's missional for me." I sighed heavily. "I can't move. Not there, anyway. Even as much as I loved it, it isn't right for me."

Anita sipped her wine, then exhaled. "So you have to talk to Dani. But now isn't the time with everything that's happened," she said, reading my mind.

"She has way too much to deal with right now. I don't know. It just seems like a fragile time. I just want to give her some space, but not too much. We have to figure this out." I rubbed my temples and exhaled slowly.

Anita put her hand on my knee. "You do have to talk about it, honey. It's going to be hard, but you have to say something. Don't wait too long."

"I won't." I replied. "I'll talk to her soon."

"Good." Anita looked at me and winked. "Jazz records, candlelight, dancing in the living room under a skylight with starry skies above," she smiled and shook her head. "Yeah, you better figure this out."

TWENTY

DANI

As the forums drew closer, my hope for making an impact grew. I focused on what winning over more hearts and minds would mean to Sebastian, Aimee, Kyle, Ja'Marcus, and Sarah Beth. I couldn't let them down. I would spend several nights in a row, joining forces with Heather to try to turn the tide in our favor. Before we started the tour, we worked at Heather's apartment to time ourselves and smooth out our transitions.

After I played a song, Heather put her notes aside. "How are you holding up? Do you feel like you are still ok to do this?"

I rested my chin on my guitar and thought for a moment, while I turned my guitar pick with my fingers. "I'm holding up. I know sharing my story and hearing others will be hard, especially right now. I just feel raw most of the time now, you know?" I looked up at Heather. "But I don't feel like I have a choice. I mean, I know I technically do, but something inside tells me that this is why I am here, the reason I came to Alabama this Summer. I have to speak up, and I have to do my part to save SASH. And maybe, somehow, that will help me, too."

Heather raised her eyebrow and patted my knee before going back to her notes. "You're going to touch a lot of people, Dani."

I hoped she was right.

Open Hearts hosted the first night. The church felt so much like home, it only seemed natural to start there. Around 150 people showed up, a good number for a weeknight. Lara gave an introduction before I played a couple of songs. After my set, I introduced Rachel.

"This summer, I met someone who created a special place: SASH. This home gives young people a chance to not be homeless, and instead find family when they need it most. Rachel created that. Please welcome her as she tells you more about why we need your help."

Rachel walked up the steps and took the microphone. After a couple of sentences, she got silent for a moment and put her head down.

"There's a stack of papers on my desk that haunts me. Kids who have asked to come to SASH. Kids who I have to say 'no' to right now because I can't guarantee we will stay open. I can't even tell our current residents with any confidence that they will have a home six months from now. That's not ok. I hope you will help us."

Heather played the Reynolds video and read a few stories from former SASH residents who gave their account of how SASH helped save their lives, gave them hope, and helped them be successful in life. Lara gave a brief talk about affirmation within the Church and a call to citizens who considered themselves Christians to act with love to save SASH.

Near the end of the night, I decided to share more than I had originally planned before I sang my final song, "Belong."

I took a deep breath and paused as I looked out into the sanctuary of the church and made eye contact with Mae. I scanned the crowd and saw people, just normal everyday people. People like me. People like my dad. People like my sister. People in between. I took another breath and swallowed hard.

"So, I know you have heard a lot of stories tonight. My story isn't that different from what you've heard. When I was seventeen, my parents found out I was gay, and my dad said some very hateful things to me and kicked me out of the house. I had a sister who helped me, but other than her, I lost my family that night. I didn't have a steady place to stay for a while, because there was nothing like SASH available for me."

I closed my eyes for a moment and took a long slow breath in so I could feel my lungs and chest expand.

"I wasn't going to share this part, but I think it's important. A couple weeks ago, my dad passed away. I was able to get to the hospital before he was gone. He was unresponsive, but I still got to say some things to him." I looked down at the neck of my guitar and placed my fingers on the strings.

"Anyway, he died without ever telling me he was sorry, without ever listening to me again after the day I left. The last thing he ever said to me was horrible, and it nearly destroyed me. And honestly, if it weren't for my sister, it probably would have. I've had to learn the hard way that family isn't the people you are related to. Family is the love that ties people together when we choose each other." I looked at the front row, at my friends.

"This summer, I added to my family. Rachel, Lara, Anita, Mae, and all of those great kids at the safe home. They are family now. My family." I looked back out across the sanctuary.

"Please make sure they keep their home. Make sure you talk to your friends and your families about helping them. And if you have been like my dad, or like me—don't wait until it's too late."

I wiped my eyes and took a drink of water, then played the opening chords.

You and I
Are made of love and light
We're made for more than splits and strife
And the falsities running rampant through our time

I believe
We hold the golden key
Of connection so it runs deep
We affect each other
Can't you see

It's love that holds us
It's love that shows us
Across the spectrum of our hearts
Inside out of all we are
We belong

As my voice rang out, I thought of Jen. I thought of the heartache I had been through starting my senior year and going on until that night, all because of my dad. I felt as though I was letting it go. I was letting *him* go. I also felt with every note that I was taking in the love I had found, sharply contrasting the loud voices of rejection and hatred we had experienced in the community.

There is a lie
We have believed for some time
Fueling the fire which divides
Your sacred heart from mine

I believe
Love's the way which we can be
Made into a new family
And there's room at the table
Can't you see

It's love that holds us
It's love that shows us
Across the spectrum of our hearts
Inside out of all we are
We belong

We're made of love and light
Together you and I
Don't believe the lie
Can't you see

It's love that holds us

It's love that shows us
Across the spectrum of our hearts
Inside out of all we are
We belong

We're made of love and light
Together you and I
Don't believe the lie
Can't you see

I closed my eyes near the end, unable to make eye contact with the people I loved as salty tears filled my eyelids. I wanted the words to be true even if I couldn't believe in all of them. Maybe they were true for somebody. Maybe they would help save SASH. When I finished the song, I opened my eyes to see Mae wiping her tears away. The audience stood and clapped as Heather walked up and hugged me, her face reddened and eyes glossy, the most emotion I had seen in her since we met.

Heather ended the night with one more story to drive the point home.

"There was a girl who grew up not far from here, just over the Georgia line. When she was seventeen, her parents found out she was a lesbian, and they kicked her out of the house. For months, she hid at school after the last bell rang and slept in the library. The sound of the doors unlocking woke her up in the mornings. Finally, one of the girl's aunts welcomed her in and allowed her to stay until the girl left for college. If not for her aunt, she wouldn't have been able to go to school, have a career, or be here tonight." She paused and took in a breath. "This is my story. I realize I was lucky enough to have someone care, and these kids don't have that. I hope you'll be someone who cares for them."

I had always imagined Heather had things easy, and in that moment, the walls I had put up toward her gave way. As I stood to the side and watched, Lara walked up to the stage and closed the night with a prayer and commissioned the crowd to be welcoming and defend those in need.

Night after night, Heather and I went to several churches and stood in front of people from the community, hoping they would hear us and take what we had to say into their hearts. We rode together, and every night, Heather assured me that what I was saying was helping and would change people. After our last forum in the series, we rode back toward SASH, and Heather pulled off onto a gravel area.

"What is it?" I asked.

She turned to me and put her hand on mine.

"You've done an amazing job, Dani. I couldn't have asked for a better person to partner with for this series. But I just wanted to check —are you sure you are ok?" she asked quietly. "You've just been through so much."

I stared out of the window at the cloudy sky, unable to look to the stars for guidance or grounding. I pushed my hair back from my face and shook my head. I looked down, barely able to see in the darkness. "Not really." My voice sounded hoarse and tired. "So much has happened this summer, good and bad, and it's hard to know how to feel sometimes, like now."

"Of course. That has to be hard, Dani," Heather said. "What can I do?"

"I don't think there's anything anybody can do." My throat burned from all of the singing and speaking, but also from all of the emotion surging through me since I had gotten the call from Jen. I couldn't hold in my worry anymore. "I go back to Missouri to help my sister with Dad's estate, and I honestly don't know how I am going to come back here. It was so hard to come back to Alabama when I got to go home for a few days. I don't see how people like us can stay here. It just feels like an uphill climb all the time. I've lived so much of my life that way, it just seems like I would be taking a few steps back to live in a place like here."

"Does that mean you are set on going back to Oregon and staying there once you're done with the album?" Heather's voice was quiet and gentle.

"I don't know, maybe." I shifted in my seat. "I'm not sure. I have a lot I need to figure out."

"What about Mae?" Heather asked.

"I don't know, but surely we can figure something out. I hope she will come with me eventually, but ... I don't know that she will." I looked out of the window again.

Heather put her hand on my shoulder. "You deserve to be happy, Dani." Then she pulled back onto the road and drove me back.

∼

MAE

I drove Dani to the airport to catch her flight to Missouri. We rode together in near silence, early on a Saturday morning. I wished that I could go with her, but with the vote coming up, I needed to help at SASH. The next few days were bound to be hard for each of us, and the cruelty that we couldn't be together to support each other tightened the tension between us. I didn't know what to say, so I reached over to touch her most of the drive and hoped she knew my heart.

At the airport drop-off, Dani pushed my hair back behind my ear as she kissed me. "Don't worry about me. Jen and I will take good care of each other. We always do."

"I know." I put my arms around her and closed my eyes. "Don't worry about me either. There's so much to do that it'll keep me busy enough to not get trapped in my mind."

We kissed again, and I watched Dani walk inside the airport before I drove away.

Along the drive back, my mind felt cluttered. Though I tried to stay hopeful, the outcome of the upcoming vote worried me. I whispered silent, open-eyed prayers that all of our work had been impactful enough to make a difference. It just had to. I couldn't allow myself to think about what would happen to the residents or to Rachel, Anita, or me if we got shut down.

Dani planned to be in Missouri for several days, but promised to be back in time for the vote. In the meantime, we had a little more work to do to try to win over the residents. Heather had some signs made with money she had received from a couple of national organizations. She had also matched the amount with her own money so that we could have twice as many signs made and cover the county. There was a selflessness in her actions that stood out to me since she had been enlisted to help us. I wondered if it meant she had truly changed from the Heather that wounded me.

I volunteered to drive my truck and help put the signs out early on Sunday morning with Sebastian and Heather. The plan was to drive to Heather's apartment and load them up there, then we would drive around the county and place them out for as much visibility as possible. I got to SASH at about 6 AM. Sebastian came outside and got in my truck. He was coughing and looked pale and exhausted.

"Oh my gosh, are you sick?" I looked at his flushed face and didn't wait for him to answer. "Just go back inside and get some rest."

"I'm sorry, Mae." He climbed out of the truck.

"Seriously, it's no worries. Just go take care of yourself." I watched him walk back inside to make sure he was alright and then headed down the gravel toward the road. I realized this meant Heather and I would have to work alone. I shook my head and sighed as I gripped the steering wheel on the way to her apartment.

I pulled into the parking lot, and Heather walked outside and waved from her balcony. I walked up the stairs to her door and stood outside with my hands in my pockets.

"Where's Sebastian?" She looked down at my truck. "Is he ok?"

"He's sick. I told him to get some rest." I looked down.

"Well, that's ok." She smiled at me and put one hand on her hip. "We can handle it."

She motioned for me to come inside, and I stepped in. She handed me an armload of signs and carried a load herself. It took us a few trips to get all two hundred of them. By the time we left, it was 8 AM, and the sun already beat down upon us as it moved upward in the sky.

We drove all over the county that morning, putting up the "save the safe home" signs. We rode in silence for about the first hour, only talking when we had to. As we approached a bigger town in the county, a bright red billboard came into our view. "Do not harbor sin and wickedness. Remove the UN-Safe Home."

I slowed down, and Heather shook her head.

"Looks like The Way isn't giving up." She stared at the sign.

"No, but I guess all of your lawsuits have scared them into changing tactics." I looked at Heather and smiled, and she grinned back at me before looking out of the window again.

"You know?" I tried to keep the conversation going. "I feel pretty hopeful about our chances. I'm still nervous, though."

"I'm a little nervous, too." She looked at me a moment. "I actually always get nervous with these kinds of things. There's just so much on the line. I'll be honest, though, I can't help but believe we've made a deeper impression on people than what I usually see. Especially with Dani's help. People gravitate to her."

"Yeah, she's pretty fantastic." I pushed my hair back and smiled.

We drove throughout the county over the next couple of hours, setting out signs. By the time we finished, it was almost noon, and the heat had exhausted both of us. I pulled into the parking lot at Heather's apartment complex, and Heather paused as she got out of my truck.

"Why don't you come upstairs and get a refill of water? It's been a brutal morning with this heat."

"Ok. Sure."

I followed her upstairs and into her kitchen. I gulped down one bottle then refilled again.

She held open the door to her fridge after she replaced the pitcher.

"Why don't you stay for a while? I'll make us some lunch."

I hesitated but then thought of how well we had been getting along all morning. "Ok. Just for a little bit."

We sat down in her living room, and between the water, the salad she made, and the air conditioning, I finally felt cooled down.

"I have some news," she said and put her hair behind her ears. "There's a good chance I'm going to accept a position at a local university, building up their LGBTQ resource center."

"Wow, Heather. That actually sounds great for you." I paused. "So you'll be moving to Alabama?"

"Most likely, yes. I mean I will if I accept the offer, and I'm leaning toward it. I want to switch from all of the behind the scenes work I've done for years and do something that directly serves our community." She winked. "I guess you really inspired me with all that you've done. And Rachel, too."

Heat rose to my face, and we sat in silence for a few moments.

"So, I guess Dani is leaving soon after the vote to go to Nashville?"

"Yeah, she is," I sighed, thankful for the change in subject.

"So, what are you going to do? When she goes back to Oregon?" She rested her chin on her hand.

"Well, I'm hoping she will be back soon to visit, and I know it would be a long time, but maybe she would even be willing to move closer one day." I looked up at Heather, and she shifted in her seat.

"I'm sorry, I shouldn't have said anything." She looked away.

A strong sinking feeling permeated my body. "What do you mean? What are you talking about?"

"I'm sorry, Mae. I thought you and Dani would have talked about it by now, as close as I thought you were." She paused. "I really shouldn't tell you, but Dani told me that she wants to stay in Oregon. She's had such a hard time here, and she can't see herself coming back. She was hoping you would leave, but I know you better than that. I know how important your family and your work are to you."

I swallowed and stared ahead.

Heather added, "I didn't say anything to her. I just let her talk, and I figured it was up to the two of you to work it out together."

I looked down, and she touched my hand. "I'm sorry, Mae. I truly am. What can I do?" She spoke in a soft voice.

I could only whisper back. "Nothing." I just stared. I felt like the wind had been knocked out of me. I knew Dani seemed down about being back and that she had seemed a little withdrawn. *Why hadn't I put those things together? Why didn't she trust me enough to tell me? Were we kidding ourselves that we could find a way?*

"I need to go," I stood up.

Heather got up, too, and walked me to the door.

"Are you ok?" she touched my arm. I looked at her and shook my head, and as hard as I tried, I couldn't hold back the tears. She put her arms out and pulled me in, and I cried on her shoulder. She put one hand on the back of my head, her other arm around my back, holding me close to her. It felt odd, but familiar, her strong arms around me, her soft dark hair near my face. The tension of wanting to push her away swirled with the comfort of being embraced.

"You don't deserve this, Mae. I don't want to see you hurt," she said softly. "And I know I hurt you, and I feel terrible for everything I put you through, and if I had it to do over again, I would love you the way you deserve to be." She put her head down closer to mine, and I held on to her a little tighter, hugging her back.

"You have to look out for yourself, Mae. SASH needs you, and you know, if Dani can't make some kind of sacrifice for you, then maybe she isn't good enough for you. And maybe there's someone else who's willing to make changes and be who and where you need her to be so *you* can thrive."

I turned my head to look away, not wanting to listen to what she was saying. I loved Dani, and I didn't want to give up.

Before I could look back, Heather turned my head toward her face and kissed me.

I froze. A flood of feelings and memories washed over me, the love, the tenderness we had in the beginning, the grief, the fury, the confusion, and for a few moments, I couldn't think or move before I finally pulled away.

"I have to go. Now." I hurried out the door, down the stairs and into my truck. I drove away to put as much distance between us as I could.

I got home and went straight to the shower. I stood and let the water hit me, feeling the cool water on my warm face. After I got out of the shower and got dressed, I saw the picture of Rebecca and me on my nightstand. *What would she have thought if she saw me?*

I trudged to my kitchen and opened a cabinet and pulled out a bottle of whiskey and stared at it.

I looked at my phone to see what time it was, and I had a text from Dani.

Things are ok here. Sad, but ok. Hope you are well. I'll call soon. I love you.

My throat felt tight, and I put the bottle back. I got out my journal, hoping that writing would help me release some of what I carried. I couldn't say anything to anyone else. As I opened to a blank page, I paused and realized for the first time in a while, I felt truly alone.

TWENTY-ONE

DANI

I stayed on autopilot as I helped Jen with boxing up and labeling Dad's things. Each room reminded me how little I knew him, and I realized I had no reference for what he was like after the day I left home, no way to know if anything I knew and loved of him had remained. In the middle of his CD collection, sat all four of my albums. I picked them up and looked over them for a moment before setting them down again. *Why did he have those? Did he listen to them? What did he think of the music I had written, the way I bled my emotions through the songs straight from the wounds he gifted me?*

Jen held one of his jackets as she sat on the sofa and looked around the living room. "Do you want anything?"

I shook my head as she took a deep breath and put the jacket down and rested her hand on it. "I think I'll keep this, but we should give the rest of his clothes to a local shelter."

"Are you ok, Jen?" I sat down next to her, and she wiped her eyes.

"What can I do?" My voice softened the silence. Where Jen felt sadness, I felt numb, so I tried to shift my focus on the opportunity to be supportive for her like she had always been for me.

"I don't think there's anything you can do, Dani. Maybe if we just sit here and talk about something else for a bit. Just anything to get my mind somewhere else. Maybe you can tell me more about how things are going with Mae?" Jen squeezed my hand and looked me in the eye.

"Sure. Well, what do you want to know?"

"I don't know. I do really like her." She pushed her hair out of her face.

"Me, too!" I said laughing. It made Jen chuckle, and I smiled at her. "I never expected to meet someone this summer, especially not in the South. But you know, she captivated me from the beginning. And as I've gotten to know her more, I've just been drawn further in. The love I have for her feels different from anything else I've known."

Jen grinned at me. "I'm so happy for you." She patted my hand. Then she looked off into the distance, thinking as her smile faded.

"Dani, will she move? Will you move? What's going to happen? I know you've faced a lot of prejudice this summer, and I would worry about you if you moved to Alabama. It just seems so harsh, and you've had enough rejection in your life. You don't need more hatred and vitriol thrown your way."

"Yeah, Dad took care of that department," I spoke without thinking first. Jen grimaced then touched my hand.

"Dani, there's so much I want to say to you, but there really aren't words. The way Dad treated you ..." she rubbed her eyes. "You know how I feel about it. It was terrible. And just because he died doesn't mean I've forgotten any of that. I love you, and I'm always on your side."

I held her hand. "And I know. You aren't just a sister, you're my best friend. The best I've ever had." I gave her hand a squeeze before letting go.

I stood and walked over to a window and pushed my hair back away from my face and forehead, holding it back while I thought.

"I can't move to Alabama," I turned to look at Jen. "It's just so damn hostile to me ... the heat, the hate, the humidity."

"You should write a tourism brochure with all that alliteration." Jen smirked at her wise crack, and I couldn't help but chuckle.

I thought a moment as I looked at my sister. "I have to talk to Mae when I get back," I sighed as I sat down again. "I want to ask her to come with me to Oregon again, just to give her some more time visiting there. If I'm honest though, I don't think it would work. I don't think she would move far away." I stared at the floor and focused on the patterns in the rug.

"You know, I talked with Lara about all of this. She encouraged me to be open minded about things that may come along we haven't even thought of, but I don't even know what that might look like, or if there even is any other way. I just want to be open if it means more of a chance. I love her, Jen. I don't know what's next, but I know I want to experience it with her."

Jen put her arms around me and held me tight, just like she had always done.

We spent a few more hours sorting through dad's house and shed, packing up the rest of what we would donate. Later that afternoon, we drove to a local bank to settle dad's finances. When we got to the bank, the branch manager took us into her office and expressed her condolences. She brought us a safety deposit box as well as printouts detailing dad's accounts and then left to give us some privacy.

Jen's mouth dropped open, and she handed me the top paper. It turned out dad had invested well since the divorce, and with my share, I was inheriting a significant amount of money. I felt shocked, a little angry, confused, and hurt. *Did he think this was a way to make up for what he had done?*

"I don't want it," I whispered, looking up at Jen. I paused and looked out the office window. I watched a woman get out of her car, then go around to the back and open the door. A little girl with braided hair squinted as she got out of the car and took the woman's hand. I watched them walk toward the bank, and I looked back at Jen.

"I know what I'm going to do with it," I said, a bit surprised at the resolve in my own voice, and Jen squeezed my hand as if she knew.

"If it's what I think you are thinking, Dani, I'm in," she said to me. I knew it would take some more talking and planning, but I hoped we could get it worked out before the end of the year.

Later that night, we drank wine and talked at the fire pit in the backyard. We would be leaving the next day, and it would be awhile until we could see each other again. Jen asked me to come to her house to stay before I started touring again. With the way my music career had ramped up in the past couple of years, the only extended time I had for visits had been around the holidays, and planning a visit with my sister was long overdue.

The next morning, she loaded her SUV with a few things she kept of Dad's. I had a small box shipped back home with a few baseball cards, some pictures, and a few books on astronomy. When she dropped me off at the airport, I held her tightly and kissed her cheek before I headed inside. She held the back of my head in her hand.

"I'm proud of you Dani."

She stood and watched me go inside, waving again as I walked to the check-in counter.

Loneliness kept me company on my trip back to Alabama. I had too much time to think. I worried about Jen, then my mind turned to worrying over the vote and whether The Way would do anything else to hurt SASH. I only had a couple weeks left in Alabama before I would head up to Nashville to start recording, and I dreaded leaving Mae. My mind swirled from one thought to the next, and before I knew it, the captain announced that the plane was landing.

Soon, I saw Lara smiling and waving outside the luggage claim, and my pace quickened to meet her. I hugged her and walked with her to her car.

"How have things been here?" I asked as she put her key in the ignition.

"Stressful," she chuckled a little. As she turned onto the road, she glanced over at me, more serious. "The local radio station has been doing polls, and it's tight. So we can't be sure of anything."

"How's Rachel holding up?" As we drove along the same path Rachel had driven me on when I first arrived in Alabama, I thought of her story. I replayed her telling it to me and the way it rubbed across the open wound in my heart as we drove to SASH that first time. It felt like a whole year had passed, even though it had only been a couple of months.

"She's hanging in there. She's quiet a lot, and she tries to put on a brave face when she's at work. But I see how broken she is over it all when it's just us." Lara shifted in her seat. "I think it's good she has Cynthia here, too. She's been so supportive to Rachel. Well, you know how she helped her back when she was homeless."

I nodded as Lara glanced over again.

She focused her eyes back on the road. "I think because of that, she gives Rachel a sense of home that keeps her grounded. She'll be ok. How about you, Dani? We haven't talked much since everything that's happened with you."

"I'm hanging in there, too. I'd be lying if I said it hasn't been hard, though." My voice faltered and I looked out of my window. "When I was a kid, he gave me this telescope for my birthday. It was a big deal to me, and when we went over his will, he had left instructions that led me to find it in his shed with a little note. He also left me half of his finances, and that's confused me. Like, I wonder if it's because he thought it would somehow reconcile the way he treated me."

"Dani, that is so confusing. I don't know of anything I can say or do to help, but I am here, and you can say as much or as little as you need."

"Thanks, Lara," I looked out of the window at the fields and trees for a few minutes. The green fullness of midsummer had started to yellow, giving way to the beginning of brown and dry.

"You want to hear something crazy?" I asked, breaking the silence. "Before Dad passed, I talked to him while he was unconscious, and I forgave him." I looked over at Lara, and her lips curled into a slight smile.

"I don't even know exactly what forgiveness is or what it means. It still hurts, what Dad did and said to me, but I was able to let him go at the end, and I let him know he didn't owe me anything. I didn't want anything from him." I paused and looked over at Lara, "But dammit, here he is leaving me half of everything." We both laughed.

Before I knew it, we were back. I saw Mae's truck parked in front of the house, and I felt my heart skip a beat. I couldn't wait to see her and have some time to talk. I got my bag out of Lara's trunk and looked at the house as I walked toward the entrance. I couldn't believe it had been so many weeks since I first laid my eyes on it, or that my time there was almost over. I walked inside, and I saw Mae walking toward the door to greet us.

She hugged me and told me she was glad I was back. I held her tightly and kissed her, and she put her head against mine. I wondered if something was wrong, but before I could ask, Rachel came from the office and hugged me, welcoming me back. We all headed for the dining room, and I felt Mae's hand on my arm, barely there and almost slipping away.

~

MAE

When Dani got back, I felt a strong urge to hide. I had to tell her what happened with Heather, but I couldn't bring myself to say anything yet. There had to be too much on her mind to handle anything else, and the fact she had been immersed in her dad's death when it happened only added to my shame. We had a limited amount of time left before she would leave for Nashville, and I wanted to be with her. Yet, the walls around my heart started to rebuild, even against my will.

The first couple of days after she got back flew by. We all busied ourselves to keep from worrying too much about the vote. Rachel paced the floor between phone calls. She knew her mood impacted the rest of the staff, so she kept to herself instead of talking. We could still see it on her face, as the lines deepened, and her eyes displayed the reddened and tired hallmarks from tears she tried to hide.

One evening, Dani and I went to the garden together to pick flowers for the dinner table. We figured it would brighten the mood a little and hoped it would bring a sense of normalcy to everyone. The air hung thick with muggy heat. I looked over at Dani as she took the zinnia stems in her hands and cut them with the garden shears. Her shoulders bore the sun-kissed look of summertime, her hairline damp with sweat, further framing her face. I wanted to stay in that moment, just looking at her, but the memory of what happened forced my eyes away.

"I can't believe summer is almost over," Dani spoke, breaking the silence. My mind churned with what I wanted to say in response, but all I could manage was a nod of my head.

"Mae, I can't stay here. I know you know that much, but I mean—I can't live in Alabama. Or Georgia. Or anywhere near here. It's just—maybe I should wait until the vote is over to talk about it, but we have to face what's ahead, and I don't know—try to figure something out. We're running out of time before I leave."

I looked into Dani's green eyes and struggled to hold their gaze.

"I know," I sighed. "You're right. We can't avoid it anymore."

Thunder rumbled in the distance, and we looked up to see a storm moving in. Dani frowned as tiny globes of water began to fall from the sky. Before we could move, the cloud erupted and pelted down on us.

"Come on," I yelled above the roar of the rain as I grabbed Dani's hand, and we dashed to the barn. It felt like ages since the first time I had taken Dani there. I unlocked the latch, and we went inside. Water dripped down Dani's face, and it trickled down my cheeks, nose, and neck.

We stood with the door open for a moment watching the storm as the thunder and rain grew louder. I shut the door, and as I turned around, Dani took my face in her hands and kissed me. My mouth mingled with the rain that dripped down from her hair as I held her close to me.

"I don't know what's going to happen." She rested her forehead on mine. She took a step back and looked into my eyes. "I do know one thing. Meeting you and getting to know you this summer has been the best thing that's happened to me in a really long time. I don't know how to explain how connected I feel to you, but it reminds me of when I write a song, and I don't play it for a while. Then I pick up my guitar years later, and somehow, my fingers go to the strings, and my voice knows every note and every lilt. Loving you is like that, Mae. I love you by heart."

My heart pounded in my chest, and I put my hands on Dani's face and kissed her again. Her hands rested on mine, and held them. Then, we held on to each other. I felt too much at once. The rush of love and wonder slowed with dread and worry. The heat of attraction cooled by shame and regret.

"I can't leave here. Not now," my voice shook. "And I don't know about the future. I need to be somewhere where I can make a difference. I don't know what the answer is."

Dani sighed and looked down, shuffling her feet. "I'm going to spend some time at my sister's house in Colorado after I'm done recording. Then I'm going back home for a few weeks before I release the record. Maybe we can just visit each other as much as we can for a while, and we can keep thinking through everything. I don't want to give up," she took my hand.

The rain ceased, and a sudden silence took its place. We walked outside to see a rainbow in the distance. We made our way back to the house, and as what-ifs filled my mind, I tightened my grip on Dani's hand.

Before we knew it, it was time for the local polls to open. On the night of the vote, I stayed late to watch the results with the other staff. We decided it would be best to send the residents to bed. We expected the results to be tight and knew it could be a long night ahead.

Just before the precincts started closing, Heather arrived with two large canvas grocery bags full of snacks for everyone. She grinned at me, and I averted my eyes. It was the first time I had seen her since she had kissed me. I walked to the kitchen and opened a bottle of wine as I avoided her stare. I filled up a few glasses, and took two in my hand to take to the others. As I walked to go to the living room, Heather stood in the doorway, leaning against the frame with her hands in her pockets.

"Hey," she said, smirking. "You disappeared on me."

I shrugged my shoulders and started to walk by. She placed her hand on my lower back and looped her finger through my belt loop, catching me. She did the exact same thing in the home we once shared, usually after an argument when I wanted to walk away, but she wanted me to stay. She would catch me and sweet talk me until I melted into the mold she wanted to fit me in, always giving what I wanted over to her desires.

I turned around and whispered, "please don't" before walking away.

I stepped into the living room where everyone else fixed their eyes on the screen as the first tallies came through. No one seemed to notice how unsettled I was. Heather walked in soon after I did, drinking a glass of wine and peering at me over the rim from time to time.

The early results were too close to call, which was what we expected to happen. As the night wore on, the tally grew larger, showing more people turned out to vote on the issue than any of us had anticipated.

Rachel leaned forward often, hands clasped and brought to her face, focused on what the night would hold for SASH and the work she had devoted her life to. Lara kept a close watch on her, staying close and checking in with her.

Around 1 AM, something surprising happened. The last precinct reported, and the final results came in with a wider margin anyone could have guessed would occur, by nearly ten percentage points. We won.

Rachel and Lara cried and hugged each other. Anita jumped up and down and danced. Dani hugged me and laughed with unbelief and relief. Heather smiled as Rachel thanked her. The others also gave Heather high fives and hugs. I kept my distance, and said, "Great work, Heather," and she smiled at me.

After the eruption of joy quieted, Dani and I went outside to the front porch and sat on the swing. Coolness filled the air, giving the sign that Fall was near. We sat there in silence, knowing goodbye was upon us. I almost asked her to stay. I almost asked her to come back to Alabama after she finished recording. I almost told her about Heather. Instead, I stayed quiet, and we fell asleep there, a blanket around us. We woke up to the greyness of dawn and a damp chill in the morning air.

Twenty-Two

Dani

As my last week at SASH began, the fact I would have to say goodbye to my new friends and to Mae loomed heavy over me. The relief and joy I had felt over winning the vote soon faded, and I spent the mornings breathing deeply before heading downstairs, my head hung low as I tried to take in the sound of the creaking staircase, the smell of the coffee brewing in the kitchen, and the sounds of the residents laughing together. In the evenings, I scratched out my thoughts in my journal and made notes on the songs I would be recording in the Nashville studio. Sleep evaded me, and I tossed and turned as my mind flurried with what ifs and Mae.

Two days before I left, I spent some extra time with the residents and went to group one last time. I looked around the room, trying to find the words I wanted to say.

"I don't think I can fully express how you've impacted me. That first day I came to group, I felt overwhelmed by how much your own stories reminded me of mine. I remember wondering if I would be able to handle being here this summer, not because you are too much, but because I realized I hadn't fully healed from all the pain in my past." I paused and looked around the room, my voice stretched. "But somehow this summer, getting to know each of you has brought a little more healing in my own life. It's funny to me now that I thought I was coming here to help you and help SASH thrive, when it turns out you've all helped me. So, thank you."

"You have helped us, Dani." Sarah Beth spoke up, smiling. "I think, at least for me, you've shown me how I can turn around the bad stuff that's happened to me into something good."

"I'd say the same thing," Ja'Marcus laughed while Aimee and Sebastian nodded and grinned.

Kyle's mouth curled to one side, and he cleared his throat. "You've given me a lot of hope. Thanks."

Before leaving the room, I gave them each a hug and asked them to keep me posted on how things were going for them. Mae stood in the corner of the room as they left, her face red and arms crossed.

On my last morning at SASH, when the light was still grey, I went for a walk with Rachel. The air felt cool, and a light mist softened the lines of the pastures.

"I'm going to miss you, Dani," Rachel held her arms close to her as we walked along the fence line.

"I'll miss you, too, Rachel." I pushed my hair behind my ears.

"I don't think you'll ever know the full impact you've made. On the residents, our staff, and our community. You've touched a lot of hearts, including mine. I can't say thank you enough," she looked at me.

"Well, I don't think I could ever communicate how much this whole summer has affected me. I've learned so much about perseverance and what it means to shine light into dark places. I've gained friends that feel like family. Hell, I've even fallen in love," I said laughing a little as Rachel smiled and chuckled back. "Thank you." I stopped walking and looked her in the eye.

Rachel put her arms around me and held onto me for a moment "I'm so proud of you. And I feel grateful I get to know you, Dani." I thought back to that first moment I shared with Rachel, walking to her car, feeling unsure of myself and whether I was doing the right thing. I knew I had made the right decision to come to Alabama, a moment somehow orchestrated beyond my own understanding.

That night, the residents and staff gave me a send-off party that took me back to my first night in Alabama. The windows of the home glowed orange as we sat around a bonfire out back. I brought my guitar outside, and we sang together. I fell silent as I played, listening to the voices of people I had grown to deeply love. I watched them, their faces bright from the firelight, surrounded in shadow behind. I closed my eyes, hoping I could hold on to the memory.

As the night wore on, Mae stayed quiet and on the periphery. Her hair reflected the glow of the fire as she stared into her cup. I knew that my leaving would be harder for both of us than we had anticipated, and as I watched her, I hoped she would be ok. I knew it was time to go home with her one last time before leaving for a while.

After I hugged everyone goodbye, I walked over to Mae's truck, which she had already loaded up with my guitar and bags. Rachel walked us over and hugged me one last time, "Let me know when you make it to Nashville. We'll see you in October for our wedding. And thank you, again."

As Mae drove her truck down the gravel road, the house disappeared from sight, and hot tears welled up inside my eyes. I knew I was ready to leave, and yet I still didn't feel ready to say goodbye. I was leaving some of the best friends I had found, my new family of sorts. The hardest goodbye was still to come.

Mae and I were mostly quiet on the way back to her place, only breaking the silence to comment on the going away party. We didn't say anything else until we pulled into her driveway. Mae stopped the engine and sat a minute before she whispered, "I need a shower from the fire."

"Me, too," I responded as I opened my door.

She set out fresh towels while I got out a shirt and pajama pants to sleep in. I walked into the bathroom, and we both stepped into the steamy spray of the water, anxious to rid our hair of the lingering smoke. After rinsing my hair, I turned and put my arms around Mae. Our bodies pressed together as we held on. I could feel her hands tight on my back as I rested my head against her forehead. She kissed me before stepping out. I stood there a few more moments, letting the water fall on my face in hopes to wake up a little more.

When I came out, I found Mae on her screened in porch, resting her head on her knees and staring into the dark of the night. I sat next to her and rested my hand on hers.

The air bore a slight early chill, and I shivered. I didn't know what to say, even though hundreds of words ran through my mind. Words like "promise, future, possibility," as well as "love, committed, trust," among a barrage of others. Instead of those, when I spoke, all I could manage was, "It's getting late."

Mae looked out into the darkness and answered, "It is late. We should go inside. You have a long drive tomorrow."

We walked into her room and lay on her bed, silent. I snuggled in close and held onto her as we drifted off to sleep.

The next morning, I woke up to the smell of breakfast cooking and the sight of Mae handing me a cup of coffee. It reminded me of when I brought coffee to her after we were up all night, worried about Kyle and his overdose. After Mae walked out of the room, I stared into my mug a few moments, remembering.

I got up and walked to the kitchen and put my arms around Mae as she stood at the counter, moving omelets onto our plates. She put her hands on mine then turned around, and we stood holding each other in silence.

"I know you have to go," she whispered. "But it's still hard. I still don't want you to."

I breathed in slowly, "I know. I don't want to say goodbye, because I don't know ..." I couldn't finish the sentence. Because I didn't know how.

After breakfast, Mae drove me to pick up my rental car. She helped me move my bags and guitar from her truck to the car. We kissed each other, and I promised to call when I got to Nashville. I got in the car, and started to drive away as I listened to Eva Cassidy's "Early Morning Rain." I looked at Mae standing next to her truck, watching and waving goodbye, her image disappearing from the rear view mirror, but etched deeply in my mind.

∽

MAE

Watching Dani drive away felt surreal. Everything moved in slow motion as I drove back home. I was thankful that it was Saturday, and I didn't have to work. Anita came by later that afternoon, so we could make dinner together, and we sat on my screened in porch and talked while we ate.

"How you holding up?" she started.

"I'm ok, I think. We've talked about visiting each other when we can, and that helps. But there's still so much up in the air—you know? It worries me."

She looked at me and touched my hand for a brief moment.

"I know you'll figure it out," her soft voice provided the ground for my thoughts to sprawl like a patch of blackberry brambles.

I took a drink of my water and stared outside at the backyard, remembering the night in Dani's backyard, when we looked through the telescope together and how perfect Dani seemed in that moment, her wonder at the stars and the gentleness of her melancholy showing through.

Then, my mind turned to Heather, and how perfect everything seemed at first, but how quickly things changed. The thought of Heather led me to the memory of her kissing me in her apartment while Dani was in Missouri, and the flood of confusion and shame nauseated me.

What was wrong with me? What if I was wrong about Dani? About Heather? Had she changed? Did it matter to me?

"What is it, Mae?" Anita asked me, as if she could see my mind chasing thought after thought.

I startled out of my thoughts, embarrassed that someone else was there while I was remembering.

"It's nothing," I said. "I just know we have a lot to figure out."

She kept her silence as she looked into my eyes, an invitation to say more, but I couldn't. I wasn't ready to talk about it all with anyone, not even Anita. She changed the subject to work, and we spent the rest of the evening reflecting on how glad we were that SASH won the vote.

When I got to work on Monday, I noticed Heather's car parked in front of the house. I went inside, stepping lightly so she wouldn't hear, and I heard her talking with Rachel in her office as I walked by to go to the group room. The group discussions that day centered on saying goodbye to Dani and on the new school year and what it might hold for each of the residents. Considering all the heaviness we had been through, it felt like a relief to have a lighter group time.

After group time was over, I looked out the window to see that Heather's car was still there. Then I made my way to the kitchen and noticed her in the dining room, helping set the table. She stayed for dinner and told everyone she was heading back home to Atlanta the next morning. Rachel thanked Heather for her work to help SASH stay open and in helping us gain so much support from the community.

Heather turned her eyes downward and shook her head, "It was you all, not me. I just helped."

My eyes stayed fixed on her as I tried to process what she said. It wasn't like Heather to be so humble. *Or was it? How could I know for sure? How could I be sure of anything?*

Once dinner was over, I went outside to the porch and watched the residents play kickball in the yard. A cool breeze blew across the fields and set the wind chimes into melodic motion. The chill in the air seemed too soon, replacing the warmth I had become used to.

I heard some footsteps next to me, and I glanced over to see Heather standing nearby.

"Can I sit down?" she asked me.

I nodded my head and turned to face the fields and gaze across the waving grasses.

"I wanted to tell you something," she said to me, her voice gentle and quiet. "Well, a couple of things. And I know it might not matter, but I need to say it."

I looked over at her as I shifted in my chair and wrapped my arms around myself.

"First—" she turned toward me "—I am sorry if I confused you or hurt you. I shouldn't have kissed you. I would say I am sorry for kissing you, but that wouldn't be true."

The back of my neck set on fire, and I looked down in silence. As I pictured being there in that moment, when she turned my face toward her and kissed me, the uneasiness filled me. I couldn't bear to look at her, but I wanted to give her the space to talk.

She continued on, "I also wanted to tell you that I am coming back. I accepted the position at the university, and I'm moving to Alabama in a few weeks. I'm looking forward to doing something meaningful, and I already talked with Rachel about using my position to start a scholarship program for SASH residents. I know it won't be immediate, but I'm hopeful I can make it happen within a year or two."

I looked up at her. "Wow, that would be incredible. Thank you, Heather. I mean that."

She leaned toward me a little more.

"Mae, I know you and Dani are still trying to figure it all out. And I don't have the best track record with you. I know that I've hurt you ... a lot."

"That's an understatement," I whispered, and she looked away a moment before meeting my eyes.

"I know," she sighed. "You're right. I am so, *so* sorry, Mae. I wish I could go back in time and be the woman I needed to be for you. I still care for you. You have to know that. You have to see it. If you ever decided it was worth trying again, I'm here, Mae. If there's one thing I learned this summer, it's that I still love you."

I stared at her in silence.

"I'll see you soon," she said, and she got up and walked to her car. I closed my eyes, wishing I had someone to talk to and thought about the weekend ahead. I needed to ground myself. I needed to get away. I knew I needed to talk to Dani.

The next weekend, I drove up to Nashville. I pulled up in front of where Dani was staying, and she met me at my truck, her smile wide and welcoming. She embraced me right away, and her softness and warmth drew me in, reminding me of what I had missed since she left.

She took me to the studio where she was working and let me listen to the recording of "Belong." It sounded full, inspiring, and it took me back to the night she first sang it, how the power of her genuineness brought our community closer together.

After we listened, we went for a walk at a park nearby. As we made our way along the greenway, Dani talked about how excited she was to finish the album and release it. While I listened, my mind turned back to Alabama, and I let go of Dani's hand and held my arms close to me.

"Dani, I need to tell you something," I couldn't hold it in another minute.

"Ok," she said, stopping and waiting. My stomach turned as I felt my eyes forced away.

She reached over and touched my arm. "Do you want to sit down?"

I nodded, and we wandered over to a picnic table and sat down across from each other. I looked at her green eyes, and I took in the sight of her gazing at me. My heart hurt, and tightness reached across my abdomen, my back, and my arms.

"What is it, Mae?" She reached across the table to touch my hand.

"I've been so confused these past few weeks. I haven't known what to do or say about it. I worried it would make things worse for you with everything that's gone on, and then there was SASH ..." I wanted to run and hide. I knew if I didn't come out with the hardest part, I might leave Nashville without saying it. "It's Heather. She kissed me."

Dani looked down then back up at me, disbelief across her face. "What? When? What happened?"

"A couple of weeks ago," I held my hands down, tight together, near my knees as they bounced up and down.

She added up the time as I winced. "When I was in Missouri?"

I took in a stuttered breath before whispering, "Yes."

Her brow cinched together as she looked away.

"How could she? And you ..." her voice faltered, but I could finish her sentence. *Betrayed me. Cut me. Made me out to be a fool while I was settling my dead dad's affairs.* I was guilty of it all. Still, she wanted an explanation.

"It was after we put out the signs before the vote. I went inside for water, and we talked for a bit. On the way out, I was crying, and she hugged me. Before I knew it, she pulled me in and kissed me. I froze. I didn't know what to do." I held my breath.

She looked at me for a few moments, and then she looked out into the distance, then back at me.

"Are you ok? Why were you crying?"

"Does it matter?" Frustration filled my voice, but I was unable to stop it. "She kissed me, Dani, and I didn't stop her. In fact, I stood there, and I thought about all the time I spent with her. I've thought about it since, and she's been trying to talk with me and get me alone ever since it happened. She finally did, and she told me she still cares about me, and she's moving to Alabama."

Dani's face reddened and her eyes darted to the trees where she stared, processing. "She took the job at the university ... I ... I just don't understand. Was that the only time?"

"Of course it was the only time," I snapped. "What do you think? That I've been playing you this whole time? And I was crying because she told me that you had said you could never move to be with me and that you were going to stay in Oregon."

"That's not what I meant. And that's not what I told her," Dani's voice was firm.

"It doesn't matter. I don't know who or what to believe anymore," I sighed and put my hands on my temples.

"What are you saying? What are you thinking, Mae?" Dani's eyes stayed fixed on me.

"I don't want to go back to Heather, if that's what you're implying." Ice filled my chest and arms.

"No, I'm not." Dani shook her head. "I know better than that."

I looked out across the park and took in a deep breath. "I think I need some time to sort through things. There was a time when I thought Heather was noble and honest and that her love for me was true. Like I have felt about you. I was wrong about her, and maybe I'm still wrong. I don't know, Dani." I bit my lip. "I think we need to take a break." I looked down and picked at my thumbnail cuticle, as tears welled up in my eyes and rolled down my cheeks. "I need some time. I need some space." I wiped my eyes and looked at her. "I'm so sorry."

Dani looked to the trees again, and she cupped her shaking hand over her mouth as she drew in a few stuttered breaths. I looked down again, the heaviness too much for me to take in.

She exhaled slowly and closed her eyes then stood up. "Ok," she whispered. "I'll take you to your truck."

She drove me to my truck, and we rode in silence. I noticed the skin around my thumbnail was bleeding as she parked the car and shut off the engine. We both looked at the floorboards before she faced me with glassy eyes and whispered, "What now? What can I do?"

"I don't know, Dani." I shook my head and shrugged. "I have to figure it out for myself. Can't you see that? You can't do it for me. Not you, or Anita, or my parents. Just me."

"I know that." She hung her head and wiped her eyes and nose.

"I'm going to head back to Alabama. Dani, I … I didn't mean to hurt you."

"I know." The look in her eyes told the story of someone who put their trust in me only to be wounded by my own failure. Someone like Esther when I betrayed her. Someone like Rebecca, who never told me, but I know. I should have done more to save her.

"Mae? Be safe. I love you. That's not habit. I still mean it. I still do."

I nodded and shut the door then walked away.

I got in my truck and drove the long lonely way home down the interstate, listening to Eva Cassidy, thinking of Dani as the songs moved from one to another. When I got to the backroads, "O Danny Boy" played, and I pulled my truck over and wept while the engine ran quietly in the background, the longing in my heart reaching into the emptiness I could feel around me.

TWENTY-THREE

DANI

When Mae told me she wanted us to take a break, my heart broke. I know people say things like that all the time. In fact, we hear it so much, it sounds trite and cliché. But then it happens to you. It takes that closeness for you to realize that a broken heart means more than just crying in the shower or sobbing into your pillow. It means endless nights of tossing and turning, wishing for sleep; but even the good dreams are painful, because they serve as reminders of what may be lost forever. It means panged breaths when the smallest things like a cup of coffee, the way your shampoo smells, or the sound of rain bring a torrent of memories and a surge of emotion. It means feeling not just that you lost something or someone, but that *you* are lost.

That's what I mean when I say my heart broke. And that's just what I can remember through the fog of tears and feelings.

I called my sister, and she gasped, as shocked as I was. She asked me to come stay with her, but I was determined to finish my album and stick with my original plan. Even though it was just a phone call, her voice brought a small piece of comfort to me.

During the daytime, I went to the studio and recorded my new songs. Somehow, my music proved to be a solace and the studio a respite of sorts, helping me escape the anguish inside of me. In the evenings, I listened to Eva Cassidy's "Autumn Leaves." As I listened, I replayed the summer, thinking of how Mae's guardedness gave way to warmth and trust. I thought of the meaningful moments we shared and our conversations while we walked in the evenings. Her smile, her hair, the taste of her lips, and the way her body connected with mine haunted me.

After the first week went by, I replaced listening to music with writing new songs. Most of them were just working through my confusion and loneliness. My fury at Heather was only tempered by my worry about Mae. One song in particular reflected my truest feelings, and I decided to record it.

One evening, I worked late into the night at the studio. We had finished recording what was already planned, then I added the new song. It took me a few takes to get it exactly like I wanted it. By the end, I was physically and emotionally wiped, and I stepped outside onto a balcony. The night air felt cool, much cooler than in Alabama.

I looked up to see the stars bright across a blackened sky. The moon was new. I never understood why the moon was called new when it's dark and absent from our view. Mae and her love for me looked absent, too, even after I had experienced her fullness. I hoped our love could somehow be made new again.

I searched the stars, and I spotted my favorite constellations, the dippers. I loved them since I was a little kid. I remembered looking through the telescope Dad gave me, seeing them in a different way, thinking of how much closer they seemed. Then here I was, twenty-eight and broken hearted, feeling lost and looking at the stars.

I took in a deep breath of the cool night air, and I did something I hadn't done in years.

I prayed.

"God? Yeah, I know ... it's been a minute. I don't know if you are there. Or what I believe." Even saying the word "God" felt foreign and hurtful after all I had endured from people claiming to speak for God. My jaw tightened as I pushed away the images I had been taught and tried to replace them with the feeling of love I felt when I spoke with Lara.

I sighed and looked out into the expanse as tears began to sting my eyes. A lump formed in my throat.

"Um ... I don't know how to do this. Right now, I know Mae is hurting. I'm hurting, too, and I could use some clarity here. I don't know what to say or do, if there even is anything I can say or do. Help me? And, more than that ... please help Mae. I don't want her to sink down like she did before."

I looked out across the night sky again, and took in deep breaths of the cool night air, and then I headed back inside.

I sat down in the studio, lights dimmed, alone. The engineer had left for the night, and the interns were in the equipment room, prepping for the next recording day. I picked up my guitar, and I listened to the sound of the room. The room sounded fantastic on its own. The wood paneling reverberated gently without adding too much echo. Sound carried through the air, sounding pristine and important. I played through a chord progression I often used for relaxing, paying close attention to the ambiance surrounding me.

I paused and took a deep breath. I walked over to the control room and set up my computer to record. I walked back into the recording room, and sat down with my guitar. My fingers ached from all the playing I had done earlier that night, but I needed to work through my pain, all of it.

I started playing the song I had just recorded again, this time stripped down to just my guitar and me, singing through the lump in my throat and the hot tears in my eyes.

"My love is always there for you,
Like the sun toward the moon.
Your love for me fades away
Like the moon upon the day"

It was incredibly raw, messy, and the most vulnerable I had allowed myself to be in a recording.

"I wonder and wander through the darkness
Of doubting and questions

And sorrow's thick forest.
It's the way I'm still here
And I still love you."

As I ended the song, I looked up, my vision blurry, and I wiped my eyes with my sleeve. I saw my co-producer, Leslie, sitting the control room, leaning forward, hands clasped in front of her nose and mouth, appearing to be caught between thoughtfulness and prayer. I looked down at my guitar, suddenly exposed in my sorrow.

She pressed the talkback switch, "God, Dani ... That was it."

I looked back up, and braved a crooked smile. "Glad I recorded it."

She chuckled in a quiet laugh then told me to go get some rest so we could work some more the next day. I knew she was right. We had a few more days to finish up at the studio, and I would need a second wind to do it well.

I went back to my room, and rested my head on my pillow. For the first time since Mae had left, I fell asleep and stayed asleep through the night. In the place of nightmares or dreams of what might have been, I dreamt of myself walking through golden fields, lit by soft moonlight, a cool breeze in my face, and the stars dotting the expanse above me, reminding me I wasn't alone.

∼

MAE

I felt like I found myself for the first time when I was sixteen. In early summer, my family took a trip out west, to Wyoming. We visited Yellowstone, and the mountains there made the Appalachians back home look like little hills. I realized how small I felt, how small Georgia seemed in the vast world. It was a few months after Rebecca ... after my childhood came to a crashing end. I know my parents wanted to get me away from the scenery, from our house, from every constant reminder of the person I had loved and couldn't save.

I woke up early one morning and walked out of the tent and stood to look at the sky above, shifting colors with the rising sun. As I took in a breath of air, I heard rustling nearby, and I looked to my right to see an eagle perched in a tree next to me close enough to see its eyes. I held my breath as I watched, as still as possible. The eagle unfurled its wings in a majestic display, and I gasped silently. It looked over in my direction, watching me for a moment, our eyes locking. It seemed like a long time, even though it only lasted a few seconds. Then, in an act of beauty and power, it took off in flight. My eyes burned with tears as I watched it soar over the mirror surface of the lake.

In times when I feel troubled, I think of that memory, and I remind myself to be still. I wished I would have done that instead of lashing out at Dani. She wasn't the one who deserved that. Yet, in my confusion and self-doubt, I pushed away one of the kindest people I had ever met, the person I loved and who loved me.

After I got back to Alabama, I isolated myself at my house. I stood in my kitchen and stared into the liquor cabinet, longing for relief but afraid of what would happen if I allowed myself to have a glass. I knew better than to become a drunken mess like I did when Heather broke my heart. *How could I numb my pain? I was the one responsible and when I knew I hadn't just caused pain for myself, but for Dani, too.* I closed the cabinet door and went to my room for my journal. Instead I sat on my bed and rested my head on my knees, unable to put my thoughts to paper.

I knew I needed to talk to someone, so I called Anita and asked her to come over. When I answered the door, she took one look at my swollen eyes and hugged me immediately. "What's wrong? Is your family ok? Are you ok?"

"Everyone's ok," I managed to say before hesitating. "Well sort of. I'm not really ok. I'm sure Dani's not either."

"What are you talking about? What do you mean?" Anita searched my face for answers. I motioned for her to follow me in, and we sat down on my couch. I took a deep breath before starting.

"You've been doing some heavy lifting in our friendship the past few months. It's been mostly you supporting me."

"And it's been the other way around before, Mae. You've been there for me, and you will again. But right now, I'm here for you."

I nodded and closed my eyes.

"I visited Dani, up in Nashville, you know. While I was there, we had a long talk, and it didn't go well. I told her we needed to take a break." I stared at the floor.

"Say what now?" She half whispered as she peered at me. "What happened, Mae?"

The taste of copper filled my mouth and my stomach felt heavy as I hung my head, not wanting to say anything, but I knew I needed to tell someone the truth, and I trusted Anita more than just about anyone else.

"Heather …" I started to say, but the lump in my throat and the heat in my face made it difficult to speak.

Anita crossed her arms and raised her eyebrow.

"She confused the hell out of me, Anita. When Dani was gone, that day we put out the signs, she kissed me." I paused to gauge Anita's reaction. She sneered and shook her head.

"Go on. What else is there? Cause I know you didn't tell Dani you needed a break because Heather is up to her old games."

"She told me she still cares. That was just a few days ago, right before she left." All that had happened replayed in my mind, and I reached for a pillow and ran my hand along the edges. *I need to ground myself.* I looked up to see Anita waiting for me to continue.

"I didn't say anything back to her, and I froze when she kissed me. I didn't know what to do. She told me that Dani would never move from Oregon to be with me, but now I know it was her manipulating me, just like old times. I know she was taking advantage of how vulnerable I felt, but I'm still incredibly confused." I rubbed my eyes with my hands.

Anita huffed. "What are you confused about?"

"I don't know. Maybe what I should believe?" I wondered aloud.

"Like if Dani is untrustworthy and Heather is honest?" Anita tilted her head and raised her brow again.

"Of course, not," I shook my head at the thought. "That's ridiculous. I know not to trust Heather."

"Sounds like maybe you aren't confused." Anita looked at me before looking down.

I nodded my head and looked out of my window. I put my hand in front of my mouth, resting my lips on my fist, searching through my heart as I watched the leaves on the trees, dancing in the wind. *Maybe she was right. There was something else there.*

"I'm afraid," I whispered as I locked my eyes to the floor.

"What are you afraid of, Mae?" Anita's voice softened as she reached over and touched my shoulder.

"I don't know if I can trust myself. What if I am misjudging again? I really lost myself before, with Heather, and I nearly fell for her lies again, Anita."

"Why do you hold on to that, Mae? You fucked up when you trusted her, ok? It's true. But Heather is the one who is most to blame. She took advantage of you, not the other way around. She is the one who deserves all that anger and distrust. Not you." Anita paused a moment and looked at me. "But it doesn't matter if I say that all day if you don't believe it for yourself."

"You're right. It is different this time. I know myself more. I know the signs." I wiped my eyes with my sleeve and looked at Anita.

I realized something and took in a deep breath. "I think I told Dani we needed a break because I couldn't believe in how good it all was, that I had to be missing something again or something would happen, like with Rebecca. I couldn't risk the pain of having my heart broken again, so I broke it this time, instead of letting love be."

"Ok, so now what? I mean, you're gonna fight for that love, right?"

"Of course I am. I just hope Dani can understand." I sighed. "But first I need to talk to Heather."

"Ok?" She looked at me before flashing a sly smile. "I mean, I can talk to her and give her a big ol' piece of my mind. But what do you have in mind?"

I chuckled at the idea of Anita letting her words fly at Heather, but I knew it was up to me.

"I'm going to do what I should have done a long time ago. I'm going to stand up to her. Then, I'm going to take some time for myself. I have a lot I need to figure out so I can believe in me again, and in love, too, for that matter. Then I'm going to talk to Dani and hopefully she will listen." I touched Anita's hand, thankful she was there. It was time to move beyond blaming and questioning myself and for once in my life, to do what I needed to do for no one else but me.

Twenty-Four

DANI

We wrapped up recording, and I stayed an extra night in Nashville just to rest a little before heading west to Colorado. Before I left, I went to the park where Mae and I had talked. I sat at the same bench and replayed our conversation, and I searched my mind for what I could have said differently, but nothing came up. I closed my eyes and listened to the leaves moving and felt the wind blow softly through my hair. I drew in a breath. It was time to leave with no answers, no resolve, like a song ending on a dissonant note.

I took a midday flight to Colorado, and Jen met me at the luggage claim. She embraced me right away, and I held tightly to my sister for a few moments. It reminded me of the other times she had held me like that. Like when I fell off my bike when I was seven, when I failed a science test in eighth grade, and when I went to stay with her after Dad kicked me out of the house. Every time, her arms let me know I wasn't alone, and that I was held more than I realized. That moment at the airport, they let me know again.

We got into her SUV and headed toward her house, nestled in the trees on a large hill. As we pulled up the drive to her house, my brother-in-law, Josh, was waiting on the deck, waving and smiling.

I smiled at him and he smirked and said, "Well, hey there stranger." I laughed and shook my head. It had been so long since I had visited, too long.

When I walked into the guest room, I noticed a basket on the bed with some of my favorite snacks and handmade lavender soap. She had thought of everything, and as I took it all in, she walked in behind me.

"Jen, you ..."

"It's the least I could do, Dani. You'd do the same for me." She patted my shoulder, and I nodded.

"Just take your time getting settled, then when you're ready, we'll be on the deck," she said as she walked out.

I washed my face and changed into jeans and a flannel shirt. The air was cooler in Colorado, and the softness and warmth of the flannel against my skin gave me the sense of coming home. I picked up my phone to look at the time, and I stared at it, wishing I could will it to ring, and for it to be Mae, even though I didn't know what I would say if she did call.

I walked out onto the deck, and I sat with Jen while Josh stood at the grill, making dinner.

"How are you holding up?" Jen handed me a glass of wine.

"As best I can, I guess." I looked into my glass a moment, and I wondered how Mae was doing.

"When do you go back to Alabama?"

"In three weeks. Just for Rachel and Lara's wedding. I'll fly back to Oregon the next morning."

"That's really soon. Do you think you'll be ok?"

I thought for a minute. "I have to be. I don't have a choice. It's for Rachel and Lara—there's no way I could back out on them. I just have to stay focused on the fact I'm there for them. You know?"

I was no fool, though. I knew it would be hard to see Mae and to be around anyone who associated the two of us with being together. That meant everyone I had gotten to know and build a friendship with over the summer. Then I thought of Heather, and a flash of anger came over me.

"Will Heather be there?" Jen must have read my mind, or maybe it was my face. I've never been great at hiding what I'm feeling.

"I don't know," my voice trailed off. I looked off into the trees, the changing colors and the way the playful nature of evening light danced on the baring branches. "I hope not, but if she is, I'll be ok. I promise."

Jen gave me her worried look, the one where I know she doesn't like the answer I've given.

"I'm just going to focus on the wedding and celebrating with Rachel and Lara. Then I'll be out of Alabama in no time. Don't worry." I gave her a half smile to try to reassure her.

"I'm your big sister. That's kind of part of the gig. No matter how old we are, right?" she shrugged and chuckled.

Over the next few days, I spent time hiking with Jen, resting at the house and finishing up my song for Rachel and Lara's wedding. With everything that happened with Mae, I didn't have the heart to finish it until then.

On my last night there, I asked Jen if she would listen and tell me what she thought. I sang the last note and looked up to see her watching me with tears in her eyes.

"I want that for you, Dani. That kind of love you've been singing and writing about and longing for all these years. I was just so certain when I met Mae." She turned her eyes downward and put her hands together.

"I know," was all I could manage to say back in a near whisper.

Spending time in the mountains and being with my sister proved to be just what I needed to gather myself and nurture my spirit. I packed my bag the morning I left and looked forward to being home again.

I hugged Jen again when we said goodbye at the airport. We had been through so much that summer, and it served to bring us closer together. I had realized through all of it, how grateful I felt for her consistency and her persistent belief in me.

As my plane climbed altitude and the clouds filled the view from my window, I exhaled long and slow. I thought of the flights I had taken all summer, and the memories replayed in my mind like a movie reel, steady and vivid. It seemed surreal to me that the next flight I would take would carry me back to Alabama, and that this time, my heart would feel heavy and confused instead of excited.

Back home, I spent time outside, looking at the stars and going on walks. I wondered at how my spirit felt more connected in some ways, even though I felt more alone and sadder than I had in years. It all seemed like a process larger than I could grasp, so I did what I always do when I don't know what to think or say. I immersed myself in music.

I sat with my guitar and even sat down at the piano for a while. I touched my hands lightly on the keys, then played the chords to Leonard Cohen's "Hallelujah" and sang out the most lonesome verses. Then, with a creaking on the bench, I turned and looked at my living room floor, where just weeks before, I had danced with Mae, stars shining above in the sky lights. The silence echoed like a dull ache. I wondered if maybe it was what I needed—the silence and solitude. Maybe for too long, I had filled it instead of listening to it. Instead of listening to my own heart.

I turned back around and closed the lid over the keys. I ran my hand over the wood, worn from years of use from whoever owned the piano before me. I glanced over at the table where my phone lay, wishing I could call Mae, but knowing I shouldn't. My eyes came back to the sheet music in front of me, and one bar in particular drew me in: a rest. I closed my eyes and whispered, "Rest, Dani." Silence was part of the song.

∽

MAE

The week before Rachel and Lara's wedding, we all busied ourselves with preparing for the celebration. The residents worked hard on helping with the decorations while Anita and I focused on nailing every detail. Everything would take place on the surrounding farmland at SASH, and we all hoped for clear weather. After everything Rachel and Lara had done for our community, we wanted to make their wedding as perfect as possible.

On Wednesday, I sat outside making centerpieces when I heard tires on the gravel. A few moments later, I saw Heather's car coming down the drive, and my stomach tensed up. I knew she planned to be at the wedding, but I hadn't expected to see her so soon. The last time we had spoken was before I went to Nashville, and though I still planned to talk to her, I had hoped it would happen at a time when things weren't so busy.

I breathed in and glanced at Anita. She looked back at me and mouthed, "You've got this" as she continued to concentrate on helping the residents with their creations for the reception tables.

I stood up and dusted off my jeans, then went inside to wash my hands. I straightened my hair a little then stood and looked into the mirror for a moment. I looked different, the lines around my eyes had deepened, and my face looked more resolved than I felt. My mind turned to Dani and all I wanted to say to her. Even though I would be confronting Heather sooner than I thought, I was thankful it would be before I saw Dani again. I closed my eyes at the thought of her, and I hoped she would understand. I remembered Heather would be walking in any minute. I breathed in and out again, and I opened my eyes.

I opened the bathroom door and walked to the living room. She wasn't there, so I looked out of the window and saw her talking with Rachel just as Rachel pointed toward the house, and Heather walked toward the steps to come inside.

As the door creaked open and sunlight filtered in, I saw more of Heather's athletic silhouette than her face, and I wondered what her expression would be. As she shut the door, I saw her smiling at me. When we were together, I looked forward to her coming in the front door, wondering what she would say, what battle she had fought and assuredly won, if she might truly see me. But in that moment, I wanted to hide. I steadied myself against the will to run, imagining my feet were full of stone.

"Hey, stranger." She smiled and winked at me, but I didn't return the smile.

"Hey, I didn't expect to see you so soon."

I put my hands in my pockets and stood in the foyer.

"Yeah, I just finished moving everything into my new place, and I thought I would go ahead and drive over so I could see everyone before things get too hectic around the wedding day." She flashed another smile.

"You look good, Mae." She took a step toward me and put her hand out to touch my side.

I put my hand out and grabbed her wrist. "Please, don't."

She frowned at me. "What's wrong?"

I sighed and looked around, searching to see if anyone else was around to hear. I wanted our conversation to be private.

"What is it, Mae?"

"Let's go somewhere else, so we can talk."

She followed me out the back door and along the path to the fields, and we sat down on a little hill, overlooking a pasture. It was far enough away from everyone else, but close enough for me to feel safe and not as alone.

"What's on your mind, Mae?" She looked over at me.

"Heather," I started, but realized I didn't know what to begin with. I took a breath and looked out across the field at the flowing movement of the grasses and wildflowers in the wind. I had felt like those flowers, pushed and pulled by the breezes—especially when it came to Heather. I couldn't allow myself to be like that again.

"Heather, I know you and I have a lot of history. The time we shared, the connection we had once was a big part of my life. I loved you when we were together, and I gave you a huge part of me." *Too much of me.* I looked down at the ground.

"But I lost myself, and I need you to know that intentional or not, you were toxic for me. I became somebody I'm not. I lost sight of who I really am and what I want, and when you betrayed me, I felt like you cut me down. I would say it broke me, but what it broke was the remnant of who I was."

"Mae," she started to speak, but I couldn't let her interrupt me. Not this time.

"No, please. I have a lot that I need to say." I looked at her and she put up her hands and nodded. "I know you've apologized to me for what you did and the way you treated me then, and I can try to forgive you for that. I wanted to believe you when you said you were trying to be better and to live your life in a more generous way. I do see you trying, and this summer, I felt like I saw you become that better person, and I still feel very grateful for all the work you did to save SASH." I paused a moment.

"I'm glad you see that, Mae. I really am trying." She reached for my hand, and I drew back.

"But you haven't changed completely." My cheeks burned as my voice became stronger. "You took what you knew was a soft and vulnerable place in me, and you made it even more raw and vulnerable. You shared pieces of conversations and thoughts of Dani's with me, and you left out just enough to make me believe what you wanted me to. You knew I would feel weak and hurt and need someone else to lean on and then you would be there. You took advantage of it. Of me."

"It wasn't like that, Mae," she tried to calm me.

"It was exactly like that! The way you have made me feel now and back when we were together –like I'm not good enough or don't deserve love and can't trust myself, has been exactly that way. Maybe I've allowed it to happen somehow. I don't know. But I do know this—you are not good for me, Heather, and you don't have my best interest in your heart or mind. I don't believe you ever have, and I doubt you ever will."

Raising my voice felt foreign. Heather swallowed hard and looked at me with glassy eyes before looking down. I looked out across the field again, remembering walking with Dani. I gathered myself before speaking again.

"I trust the love I've shared with Dani. And I trust myself to know what's good and what's right for me. I'm not falling for your lies or your manipulation anymore. I mean that." I took in a long breath and sighed before looking at Heather again.

"I still hope you continue to change and that you become a better version of yourself—in every way. I really do. But it's not going to be with me, ever. I know you'll still be involved here, and it is what it is. Please just stay away from me and keep your distance. I'm done with giving you second chances."

She looked at me then looked down at the ground in silence.

I got up and walked away, my chest expanded as breath filled my lungs.

As I headed back toward the house, I thought of how proud I was of myself and how much I had needed this moment. Anita looked at me as I walked by and I gave her a thumbs up. I needed to go breathe a bit, so I took my truck and drove to the lake.

I pulled onto the gravel and turned off the ignition. I closed my eyes and recited a silent prayer for my own second chance. As I opened my eyes, the changing colors of the leaves across the lake caught my eye. The amber mixed with crimson and flaming orange, and a gentle breeze loosened some leaves from limb.

I thought of how good it felt to let go of Heather, and then the thought of Rebecca filled my heart. My voice came up in a whisper. "It's time I let go of that guilt, too. Is that what you're telling me? And that love isn't something to be afraid of? I promise you, I'm trying."

TWENTY-FIVE

DANI

I got back to Alabama on the Thursday before the wedding. I couldn't help but smile at seeing Lara waiting for me. She beamed with excitement for the wedding, and I couldn't help but feel overjoyed for her and Rachel. On the way to SASH, Lara filled me in on all the wedding details and how relieved she was that everything seemed to be coming together for the celebration.

"Enough about the wedding, or I might get nervous again," she laughed a little then glanced at me. "Tell me about recording. How did it go?"

"Good. We actually wrapped up a couple days early because it went so well. After this weekend, I'll go back home and start prepping for the night of the album release. I just have to get ready to live on the road again for a bit. You know I needed a break from music this summer, but after everything that's happened, I feel more connected with it again."

I looked at Lara, and she met my eyes for a moment and gave me a half smile.

The closer we got, the more inward I retreated. We made our way along the same highway Rachel had driven me down back in May, and I thought of how different it felt this time. How was it possible that in just a few months, I had connected that deeply? Heading to SASH felt, in so many ways, like heading to a family gathering, or a holiday, or even home. Surrounded by everything that stole mine, but still a home. My anticipation grew as we passed the fields and the Antebellum homes flanked by great trees decorated with Spanish moss.

Lara broke the silence with her quiet voice.

"Dani? How are you doing? With everything that's happened with you and Mae, I mean. Are you going to be ok this weekend?"

I looked down at the floorboard. "I think I'll be ok. I know it isn't going to be easy ... seeing her and wishing things were different." I swallowed back the pain. "I still love her, and I'm trying to make sense of it. I know she needs time." I ran out of words, not knowing what else to say.

"Have you talked to her since?"

"No," I whispered.

I looked out the window, recognizing the road we were turning on would take us to the house.

As we pulled into the gravel drive at SASH, I straightened up in my chair and ran my fingers through my hair. I saw Rachel's beamer and Anita's Jeep, but not Mae's bike or truck. I breathed a small sigh of relief. I wasn't ready to see her in that moment. I wondered if she had planned to be away on purpose—to give us both the space we needed or if she was afraid. My thoughts were interrupted by the sight of everyone smiling and waiting for me on the front porch.

I got out of the car and put my backpack on my shoulder, to be greeted by a barrage of hugs. Rachel embraced me, and we walked arm in arm inside the house while Lara and Anita grabbed my bag and guitar.

Once we were inside, I told Rachel I wanted to give something to her as a wedding gift, but I needed to do it in private. We went to her office, and she closed the door behind us, and I put my pack on a chair.

"Dani, your singing at our wedding is gift enough." She smiled at me and shook her head.

"I know, but there's something I've been wanting to give to you for some time, and this seems like the best time to do it," I said, smiling back as I pulled an envelope from my backpack.

I paused and looked down at it. I had written a letter inside, but I needed to say some things out loud.

"Rachel, getting to know you over the summer, and being part of this work you are doing ... well, it changed my life. I mean that. I know that a lot happened this summer that neither of us planned or even saw coming."

"You can say that again," she laughed and sighed, and I noticed the lines next to her eyes and mouth as if they marked her hard work, deep compassion, and determination.

I laughed back and looked down at the envelope in my hands.

"Rachel, what you do for these kids and the community is special, and it's so needed. I know firsthand what it's like to be rejected by someone you love, just because of who you are, and I know you do, too. But you took your heartache and built a home with it, and you filled it with safety and love for people who've been neglected or cast away." I swallowed hard and took a breath.

"I know you know how my Dad rejected me and how all that hurt came to a head this summer. What I haven't told you is that when I went to settle his estate, he left a pretty large inheritance to me and Jen. At first I told her I didn't want it, but then I realized how much good I could do with it, good that he could have and should have done in life, but chose not to. But I choose to do something good with what's left, and maybe take some inspiration from you and build upon the heartache to make shelter and goodness for others. I told Jen what I was going to do, and she chooses to join in, too."

I handed Rachel the envelope as she looked at me with tears in her eyes. She opened it up, then embraced me. "Thank you so much, Dani."

"We don't have any special requests or requirements for what you do with it. Just do something good."

"This means the world to me. I am so thankful for you. I promise to do the best I can with this."

The next day, I saw Mae. I was sitting on the porch, tuning my guitar for the wedding rehearsal when I saw her truck coming up the drive. I wanted to get up and go inside, but I decided staying would be the best thing I could do. There was no way to avoid her the entire weekend. I watched as she got out of her truck. She pulled on the bottom of her button down shirt and put her hands in her jean pockets as she walked with her head down. Her hair fell in front of her face obscuring her eyes, and I looked away, afraid she would see me watching.

I heard her feet on the steps and looked over, and she stared at me as she tucked her hair behind her ears and said, "Hey."

"Hey," I made eye contact a moment and looked away at the field.

I turned back toward her as she scanned the landscape with her eyes.

"Everything looks like it's coming together nicely." It was all I could think of to say. It felt awkward to be in space with someone I had felt so at home with just weeks before. I wanted to say more. I wanted to know more, but I knew I needed to wait.

"Yeah," she said. "The residents did such a great job. And Anita, well you know."

We both laughed.

"Yep, she's pretty awesome," I smiled and looked down.

"Speaking of, I have to go inside and find her. It's good to see you, Dani." She offered a timid smile as her hair fell across her face again.

"It's good to see you, too."

At the rehearsal that night, I played Eva Cassidy's "You Take My Breath Away," saving the song I wrote for the wedding itself. I stayed close to Lara and Rachel and caught up with Cynthia and Sebastian. I barely saw or spoke with Mae, even though the group was relatively small. Still, there were moments I caught myself admiring her gentle beauty and noticed my breathing quickening as I took her in my sights.

Before we knew it, it was time for the ceremony. Cynthia served as the officiant. She read a poem and talked about the love Rachel and Lara had for each other and how their love overflowed into helping others. After they exchanged their vows, I stepped forward to sing the song I had written for them.

Shamelessly reveling
In loving and beauty
Practicing promise
From morning to morning

I love you I love you

In words thoughts and actions
And even in silence
May you hear my heart sing

Be, Be right here
Be here now with me
And I will be here with you
In the sunshine and rain
As long as breath fills up my lungs

Your hands are tiny
But they hold my heart therein
And I'm such a small girl
To hold such great affection

I hold you in my heart
And I pray for you always
You're my smiling and laughter
You're the love of my life

Be, Be right here
Be here now with me
And I will be here with you
In the sunshine and rain

As long as breath fills up my lungs
And I love sharing a life with you
And I love building a life with you
So that others can dance in our love

Be, Be right here
Be here now with me
And I will be here with you
In the sunshine and rain
As long as breath fills up my lungs

As I finished the song, I looked up and saw Mae watching me from the front row, her eyes locked on me. I looked away, afraid that I may have lingered too long, and I turned to hug Rachel and Lara. Cynthia wrapped up the ceremony, and when she announced Rachel and Lara as married, we all stood and applauded.

As we headed to the reception area, I felt a tap on my shoulder and turned to see Heather. She was the last person I expected and certainly the last person I wanted to see in that moment.

"That was a really lovely song, Dani."

"Thanks." I continued to walk and picked up my pace, desperate to put distance between us.

"Dani." She caught my arm. I smiled uncomfortably as I stopped and turned. Others walked by us as we stepped to the side.

"Dani, I'm sorry." She held my arm. "I owe you an apology, and ..."

"No," I pulled my arm away and hoped no one was watching us. "Just don't. I don't want to do this with you, especially not now and not here. You broke my trust, and I could forgive you for a lot of what you did, but not for what you did to Mae. Not right now, I can't. I need you to keep your distance, ok?"

She swallowed hard. "Dani, I ..."

"Look, Heather." I closed my eyes and sighed. "I thought you were better. I gave you a chance and tried to see the best in you. I shouldn't have trusted you. I hope you realize what you could be like instead. Like the person I thought you were."

I walked away from her and didn't look back. Later that night, I saw her saying goodbye to Lara and Rachel, and she made eye contact with me as she left, straightening her suit jacket as she walked away.

MAE

The wedding went off without a hitch. I felt overwhelming joy and love for Rachel and Lara. They deserved every bit of happiness and celebration, and being part of their day filled me with pride.

Anita and I had much to do for the reception, so we were behind the scenes for a good while, making sure everything was perfect for Rachel and Lara. I finally had a chance to sit down and rest, and I looked out to see everyone happy, many dancing together, and I felt content with how everything had gone. I saw Heather saying goodbye to Rachel and Lara, but she kept her distance from me the entire night. I hoped she would continue to stay back and respect my boundaries in the months to come.

I thought back to the past day and a half, since I had first been around Dani again. I had done my best to give her space. I made sure I wasn't around when she arrived, even though I wanted to see her. We hadn't spoken since that day in Nashville, and I wondered what she thought of me.

When I drove my truck up the driveway that Friday, I thought I caught a glimpse of her on the porch, and I bit my lip and gripped the steering wheel as I pulled around to park. I sat in the truck for a minute before getting out, breathing and trying to calm myself. I wasn't sure how she would receive me, or even if she would talk to me, but knowing her heart, I mostly believed she would.

I walked up toward the porch, and I could barely look at her, even though my heart was leaping inside my chest, shouting at me to get it together. I knew I had to stay calm and take it slow. The last thing I wanted to do was make a scene or hurt or confuse her.

After getting past the initial awkwardness of walking up to where she was, just telling her I was glad to see her felt like a relief to be able to say. There was so much I wanted to tell her, and to ask of her, but I knew the time wasn't right. There was too much going on. So, I hid away my thoughts in my heart.

When Dani stood up to sing, I determined to keep my eyes down, but instead I couldn't take my eyes off her. When I heard her voice, I felt my heart beat harder. I thought of all I wanted to say to her, and how afraid I felt, yet still hopeful for understanding. When she finished the song, I saw her eyes meet mine, but I still couldn't bear to look away.

I was taken from my thoughts when I noticed Dani sitting alone at another table, chuckling at the residents as they danced and laughed with enough energy to wake the dead. It felt good to see them at ease again.

I stood up and walked over to Dani's table, and she looked over at me.

"Can I sit with you?"

She nodded and the corner of her mouth lifted up ever so slightly.

"This is one of the most beautiful weddings I've been to. You and Anita did such a great job," she offered a half smile.

"Thanks, Dani," I smiled at her and tucked my hair behind my ears. She looked away again.

"Um," I took a deep breath and looked at her, making sure her eyes met mine. "How are you?"

"I'm ok." She leaned in a little. "The recording turned out great."

"Oh, that's good." I leaned in, too, hoping she would give me more to go on, something other than music. Something other than the surface she had once told me people only see her for. Now here she was, only allowing me to the shallow.

"We're planning on having a release party at a local record store back home, so I fly back tomorrow and start getting ready for that. Then there's the tour. I'm excited to get back out on the road and play music for people again, especially with these songs. But I'm also kind of nervous about how it's going to be to play these songs night after night. They came from such a deeply personal place, and I feel protective of them, but also ready to share. If that makes sense."

"It does," I nodded, knowing everything she had been through in the past few months. "I can't wait to hear them."

She nodded at me and looked away for a moment.

"Dani?" I had to call her attention back to me again. Her eyes met my gaze.

"I know that this isn't the setting to say all I need to say. But, I also know you have to head back home tomorrow."

"Yeah." She tapped her finger on the bottom of her glass and kept her focus there.

"I guess maybe the best thing to say to you tonight is that I'm ready … to talk, I mean. But I understand if you're not. Or if you don't want to."

"I want to." She answered as she looked back up at me. "I do. But you're right. Tonight isn't the right time."

We sat in silence for a few moments.

"Can I call you?" I watched her eyes and waited for an answer.

"Of course, you can," she said. She reached across the table and put her hand on mine. We sat that way for a few minutes, just looking at each other and then out at everyone else.

An old jazz standard, "The Nearness of You", started to play, and I felt Dani squeeze my hand. I looked up at her as she stood and put her hand out.

We walked over, hand in hand, and we danced. I rested my head against hers and with one hand I held her hand, and wrapped my other arm around her. We moved in silence, holding on to each other in the glow of the moonlight and lights hanging from the trees.

For just over five minutes, my mind stopped turning over the words I wanted to say. Instead, I drew in the air we shared and held on to Dani's body, my heart close to hers. The ache in my soul met with a taste of assurance, and when the song ended, we stared at each other for a moment before her hand slipped from mine.

It was time for the reception to end, and we lined up to see Lara and Rachel off to their car, holding paper lanterns to light their path. Once they were gone, we all pitched in to clean up most everything so we wouldn't have much to do the next morning. Dani helped Aimee and Ja'Marcus in the ceremony area, while Anita and I headed up the reception area.

At the end of the night, I noticed Dani looking out across the moonlit fields, resting against the fence post. I walked over to stand next to her.

"Well, I think everything is done. I should probably head home."

"Yeah, it's late. Thanks for sitting with me, and for the dance." Her eyes caught the moonlight as she looked at me and truly smiled for the first time since I had seen her again.

"Thanks for letting me, and for asking me." I tucked my hair behind my ears and pulled my jacket closer around me. "I'll call you. I promise."

Dani stretched out her arms to hug me, and I held her close.

As I drove away, I looked in my rearview mirror and saw her standing with her hands in her pockets, watching me.

By the time I got home, it was nearly 2 AM, and though I was exhausted, I couldn't go to sleep. I made myself a cup of tea and sat on the back porch with a small notebook and pen, lost in writing my thoughts for a while. I looked up at the night sky and closed my eyes and replayed the night before finally coming inside to go to sleep.

When I woke up the next morning, I checked the time. I knew Anita and Dani would have already left for the airport. I picked up my notebook and read over the thoughts I had written in the night. My words had flowed as a stream of consciousness, and my filter had been down. After I read back the words, some in poetry, most in prose, I sat and looked out the window. My mind turned to the night before, and I smiled remembering how good it felt to be close to Dani again. I remembered what she said about her album release and I looked up the record store so I could see the announcement. I looked at the album title, and breathed in a stuttered breath.

"Belong"

In just one word, she captured the theme of the summer. Not just for her, not just for SASH and the community, but also for me.

I looked out of my window again and watched a wren sitting on a branch. She sat there a few moments, ruffling her feathers and gently preening her wings. Then she looked out across the yard and flew away. I thought for a moment, and then I realized what I most wanted and needed to do.

TWENTY-SIX

DANI

I slept on the flight back to Oregon. After seeing Mae and talking about reconnecting and then dancing together, my mind and heart wouldn't calm down enough for sleep, and I spent the entire night thinking and in wakeful dreams. Would things be ok between us? Was I a fool to trust her again? Would I be a fool to let her go? Once I got home, I started planning my set list for the album release. I had scheduled a couple rehearsals with my band, and I knew it would be a busy week leading up to the event.

After the first rehearsal, I went home and made a nice dinner. Cooking my own meals was one of the things I would miss the most when on the road. After I ate, I sat down in front of my wood stove with a mug of mulled wine. Then, my phone rang.

It was Mae.

"Hello?"

"Hey, Dani. How's it going?"

"Good. It's getting busy with rehearsing for the album release. The next few days will be pretty crazy."

"I would imagine."

We both fell silent.

"Dani, it was so good to see you. I ... I don't even have words."

"Me, too." My words came out as nearly a whisper.

"I know I still have a lot of explaining to do and so much that I need to be clear and open with you about, but to start with, I want to tell you I am sorry. I'm so sorry, Dani. I didn't mean to hurt you." Her voice cracked and she paused.

"I know." I wished she could see the understanding on my face, the empathy I felt that surprised me. I leaned forward and rested my arms on my knees.

"Can we try again? Or keep trying? I don't even know what the right words are. But I do know that I love you, and what I feel with you and what we are together, it's right. And it's good. And I want it. I want you, Dani. If you'll have me."

"Mae, I ... I don't even know what to say," I found myself fumbling for words. "What I am trying to say is yes, of course I want to try, too. I love you. But it's been a hard few weeks since ... I know we still have a lot to talk over and try to figure out together."

"Just knowing you are willing to try and sort it out and knowing you still love me gives me a lot of hope, and that's enough for me.

"Listen. This week is a bit crazy, but maybe we can talk more in a few days? Give us some time to think and me a chance to get through this album release so I can give my full attention to us?"

"Of course, I can't wait to talk more."

"Me, too," I smiled.

"And good luck, Dani. I know you'll be great." It felt like her voice was wrapping around me, even over the phone.

"Thanks, Mae."

The night before the release, Jen flew in and stayed in town so she could help me with getting ready and to support me and celebrate, just like she had with every release party I ever had, even for my first demo.

I filled her in on what had happened with Mae. I could tell she was happy for me by the grin on her face. Still, she wanted me to be careful.

The day of the release, we headed to town and started getting everything set up at Backwater Records, an independent record store in Eugene. They had hosted every major album release of mine. Jason, the label owner, was there, along with my co-producer, Leslie, my manager, Tee, and my bandmates.

Fans started showing up early, and I chatted with a few before I had to circle up with the band just before we took the small stage. Ever since I started playing with a band, I made it a point to get in a circle and give a little gratitude before we played together. It always helped us be on the same page, no matter who I was playing with. But this group of musicians had been with me for about three years, so we were more intuitive and connected than I had been with just about any other group I had played with.

We met in a small back office and they turned the tables on me a bit. They talked about how thankful they were for me and how much the new songs mattered. I told them how honored and glad I was to have them all with me.

I looked at the clock on the wall, and Tee told me it was time to go out. I could hear Jason and the owner of Backwater Records talking about the new album and introducing me. Tee opened the door and we walked out to the applause of a packed out room. We made our way through the crowd, squeezing by and getting up to the stage to take our instruments.

"Hello, everybody! It's good to be back tonight!" I called out with a smile, and the crowd cheered. "Thank you," I called back out. I started playing the chords to "Belong."

"Thanks so much for coming and for listening all this time."

Over the next hour, I sang a few more songs, shared stories and talked about my experience of SASH and what I had learned about perseverance and resilience.

When we played "Still" a hush fell over the room, and I could feel the same weight as the night I recorded it after saying my prayer under the stars. In that moment, I realized the power to putting all of that pain into a song and how much it resonated with others.

When the song was over, I breathed deeply and sighed. I felt tired from the emotions and the flood of memories the song brought for me. But there was more to share.

I sang a more upbeat song, and I couldn't help but smile back at the people smiling at me.

I talked again, thanking everyone for coming out, and the crowd chanted for more. I had one more up my sleeve, just in case. It was still a little rough around the edges to perform live, but I was willing to give it a go anyway.

"Ok, ok," I laughed. "Just one more."

I took a step back and nodded to my band mates who readied themselves for the final number.

I started playing a soft chord progression and stepped up to the microphone.

Little did I know
That the dream that I had dreamed
Lay across the world
In fields of gold and green

But then you appeared
And then the moment was gone
Left me in my tears
Singing sorrow's lonely song

But I will wait for you
Hoping the promise will still ring true
And you, Mae.

Mae be the one
The one that I adore
It was you all along
That I'd been looking for

And you, Mae, feel scared
And just a little bit off guard
Or think I wouldn't stay
Once you've bared all your scars

But I will wait for you
Hoping the promise will still ring true

All for you, Mae

Mae, all the stars point to you
And may the sun remind us too
The distance is long,
But my heart belongs to you

I will wait for you
This promise from me is still true
And you Mae

As I played the final notes on my guitar, I opened my eyes and looked up at my bandmates. They smiled at me, and I looked out at the crowd. Everyone was clapping, some whistling, and some calling out things like "we love you, Dani!" and "you're awesome!" I saw Jen smiling over at the side of the stage. I looked out again, thanking everyone for coming out and encouraged them to buy the new album.

Just before I left the stage, I took a bow, and held up my guitar like I always do, then pointed to the band and called out their names. I bowed for a final time and waved as I looked across the crowd. It did my heart good to see my new songs so well received. Then my eye caught another familiar face, standing near the back. My heart skipped a beat. It was Mae.

~

MAE

The more I thought about her, the more I knew I had to fly across the country and surprise Dani. I had no idea how things would go, but I had to take the risk. So I found myself packing a backpack and hopping on a flight to get to the show.

I had slipped into the back just before her show started, hoping I would be unnoticed. Jen saw me early on and smiled as she waved at me. I smiled back and motioned for her to keep it secret.

When Dani took the stage, it felt electric. I had loved her music for a while, and I always thought it would be great to be at an album release. A special energy filled the record store, and I immersed myself in the experience of it.

Every performance rang out with authenticity and fervor, but when Dani sang, "Still," I could barely breathe. Though I knew the song was probably complicated and about many things, my chest tightened with the knowing I had caused her so much pain. Especially when she sang the chorus:

It's the way we said goodbye
It's the way you left me with no tears to cry
As I wonder and wander
Through the darkness
Of doubting and questions
And sorrow's thick forest
It's the way I'm still here
And I still love you

When she finished, a collective breath rippled through the audience. Everyone had been still throughout the song, and I found myself needing to breathe again. I wondered how she felt singing those words and if the feelings would come back and make her think twice about giving me another chance.

Soon she announced what would be her final song, so I looked over the room for where I should go to find Jen and go see Dani. Paralysis hit me as I heard her sing my name.

I smiled at her cleverness, weaving my name throughout the lyrics. The song held tenderness and simplicity in the best of ways. Just like Dani.

The song ended, and the crowd erupted with clapping.

I whispered "Damn," and wiped away a couple of tears before joining the applause.

As she was bowing for the final time, the house lights came up. I stood still and watched her waving and smiling to her fans. She looked across and to each side, being purposeful to give attention to the whole room as much as she could.

Then, her green eyes met mine, and she paused for a few moments before heading down the stage.

I walked along the back wall and quickened my pace hoping to find her, or at least Jen. I turned the corner to move along the side wall and push through the crowd in an effort to get closer to the front. Most people made their way toward a table set up near the front for Dani to greet fans and sign autographs. I didn't see her there. I stood on the tips of my toes and scanned the room for Dani, unable to find her.

"Mae." I heard a familiar voice say, then I turned to see Dani standing right next me.

She put her hands on either side of my face and smiled at me. "I can't believe you're here."

She pulled me in, and our mouths connected in a long, impassioned kiss. I held her close to me as she wrapped her arms around me. The people around us cheered, and for a moment, I felt like I was in a movie.

We looked at each other and laughed as Dani held my hand and then motioned a thank you to the crowd.

"Are you sticking around? Can you I mean? I'll be at the table for a bit, signing autographs and taking pictures."

"Of course I am. I'll be here when you are done."

She grinned and kissed my hand before she walked over to the table.

I found Jen, and we stood off to the side while Dani greeted fans and took pictures with them. Every now and then, she looked my way and smiled. Jen and I talked about Dani's show and how amazing her performance was.

A couple hours later, the last fans had gone and the store owner, musicians, and others in Dani's entourage said their goodbyes, complimenting Dani on the show, and thanking her for her music while she thanked everyone else for their part.

Jen touched my shoulder. "It was good to see you, Mae."

"You, too." I hugged her before she walked over to say goodbye to Dani and talk about meeting up the next morning before she flew back home. After they decided on a plan, Dani shuffled toward me with her hands in her pockets and a sideways smile.

She kissed me again before touching my face and looking me in the eye. "Will you come stay with me?"

"Are you sure?" I wanted to, but I didn't want to pressure her. She nodded and held out her hand for me to take and I smiled as we walked to her truck.

On the way back to her house, Dani grinned at me, "I can't believe you are here. That you came so far, just to be here tonight."

She held the door open for me as I walked inside her house.

After she put her guitar down, she walked to the kitchen and asked if I wanted anything to drink, and she brought us both some water.

Though it was late, the night energized us, and we went to her living room to talk. Dani got a fire going then sat down next to me. She touched my hand, and I turned my hand over so I could hold hers.

"Dani, you were incredible tonight," I said. "You are always incredible. You just are," I felt myself stammering and I looked down, warmth filling my cheeks.

"Thank you. I'm just so glad you are here." She squeezed my hand, and I met her eyes. I took in her love and kindness and I took in my breath.

"Dani, I love you." My grip on her hand tightened. "I could tell you I'm sorry a thousand times over and still feel like I needed to say more. When you sang that song tonight, I knew just how deep that pain went. The pain I caused you. I want you to know just how sorry I am."

She nodded at me and whispered, "I know. I forgive you. I did a long time ago. I could see how confused you were, and it confused me, too. I knew you were hurting. I just wish I could have helped you somehow."

I touched her cheek and met her lips with mine for a few moments before I held her hand and looked at her again.

"I want you to know what happened. Why I felt like I needed some space and where my head and heart have been. I know it'll take more than one conversation, but I'm ready to talk about it, and I'm more certain now than ever of how I feel. I took the time I needed and sorted things out. For myself. For us, and for you." I looked her in the eyes. She nodded and put her hand on my back.

I took a deep breath.

"I know you know the history of what all happened with Heather, and I know you know how confused I got when she appeared back in my life. Even though she helped save SASH, her being around did me more harm than good. It reminded me of all the ways I felt before, when I was with her. I started to feel inferior, uncertain, and unworthy again. Then when I saw her doing good and thought she was changing, I felt like I had done something wrong or had believed something wrong before. It made me feel like I couldn't trust myself. I know now that she manipulated me, and she took advantage of the little inch I gave her."

"I can't imagine how confusing that had to be."

"I want you to know that I stood up to her just before the wedding."

"Seriously?" She raised her eyebrow then smiled at me.

"Yeah." I laughed a little at how long that conversation with Heather had been coming. "I finally set the boundaries I should have a long time ago."

"I wish I could have overheard that." Dani laughed. "She tried to talk to me at the wedding, and I told her to stay away."

Of course she had. I shook my head at the thought of Heather trying to talk with Dani, then I focused back on what I needed to say.

"Dani, back in Nashville, when we were at the park, I got so angry with you."

"Yeah, I know."

"I think I reacted in anger because you startled me. I just couldn't believe someone would care that much, to see past a huge mistake and what I felt like was a betrayal, and that you would want to know what was wrong. I realized afterward, that I was feeling unworthy on top of all that confusion, and I lashed out at you. That was wrong of me, and you didn't deserve that anger." I looked down for a moment, and Dani touched my hair. I reached up and held her hand.

"The way I withdrew wasn't right, but I did need that time to be more certain of my feelings and to figure out for myself what I wanted to trust and believe."

"Of course, Mae. That makes perfect sense. And we do still have a lot to figure out, especially with where we could be together."

I intertwined my fingers with hers and looked her in the eyes. "I trust you. I trust the love between us, and I believe in the love we have shared, and I believe that we will continue to share. We'll figure it out. We have to."

Dani put her arms around me and held me close to her. For a few moments, we stayed in that embrace. She kissed me, and the scent of her hair and the softness of her skin intoxicated me. I caressed her hair and leaned into her, breathing in her closeness. We moved to Dani's bed, and our bodies together felt familiar and comforting, yet somehow bold and new. Late into the night, we fell asleep in each other's arms.

I woke up first and looked at Dani. I couldn't shake the feeling that waking up next to her felt like home. We had to find a way to be together and both be fulfilled in our work and where we live, even if we couldn't see it.

Soon, Dani woke up. She had planned to meet up for brunch with Jen, and I encouraged her to go without me so I could rest and so they could have some time just the two of them. I knew Dani would need to process our reconnection, and I wanted to give her the space to do that.

While she was gone, my phone rang, and I saw it was Anita.

"Hey, Anita."

"Hey. I hope I'm not interrupting."

"No, Dani's out with her sister before she leaves. Things are going really great though."

"Well, that's wonderful news!" Anita laughed then got serious again. "Can you talk? And are you sitting down?"

TWENTY-SEVEN

DANI

As soon as I got back from seeing Jen, Mae was waiting for me at the door. Her smile stretched across her face and she kissed me.

"What's going on? You look like you won the lottery." I laughed.

"Well, I kind of did. I think. I got a call from Anita, and something super exciting is happening. We need to call Rachel."

I sat down with Mae on the couch, and we made the call. Rachel answered right away.

"Hey, Dani. Congratulations on the album release. How did the show go?"

"Thanks! It went really well. And Mae being here was quite the surprise."

She chuckled. "I'm so glad. About both of those things. I have something I wanted to share with you that I wanted to make sure you heard from me and not anybody else. Are you sitting down?"

"Yeah, we're sitting on my couch and I'm ready to hear all about it."

"Lara and I just got back from North Carolina for our honeymoon. We spent a good amount of time exploring the areas around Asheville, and we stumbled on something. Something we weren't looking for yet, but it's too perfect to pass up. I called the board, and we were able to move on everything immediately. Dani, with the gift from you and Jen, we are buying a small farm to make a second safe home."

"What?! Are you serious?"

"I sure am. Your generosity was enough to make expanding the work we do turn from dream into reality. All of the pieces fell together at the right time, and when we saw this place nestled in the mountains, we had to jump on it. This means we'll be able to help more people. We have enough to cover costs for the first couple of years, and we feel confident we can get more support to keep it going and hopefully expand again in a few years."

I couldn't speak for a moment. It turned out that Dad's money would give shelter and safety to people like me.

"Dani, are you there?"

Mae smiled and nudged me to speak.

"Yeah, I just. Wow. That's incredible, and I can't thank you enough for telling me. I'll be sure to tell Jen. And if there's anything else I can do to help out, don't hesitate to ask. This is incredible."

"Thank you, Dani. We'll talk again soon."

We ended the call, and I sat a moment staring in wonder.

"Well?" Mae put her arm around me.

"I can't believe it. This is going to accomplish more than I ever dreamed. And to think it came from Dad." I shook my head and looked back at Mae. "It feels weird but right, if that makes sense. Like some closure for me, maybe."

Mae smiled at me and took my hand.

"Dani, there's more, and I asked Rachel if I could be the one to tell you this part."

I turned toward Mae and wondered what else there could be to tell.

"Rachel asked Anita and me to go to Asheville and get everything set up, and she wants us to stay there and direct the house together. And, well, we both agreed to it."

"What?!" I threw my arms around Mae. "That's incredible. I'm so proud of you right now. You and Anita are freaking rock stars. You're going to be so great!"

"Thanks, babe. I just can't believe it. We're going to view the place in a couple of weeks." She paused a moment. "It's going to be good to be in the mountains again."

Mae stayed with me for a few days, and we hiked some of my favorite trails, talked for hours, and laughed. God, we laughed so much. We spent hours reconnecting our hearts and our bodies.

On the day she left, I took her to the airport early in the morning, and we kissed goodbye. She held my hand to her heart and put her forehead against mine, "I carry your heart with me"—one of my favorite lines by e.e. cummings.

I answered back, "I am never without it."

We embraced again before she walked toward the terminal to go through security.

MAE

Knowing Rachel believed in Anita and me that much made me determined to reach my fullest potential and do her proud. It encouraged me to know our work was expanding more, and that the mission was getting bigger than we had dreamed for ourselves and the community.

When I got back to Alabama, I sat down with Anita.

"Can you believe it?" I poured her a cup of hot tea as we sat on my back porch.

"Yes, girl, I can. I done told you the Lord works in mysterious ways." She cackled, and I couldn't help but join her.

"Ok, for real though, Mae. I think it's good. I didn't expect something like this so soon, but it feels right. You know?"

I sighed and looked into my tea. "It does."

"Ok enough about work for now, you gotta tell me about you and Dani."

"What's to tell?" I gave her a coy look, and she raised her eyebrow at me.

I took a moment and a sip of my tea.

"It's good, Anita. It's really good. You know, for the first time in a really long time, I feel like I can trust myself. I feel like I can trust when I feel something is right. And she feels righter than anything I've felt."

Anita flashed a sly smile at me and took a drink.

"What?" I chuckled.

"I'm not saying anything. You know I think you two belong together. I'm not saying anything else."

"Ok good, cause maybe we can talk a little more about work now." I smiled back at her.

Everything moved forward at a quick pace, and Anita and I made plans to move in the spring. I felt thankful that I would have time to say goodbye to the residents and the other staff, and I was incredibly grateful for the change in scenery. After all that had happened over the summer with Heather, putting more distance between us felt like the best idea.

The more time I spent in our new location, helping with plans and making community connections, the more I felt at ease and excited about the new environment. I didn't realize how much I had missed the mountains until being around them again felt like home.

The potential for a real future there stayed at the front of my mind. There were more accepting and open-minded people around, and a local artist scene thrived. Connection to nature abounded with waterfalls, places to hike and fish and get out on the water, outdoor concerts and festivals, and agricultural classes. In some ways, I thought it bore similarity to Eugene, in its loveliness, simplicity, and love of the arts. I couldn't wait to share it with Dani. I knew she'd love it just as much. At least, I hoped so.

After my second trip to the new site, I went home to stay with my parents for a couple of days. I sat on the porch with my mom on my last night there, drinking hot cider. We sat on the porch swing and talked about my move for a while before the conversation turned.

"How are you and Dani?" My mom looked at me and touched my arm.

"We're good. Really good, actually. She's still planning to visit in a few weeks, after Thanksgiving. I'll still bring her here if that's still ok with you and dad?" She nodded, and I looked out in the dark before looking back at my mom. "Momma, can I ask you something?"

"Of course."

"You've always told me to let love be. I always thought it meant to be still, to rest in love and not force anything."

"Mmmhmm."

"But after everything that happened this summer with Heather popping back into my life and the way it affected me ... well, and falling in love with Dani, I think it maybe means something different."

The hint of a smile touched her face.

"I think it still means those things, but maybe it also means letting love be *in me*. That I need to love and trust *myself* and that we all come from love, that love holds me, and won't let me down. And then that same love will pour out of me when I love others."

Mom looked at me with glassy eyes. "It's what I want most for you, Mae. You've been through so much this summer, and you've been to hell and back with what happened with Rebecca, and then how lost you were with Heather. But you came back around. Just like I knew you would. Love is in you. Love holds you. Yes, let love be."

TWENTY-EIGHT

DANI

I busied myself with more rehearsals for the upcoming tour, and I made plans to stay with Jen for the holidays. Mae invited me to spend some time after Thanksgiving with her family in Northeast Georgia, so I found myself flying to the south again, excited to see Mae for the first time since she surprised me. We had talked nearly every day and sent each other letters in the mail. Though I was excited for my tour, I knew I only had time for a couple more visits before things got hectic for a while. We still didn't know what would lie ahead, but we knew we couldn't give up.

Being with her parents felt relaxing as always, and I was glad for the chance to spend some time with them. One night, Mae asked me to trust her and go with her on a little road trip the next day. We left early, just after the morning light had turned the sky from midnight blue to grey. As we drove, I took in the aroma of fresh coffee mingled with Mae's perfume.

Over the next few hours, we drove through the mountains, and peaks and conifer trees filled my view.

"Now these are mountains," I sighed while looking out of the window. "No offense."

"Ha ha ha," Mae looked at me with a grin.

Soon, we came into a small town, and Mae pulled her truck into the lot of a small café. We got out of the truck and walked up to the door to go inside.

A small rainbow flag and sign about being welcoming to all people greeted us, and for a moment I wondered if I was seeing things right or if my eyes were not adjusted to the light. A waitress with dreadlocks and a nose ring walked up and grinned at us as she grabbed a couple of menus.

As Mae and I sat down at a booth, I looked around to see people who looked more like they belonged in Oregon than the South. I looked at Mae and smirked. "Where are we? Did we leave the South?"

She laughed at me and shook her head, "The new home will be about ten miles that way." She pointed to her right.

"You're kidding. Is it really this cool and accepting around here?"

"No," she said sighing. "I mean, this particular town is, and a lot of the area in and around Asheville is, too. But as a whole, there's still a lot of work to do, especially on a state and regional level."

"Still, this beats south Alabama by a landslide. Seriously, even having pockets of safety like this and knowing there's some real support nearby … wow, this is going to be great."

She smiled and took a drink as she raised her eyebrows at me.

After lunch, we went to the site of the new home and walked around. Mae showed me all the buildings on the farm, even an old barn she planned to convert into another hideaway. We spent the day talking about the new home and how happy Mae was for the change in environment and the work they were going to do.

As we walked to her truck to head back, she held my hand. "What do you think, Dani?"

"I think it's perfect." I looked at her and smiled. "I see how happy you could be here. Plus, it's a much nicer place for me to come see you." I leaned in and kissed her.

We made plans for me to come back to her parents' home for the New Year. It would be my last visit with Mae before my tour started, and then I would be traveling more days than not for a few months. It would be April before I had a lengthy amount of free time.

Around Christmastime, I stayed with Jen and Josh, and we celebrated the holiday together with mom. Jen and I stayed up late on Christmas night, and we talked by the fire.

"So you're going to see Mae again next week?"

"Yeah, it'll be the last chance I get before I head out on tour. We're going to stay with her parents and then go to North Carolina for a couple of days."

"I'm so glad they are using Dad's money to build a new home. From what you've told me, it sounds great. And sounds like you really like it there." Jen winked at me, waiting for an answer.

I looked at the glow of the fire and the lights on the Christmas tree.

"I do. And, I think I figured out something."

"What's that?"

"When dad kicked me out of the house, I spent years looking for something I could hold. Looking for love and belonging, looking for home, really. I found a lot of heartache, outside of you, of course."

"I know." She gave my hand a squeeze.

"But this summer, when I was in Alabama, in the middle of all the vitriol and the not knowing and the questions, I found something special. Something I didn't expect."

She looked at me again, and touched my shoulder.

"I found love. I found family. I even found a sense of home with Mae. That's why it hurt so bad when I thought I had lost her." I turned around to face my sister.

"But Jen, what if belonging isn't something we find? What if it's already there, and we just have to trust it? Even if we are broken? And maybe what we can do is make the space for it to just be. I want to make that space, wherever I need to. I want to create more belonging and love."

Wherever I can, and if I can help it, with Mae.

Jen smiled then pulled me in close and held me.

～

MAE

I knew we would only have one more visit together before Dani would leave to go on tour. I wanted the time to be special, and I planned to take her to North Carolina with me again, this time to take her to one of my favorite new trails so we could have some low-key time together.

I picked Dani up from the airport and drove her to my parents' house. We rang in the new year together, and seeing Dani connecting with my parents again felt natural and right. A couple days into her visit, we packed a small bag and some camping supplies to stay in North Carolina for a couple nights. We planned to drive out to see the progress made, stay in a small camping cabin, then spend some time hiking before coming home.

We went to the new home site, and I showed Dani the paint that would go on the walls and the new doors, cabinetry, and bath fixtures. Then, we went into town for water, coffee, and food to take back to the cabin.

The next morning, we awoke to a breathtaking scene of white branches and falling snow beginning to blanket the ground. We made ourselves a light breakfast and coffee then decided my truck wouldn't be able make the drive out of the camping area to go to the trail. I remembered there was another trail within walking distance. We bundled up and made our way to the trail together, hand in hand, boots crunching on the snow.

Leafless branches arched above us, with a thin layer of fresh snow. Cardinals chirped in the trees, and the gentle babbling of the nearby brook made its way over stones and bunches of leaves and twigs.

We reached a place in the trail that had a large stone to the side and a little lookout over a small ravine. I asked Dani if we could take a rest and look for a while.

"It's so serene," she spoke in a near whisper, as if she didn't want to speak over the delicate sound of the snowflakes.

I lay my head on her shoulder and nodded. I put my hands in the pockets of my jacket and looked out across the ravine at the trees and the crevices in the hills. I inhaled the cold air and listened to the gentle melody of snow falling on the evergreens.

"Dani," I said softly, "I'm so glad we are sharing this together."

"Me, too."

We kissed and then put an arm around each other, sitting and looking in silence.

I took in another deep invigorating breath. "So much has happened this year. Good, hard, challenging, and life-giving. I've been stretched and loved and tested—pushed to my limits, really. But I feel like I wouldn't trade any of it."

"Yeah, for sure." She rubbed my side. "I feel the same way."

I looked out and back over at her. "I finally understand more of how I've struggled and why. And I feel like even though it was painful, I have more clarity and strength now."

Dani hugged me a little tighter.

"I know now what I want more than ever before, and I realize how precious that is. Just to know and be sure of it. To be sure of myself."

Our eyes met as I spoke. "When we first met, I felt like I was too wounded and too broken, not just to love again, but to receive love. I didn't want it, and I certainly wasn't looking for it or even feeling open to it. But then here you came, Dani Williams. Straight from the albums I had loved and then for real into my life." I smiled and then swallowed hard and took another deep breath before continuing.

"I've never dreamed all that much for myself. I've always just wanted life to be something simple and true. But then I started giving up on that dream, too. Until now." I touched her hand.

"The best dream I've ever dreamed for myself is the one where you share that dream. It's the one where we're together and happy. You're the dream. You're the one I've most hoped for, even when I didn't know it. Your love, your kindness, and your light are the love, kindness, and light I want to rest in. And I want to shower you with mine. What if we split our time? You come stay in Asheville some, and I can spend time in Oregon."

"I was going to ask you the same thing," she laughed as my eyes filled with tears. "I even thought, if you want, you could come on the road with me some to raise more awareness and money for SASH."

I hugged her for a while and then she leaned back and looked me in the eyes.

"Since I've met you, I found love and a sense of home where I never expected it, or even thought to look for that matter. It's in you, and it's somehow even inside of me. I can't think of anyone I'd rather do life with. I keep thinking you're the melody I've always hummed, the song I've penned time and time again, the one I know by heart."

We embraced each other and kissed, snow falling around us, like a chorus of celebration.

Then, we trudged through the snow, back to the cabin, hand in hand, heart to heart, with snowflakes melting as they lighted upon our shoulders.

ACKNOWLEDGMENTS

I want to give gratitude to the good people who helped this book come into the world.

Deb, thank you for being a wonderful critique partner and for your encouragement to me to keep going. Alder Van Otterloo, your early wisdom and insights helped me immensely in further developing the story. I've always admired your parenting wisdom, and having you as copyeditor on this book was another moment of feeling I'm getting guidance from a great.

Cat, the cover you created blows me away. Your attention to detail and care are exemplary. Thank you for creating such a gorgeous work of art for this story.

Kate, Stephani, Tiffany, and Jessica – thank you for giving me great feedback that helped bolster me and helped me make this book better.

To Betty Woomer, Carolyn Goss, and Kim Eckert: of all my teachers, you encouraged my writing the most, and you cheered me on in ways that helped me believe more in myself. Thank you.

Sarah, thank you for being one of my biggest cheerleaders in this creation. Your enthusiasm for this book has been delightful. I love you, sistor.

Deanna, thank you for the early conversations and your spark of an idea that became this story. From mugs of tea at my writing desk, to begging for the next chapter, to reading the story through every revision, you've been with me every step of the way. I love you forever and always. Willow and Sycamore, I'm so proud of the people you already are. I am so thankful to be Momma C to you. My family, found and kept, thank you for all of your support and love.

And to my readers, thank you. May you always find belonging wherever you are.

About the Author

Charity Muse is an emerging author of lesbian centric women's fiction and nonfiction works on connection. *Broken to Belong* is Charity's debut novel. Her poetry has been featured in the anthology *Smitten: This is What Love Looks Like* by Indie Blue Publishing. Originally from Chattanooga, TN, she currently lives in Northwest Georgia with her wife and children.

You can find her and a discussion guide and original music for this novel online at http://charitymmuse.com.

facebook.com/CharityMMuse

instagram.com/charitymuse

CPSIA information can be obtained
at www.ICGtesting.com
Printed in the USA
LVHW050309240522
719535LV00007B/243